Jump Off:
The Deep End

A Cautionary Tale

§

Traci Morris

The Java Tree Press *paperback edition:*

Copyright © 2017, 2020 Traci Morris

All rights reserved.

Published by The Java Tree Press

Olympia Fields, IL 60461

Printed in the United States

ISBN-13: 978-0692366103
ISBN 10: 0692366105

Book design by Traci Morris

DEDICATION

To my mother, Dorothy,

who always believed in me and encouraged me to

use all of the creativity God gave me.

Thank you, Mom, from the bottom of my heart.

I love you.

PROLOGUE

Don't ever judge someone for doing something you say you would not do. A person on drugs or a person who cheats. An alcoholic or a sex addict. I used to say, *Oh, I would never do that. How they could get themselves into that situation?* But unless you're in that person's shoes, you honestly don't know the circumstances that led them to that decision. And you don't know the addiction that made them stay in it. *Addiction.* I'd always associated the term with drugs or something that could be overcome if the person just "tried harder." Tried harder to acknowledge their problem, solve it, stay away from the temptation, and be good. Just like that...

Well, easier said than done. In my short time on earth and with some unlikely, firsthand wisdom, I could honestly say that I will never again judge a person for being addicted and making poor choices. Because, I became that person. I threw all of my morals and positive family values out the window when I came to this town. Don't judge me until you hear my story. My story on how I, Merci Townsend, good girl, exemplary student, and straight-laced overachiever, became a symbol of degradation by obtaining the status of a *Jump Off*.

Urban Dictionary: *Jump off: A casual sex partner. A mistress or a person that is usually only being used for sex while in marriage or serious relationship; The chick (or man) on the side. See also (Booty Call)*

"My Jump Off never has me going out of my way, and she don't want nothing on Valentine's Day" - Joe Budden

IN THE BEGINNING, THERE WERE WORDS:

PART I

CHAPTER ONE

Six Months Earlier

"Teresa, you look great, but maybe you could loosen up a few buttons," I said, frowning at the blouse that was buttoned all the way up to her neck.

"You think? Good idea."

I couldn't believe I was telling my roommate to wear something a little less conservative. Who would've thought? I knew if Layla were here, she'd be trying to get me into something crazy, but Teresa was a lot like me…

§

My first year at the University of Chicago was a productive one. I absolutely loved my school and the history that came with it. Moving from small-town Stevensville, New Hampshire to Chicago seemed daunting at first, but I adjusted pretty well at the prestigious university. Our grounds were beautiful with new and old historical buildings, and charming, ivy-covered housing. The courtyards reminded me of New England, so I felt right at home.

At nineteen, I was just finishing up the spring semester and excited to have the early opportunity for an internship at a corporate firm downtown. Instead of going home this summer, I thought acclimating myself into the business world could be a great experience for me. I was always an A student in high school and prided myself on my ability to comprehend most things pretty easily. I wasn't a total nerd, though. While I loved to be involved in school activities, I also didn't mind being sociable either. Hanging out with friends at a party and dancing was not something I rejected, but neither was it a priority in my life.

My parents, George and Sheila Townsend, were active in the church and I usually went with them every week. I come from a religious (here - my parents would quickly correct me and inject "spiritual") family. They prayed a lot, but I admit I wasn't that into it. Don't get me wrong, I believed in God and everything, but being so self-reliant, I thought I was doing pretty good on my own...

It was always said I was more mature than my friends. My parents said I had an old soul. They weren't really worried about me being here on my own, although my pops, being the overprotective ex-military that he is, made sure I got a refresher on self-defense and even tried to push a .45 my way. I adamantly refused. He laughed it off because deep down he believed I would be fine and told me to go "handle my business" regarding school and my new life. My mother tearfully kissed me goodbye, made sure my Bible was packed and told me how proud she was of me. They just knew I would make them proud and become the successful daughter I was brought up to be and had always been. You see, I was never one to disappoint my parents...

Late last August, I drove from Stevensville in the new, compact Ford Focus my folks bought me at graduation. Since I got good grades and received a full scholarship, my parents splurged on me. My car was filled to capacity with all of my stuff and I wondered if everything would fit, but it did. There was parking outside of the dormitory, so that worked out well.

While I never looked at myself as "hot," I wasn't naïve enough to overlook the fact that I had blossomed in my last years of high school. At five foot six, I had finally acquired some major curves. I had thick wavy hair, my mom's creamy smooth complexion, and was told my almond-shaped, brown eyes were exotic. As a freshman, I was all bones and long limbs, had acne and braces, and hadn't yet started wearing contacts. Once that changed and I started to fill out, I received a lot of attention. I brushed most of it off, though. My blasé' attitude could probably be attributed to my awkward beginning. As a journalism major, I was most concerned with my books.

At one time I dated a guy from back home, Brandon. We were close friends growing up and it just evolved naturally into something else as we got older. We kind of grew apart romantically, but remained friends. We had "relations" for my first time when I was seventeen. It was okay, but I couldn't really say I'd be missing him in that or any capacity. We parted ways with no hard feelings on either part.

Layla, my best friend from back home, was a spitfire who was the opposite of me in so many ways. Because of her I was dragged into a social life in high school. She was loud and shrill where I was quiet and cool. She was fashionable and outgoing in contrast to my subtle demeanor regarding style. But I learned a lot from her on how to dress, apply makeup, and I brought her fashion pointers with me. She taught me how to transform myself into understated elegance my last year in high school. Of course, Layla wanted me to have a more pseudo-slutty look, but I wasn't having it. Especially if she wanted to have any input. So we compromised on my look. I now paired up clothes to bring out my newly acquired confidence without going too far. If I wore a small skirt or skinny jeans that emphasized my "assets," then my top had to leave something to the imagination. If I wore a tank that showed some cleavage, my bottoms had to be a bit more conservative. That was my rule.

I became really good friends with my roommate, Teresa Rothschild, first semester. She was actually from the Chicagoland area and showed me the ropes in the Hyde Park neighborhood. We even tried to sneak a peek at the president's Chicago home, but the police weren't going for it. We applied for summer internships together and when we both got accepted at Jansen Worldwide Capital, we squealed in excitement. Although it had nothing to do with either of our majors, internships were hard to come by in Chicago and we jumped at the opportunity. The thought of working together at a prestigious firm downtown, having lunch at the cool eateries and browsing Michigan Avenue shops sounded awesome. Maybe I could get inside of that massive Harold Washington Library on a lunch break one day.

§

Today, Teresa and I were trying on outfits and couldn't wait to start our internship on Monday. Although very pretty with long, blue-black hair and trendy specs, she could be a bit timid. Because of my experiences with Layla being pushy, I gradually tried to give her a few fashion tips that wouldn't scare her away.

I bought a small group of coordinates on sale last week through a Victoria's Secret catalog. I loved their work clothes because they were sexy and could be conservative at the same time. Because I was on scholarship, my parents were able to give me a nice allowance for a work place wardrobe. I bought some pencil skirts, mini-skirts, a few dresses and romantic blouses along with four pairs of heels at different heights, ranging from two to five inches. Five was really too high for me, so they were for special occasions if needed. Teresa was not moved by shoes and anything higher than three inches was a deal breaker for her. Maybe I *was* becoming more adventurous…

§

Monday arrived, and we took the Fifty-fifth street Metra train to the firm that was set just at the northern tip of downtown. There was no way I would drive and pay for expensive downtown parking. We would be working at a business investment firm called Jansen Worldwide Capital or JWC for short, as assistants. While I'm sure they had administrative assistants to the managers, we would be assisting everyone when needed. I was curious to experience the dynamic of working in an office, not to mention a high powered company in the third largest city in the United States. A nervous anticipation settled over me.

After exiting the train at Randolph and Michigan, we crossed over the Chicago River to a building right on Michigan Avenue. The building was ideally located right before you get to all of the cool shops, otherwise known as the Magnificent Mile. As we arrived, a fancy plaque on the outside of the building read, *Jansen Worldwide Capital*. Wow, they owned the whole building?

Once we reported to human resources, we filled out the necessary paperwork and were assigned to cubicles on the next floor up. My cubicle wasn't in the same area as Teresa's, so we regretfully promised to find each other when lunchtime came.

In my area, plenty of people were working steadily at their stations. On the other side of a wall were offices with doors where I assumed the managers worked. I was introduced to a few folks in my area and they all seemed pretty nice. A guy named Lance and another named Darren, who kept leering at me, let me know they were also interns. I was informed that some of the bigger desks up towards the front were held by administrative assistants.

One assistant I was introduced to was a perky blonde named Jessica who seemed friendly enough. Across from her was a gorgeous redhead introduced as Jasmine. Apparently, she was too busy with her work and couldn't be bothered to greet me. *Okay.*

I settled into my desk after being led to the supply closet by Lance to get the necessities. As soon as I had everything arranged and in order, the redhead sauntered over with a huge stack of papers and dropped them onto my desk.

"Hi, *Marci,* can you please sort all of these invoices into alphabetical order?" she asked with a purr and looked away at her overly long, fake nails.

"No problem, Jocelyn."

Her eyes cut sharply back to mine while her mouth opened in astonishment. I stared back in challenge.

"My name is not Jocelyn, its Jasmine," she said through gritted teeth.

"Oh, sorry about that," I said insincerely. "By the way,

my name is Merci." I gave her a sweet smile.

That should nip that in the bud, right? Was this junior high? Although I could be quiet, the Townsends didn't raise a punk. She abruptly turned around to strut away, her hips swaying ridiculously. Was she doing that for me? Not impressed nor interested. Shaking my head, I chuckled to myself. I could tell it was going to be fun here.

Luckily, Teresa and I had the same lunch hour. We went to Potbelly's and laughed about the colorful characters we'd met so far. She shared a story similar to mine about a persnickety girl from her department.

"She comes right over and tells me her name is Amanda - doesn't ask for mine, and starts right in. So, she's making a big deal about the Rothschild method of classifying and how it may be *quite* difficult for me to catch on. I told her I knew it *quite* well because my great-grandfather, Linus Rothschild, invented it!" We doubled back in laughter. Teresa's family was pretty wealthy and well known in Chicago. "And then I reached out my hand and said, 'By the way, I'm Teresa Rothschild.'"

I laughed so hard. "Wait, wait - how did she look when you said that?"

"She just started sputtering and looking around with these big, bug eyes. Then she says, 'Um - well, then I know you'll do a good job.' She couldn't get away fast enough!"

We both hooted so loud, a couple of folks a booth over were looking at us like we had lost it. We brought it down a notch.

"I think this summer is going to be a blast," she said.

"Me too."

CHAPTER TWO

In the afternoon, I settled into finishing up another five hundred stack sorting job. For some reason, Jasmine didn't seem too happy when I returned the sorted papers from this morning. Was I too fast? Right away, she unceremoniously dumped another pile in my arms. No problem. I was already through the first one hundred when all of sudden, a hush came over the room. All typing and low chatter ceased.

The outside glass door opened and in came a tall, good-looking guy with dark hair followed immediately by three other guys. They all had on dark suits, but the first guy had on a custom Armani suit. I spotted it right away due to the fashion magazines Layla insisted I look through. Looking a little closer, the men following him seemed to be either security or his assistants. I think I spotted a few walkie-talkies. They were speaking in hushed tones as they surveyed the area. The main guy seemed to be giving instructions to the others who were furiously writing them down.

Out of the corner of my eye, I spotted Jasmine flipping her hair and preening in her seat. Was she...trying to get his attention? Laugh out loud. As I zeroed in, I could see her batting her eyelashes - and he wasn't even looking in her direction. Was she serious?

I refocused on my work until the men came closer to my station. My eyes shifted and I saw that main guy's shoes were sleek and expensive as opposed to the others which looked a bit scuffed. When I looked up, I was face to face with the most gorgeous man I had ever seen.

If I thought he was good-looking from a distance, it couldn't begin to compare up close. He was at least six foot three with dark, curly hair, a swarthy complexion and a strong, chiseled jawbone. I couldn't help but notice his high cheek bones, perfectly sculpted dark brows, full, pouty lips and his dimpled chin. It also seemed as if he had a muscular, athletic build under his suit as indicated by his broad shoulders. His eyes centered directly on me at this time. They were darker than hazel but lighter than regular brown. I would call them chestnut brown. And they were cold as ice.

He seemed to look right through me and directly at my soul. It was so unexpected that I was startled and I quickly looked back down at my work. Um, what was his deal? That was weird. When I ventured to look back up, the men were moving on to survey another area or whatever they were doing. Meanwhile, nobody in the office was moving a muscle. Except Jasmine, of course. She was turned completely around facing them while pretending to be looking at a document on her lap. Sadly, they still had their backs turned away. How desperate could you be? The men were oblivious to her siren call and within a minute, they smoothly exited. Chatter began as soon as they left. I was curious. I didn't have to wait long.

"OMG, he is gorgeous, who was that?" gushed Samantha, a new intern.

"Well, I guess you all would find out sooner or later," Jasmine stated in a loud, snobbish tone. "He is James Jansen III, heir to the Jansen Worldwide Capital fortune and acting CEO. He's worth a quarter of a billion dollars and completely off limits to the likes of you. He's engaged," she said with what I detected was a slightly disappointed tone. Apparently, I wasn't the only one.

"Hey, Jasmine, that means he's off limits to you, too!" Darren taunted, which had the office in titters. I silently giggled because she deserved it. What she said was nasty and unnecessary.

She waved her hand in dismissal. "Whatever...I meant you interns..."

As I got back to work, I thought about my brief eye contact with this James Jansen guy. He seemed to have a distinctive effect on people. Not just because of his wealth or status - after all, I didn't know who he was at first. I believe it had something to do with his eyes. They were so spellbinding, like they could penetrate your very being. It's hard to describe, but they were cold and intense at the same time. I was intrigued.

§

The next few days were relatively the same. Teresa and I had lunch somewhere new every day that week. We were trying to determine which places would become our regulars. Most of the food was absolutely delicious, yet a bit pricey. I could appreciate Teresa's upbringing because even though she came from an affluent family, her parents raised her to be practical and self-sufficient. After all, she still didn't have her own car. She told me her father always preached, "That's my grandfather's money, not mine," so they gave her a modest allowance like I received. I was thinking maybe we should bring our lunch on some days. But this week, it appeared we were splurging.

I couldn't help but think about James Jansen, periodically.

For some reason I had been curious about where he worked in the building and what he was up to. I mentioned him to Teresa.

"Have you seen the acting CEO of JWC yet?"

"Yes, he's *fine*, right? I heard a few things about him."

"Oh, like what?" I asked casually, when inside, I was bursting to find out more information.

"I heard he's twenty-nine, engaged to the heiress of Sampson Electronics, Lorelei Sampson. That she's called 'The Ice Princess' in inner circles because she's rumored to be frigid - that he cheats on her constantly and they can't stand each other, and that their marriage is actually going to be a merger of sorts between their entities."

"Wow," I said in awe, "you found out a lot." I leaned forward, clasping my hands under my chin. "What else?"

"That's about it. He works up on the fortieth floor and they're priming him for takeover because his father, President Jim Jansen, is about to retire. That's why James has been more visible recently. I heard he's making changes to the aesthetic of Jansen - hates the way it's designed."

"Really? Where do you hear this stuff?"

"My mom knows some things and..." she paused and smiled.

"And?" I asked impatiently.

Teresa laughed. "Well, I guess when I checked Amanda that day, I gained her respect. She tells me all of the inside scoop. She's actually pretty cool now."

"Shut up!" We both cracked up.

§

On my way back to the office from lunch, I was running a little later than usual. I wasn't looking forward to seeing

Jasmine's face scrutinize me and the clock like she'd been doing all week. I knew she'd been keeping an eye on me, but I usually didn't have to worry because I was typically impeccable with my time.

As I was rushing through the lobby of JWC, I forcefully bumped shoulders with a large frame while trying to make it to the elevator before it closed.

I knew it was rude, so I mumbled a low, "Sorry," and kept going.

I didn't make it.

"Shoot," I whisper-shouted. I was so embarrassed because whoever I just hit noticed I didn't make it. No doubt, I would be confronted by them. I looked straight ahead at the elevator and waited. I was hoping they wouldn't say anything, although I knew I should sincerely apologize. *Yes, Merci, that's the right thing to do*, I told my-

"Excuse me, miss, you need to make sure you're on time so you won't have to rush off and *kill* everyone in the process," a deep, almost baritone voice drawled softly from behind.

I meekly turned around to offer an apology and was shocked to find that it was none other than James Jansen III, in the flesh. He was staring down at me through flat, unfathomable eyes. At this point, I was so completely mortified I couldn't speak, but I quickly tried to recover. I was usually cooler than this.

He looked at me expectantly, his chestnut eyes arctic cold. Involuntarily, I shivered.

"I'm so sorry. Yes, you're right. I didn't leave from lunch on time and I surely don't want to *kill* anyone." Acknowledging his authority, I added, "sir," as I remembered he would be the "big boss" soon.

Still regarding me coolly, he seemed to really take a look

at me for the first time. I wanted to look away from his disconcerting eyes which were vacillating between impassive and intensity, but I couldn't. Then, they flickered as he seemed to settle something in his mind. He walked up to me closely. All I could do was look up at his ethereally handsome, clean-shaven, chiseled face as he towered over me, even in the three and a half inch heels I had on today. My heart was beating so fast I was sure he could hear it, but I stared back with resolve. I would not wither under his intimidating glare, I told myself. He smelled so good, though. The hairs on my arm stood up and I couldn't breathe. His eyes...

Then he did something totally unexpected. He smiled. He was beautiful. His eyes thawed marginally and he chuckled. He had the whitest, straightest teeth. *He really should be in Colgate commercials,* I thought.

Still too close for my sanity, he said, "Just make sure you get back on time, Miss...?"

"Townsend," I stepped back a bit and offered my hand, "Merci Townsend." I was proud of how confident I sounded.

He looked down at my hand for a moment and took it in his. Not shaking it, just holding it. My smaller one was engulfed in his cool one, yet I was on fire.

"Merci Townsend," he said slowly, as if testing it out. "That is a unique name. Okay, Merci Townsend, I'm James."

Oh, I know, I know... Of course I played it off.

"Nice to meet you, James," I managed rather smoothly. He slowly let go of my hand. I noticed he intentionally omitted his last name. Probably because he figured I knew who he was.

The elevator came back and we got on. I pushed thirty-one and he pushed forty. We rode in a totally awkward silence on my part. I glanced at him from under my eyelashes and he, on the other hand, looked totally relaxed. He was silent and looking straight ahead. As I exited at my floor, I expected him to say bye, at least. Nothing.

§

My lateness completely disregarded, I walked to my desk pondering his odd behavior. Jasmine piped up and caught me off guard.

"Merci, please be on time coming from lunch," she sang without looking up.

I muttered, "Okay."

Was she my boss? Not formally, but evidently, she felt entitled to be in charge of us lowly interns. Whatever. My brain was too scattered to give her any more thought. I was still frazzled by my encounter with James Jansen III.

After working for a half an hour, an email came in. My heart rate triple-timed when I saw who it was from.

To: Merci Townsend
From: James Jansen III
Subject:
If you have any problems with anyone due to your tardiness, let me know.

What? Oh my goodness, how should I respond?

To: James Jansen III
From: Merci Townsend
Subject: Re:
I will. Thank you, sir.

I didn't know what else to say so I left it at that. I couldn't believe the future CEO just emailed me. He remembered my name. I waited but heard nothing back. Well, what *would* he say after that?

Teresa was meeting a relative after work, so I rode home on the train alone. I contemplated my exchange with James today. What made him decide to be somewhat cordial after reprimanding me, cold on the elevator, and back to cordial through email? Was he crazy? I thought that this was a distinct possibility. I continued to speculate on what his problem might be all the way to campus.

As I neared my stop, another theory surfaced. Could he possibly be interested in me? I was looking pretty decent today in a fitting, black knit-weave pencil skirt and a conservatively low-cut cream, chiffon blouse with faux pearls to match. My thick hair was slicked back in a chignon; I wore light coral lipstick to look natural, but played up my eyes in a light, smoky effect…

Get real, Merci. Yeah, I looked okay, but there were way more glamorous girls at the company than me. For instance; although a nut - Jasmine was a gorgeous redhead. Jessica was blonde and slim like a swimsuit model. So no, I didn't think he was interested since, in my opinion, there were more viable options right under his nose. Plus, although a rumored player, he was engaged. I couldn't figure him out…

CHAPTER THREE

The next week, I didn't run into James at all. I tried to erase all encounters and write them off as weird, meaningless exchanges. However, I couldn't lie that I didn't check my email occasionally hoping for more correspondence. Maybe he was out of town. Should I have emailed him a lengthier response? Why was I thinking about him at all? *He's engaged and not interested in you, sweetie - move on.* I'm not interested in him, just curious. I couldn't believe this guy was making me talk to myself.

After a week and a half of busy work, Lance asked if I was interested in going to lunch with a few fellow interns. Teresa was working through her lunch today, so I agreed. We went to California Pizza Kitchen, located further north off Michigan Ave. Four of us were eating at a booth when none other than James Jansen walked in to the take-out counter. He had on a charcoal grey suit, white crisp shirt - open, no tie. My, he was *hot*. As he was waiting, he was checking his watch and looking at his phone. After a minute as he was grabbing his bag to go, he glanced in our direction. No one else seemed to have spotted him but me. He was stock-still for a moment, staring at me with those...eyes and began purposely making his way over in our direction. *What the?* Finally spotted by the others, they fell silent and then piped up together.

"Hello, Mr. Jansen."

He glanced over the group as if just becoming aware of their presence.

"Hello, how are you guys?" He didn't smile and didn't look like he really wanted an answer. He was so cold.

Samantha, who had a dreamy look on her face, answered first, "Fine, just like you - I mean," she sputtered, "fine, *how are* you?" The others laughed. I looked down.

"Great." Then just like that, he was taking off. "You all take care." Pausing, he turned around and his incomprehensible eyes zeroed in on me. With a nod, he acknowledged, "Ms. Townsend." And then, he was out the door.

The group was in shock and I was extremely uncomfortable.

Then, it began.

"Ooh, Merci, he knows your name!"

"Girl, you must be next on his list."

"He has never spoken to us before."

I warded off their innuendos and speculations with a shrug.

"I literally ran into him last week and he's just being friendly," I explained.

"He is never friendly and especially never speaks to anyone on our level or even in our department," Lance said. In deep deliberation, he raised a finger. "He must want something."

"I'm telling you, you're next..." Darren teased. "I heard he is a major playa and what dude wants - dude gets."

"Puh-leaze," I countered.

§

The next few days passed uneventfully, which was fine with

me, I told myself. Teasing from the others regarding James had quieted since we hadn't seen him around.

Being early to work this morning, Teresa and I decided to go to Starbucks to get drinks. We stood in front of Jansen Worldwide, chatting, drinking and joking before going up. While laughing, I noticed a black limousine sitting on the corner. My eyes lingered as I wondered if the limo belonged to James or somebody like his father. Of course since the windows were tinted, I couldn't see who was in there, if anyone. Teresa and I turned away and headed in to work.

As I was quickly sorting another stack of invoices, my computer let me know with a ghostly apparition that I had an email. Expecting more tasks from Jasmine and Jessica, I clicked.

To: Merci Townsend
From: James Jansen III
Subject: Assistance Needed
Please come up to our 40th floor offices right away. My assistant and I require your help.

What? Why did he want me? I was totally confused and a little nervous.

To: James Jansen III
From Merci Townsend
Subject: Re: Assistance Needed
Okay, I'll be right up.

I really had no choice but to do what the future big boss said. I pulled out my compact to straighten my hair and apply fresh lipstick. I grabbed a legal pad, pen and my key card to get back in the office. As I passed by, Jasmine looked curious as to where I was going. I guess I needed to tell someone.

"I've been summoned upstairs to the executive offices by Mr. Jansen to assist him and his assistant."

"Really? President Jansen called and requested you?" She asked, her expression one of a deer in headlights.

"No, Mr. Jansen III emailed and requested me."

If possible, her eyes bugged out even more in disbelief. It was comical to see.

"What? James Jansen emailed *you*?"

"Yes, and I better not keep him waiting," At this point I was getting exasperated because I was already a bit nervous. I really didn't need this now. "I just wanted to let someone know in case anyone was looking for me."

I waited a moment for her reply, but she was stunned into silence. As I walked away, I could feel her eyes shooting daggers into my back, so giving her a taste of her own medicine, I swayed my hips in retaliation. She was obviously mad it wasn't her, but really - I didn't know what was going on - just following orders.

Once in the elevator, I got nervous again. I was reminded of the last time we were in here together. Once I reached the fortieth floor and the doors opened, it was like being at another company altogether. All of the surrounding areas were decorated in deep walnut accented with blue. I noticed there were three sections with huge walnut double doors that went all the way to the high ceiling. I walked across the foyer towards a large matching desk where there sat a lovely woman in her sixties with cat eye glasses. Her grey, streaked hair was pulled severely into a bun and her makeup was perfection. Did she use that new air brush makeup? She looked up at me expectantly, although indifferently.

Speaking through bright, pink lips, she said, "Hello, you must be Merci, whom Mr. Jansen is expecting."

I took a deep breath to calm down. No need to get ruffled about whatever this was.

"Yes, thank you," I answered brightly. "How are you?" I smiled as she seemed to consider my question while tilting her head to the side as if to study me. Her face softened. What? People didn't ask how others were doing up here? Slowly, she smiled.

"I'm fine, thank you. My name is Marguerite." Marguerite stood and came from behind the massive desk. She was barely taller than when she was sitting and was dressed smartly in a light grey suit.

"Hi, Marguerite," I said.

"Come right this way, Merci."

She led me to the left set of double wood doors. As she opened them, I was braced to see James Jansen, but apparently this still wasn't his office. A young man in his mid twenties was standing behind a large desk. There were papers and boxes everywhere around him. He was about five foot seven and had stylishly cut blonde hair. Super Cuts? He was dressed in one of those tight fitting suits that I'd seen male models in fashion shows wear nowadays. He had on long, pointed shoes that looked a bit outrageous in contrast to the tight fit at the bottom of his pants. For all of the physical work he had to do, he didn't look too comfortable. He eyed me with curiosity first, then a look that I couldn't identify - but it wasn't a pleased one. I began to doubt myself. I knew my clothes weren't as fabulous as his, but I thought I was looking alright today. My thick hair was down and a bit on the wild side, but most of the time it worked. I wore a wine red lip color and had given my eyes a smokier look than usual. My grey and black leather, Rachel

Roy shift dress showed off my long legs. On my feet were my coveted, four-inch knock off, Louboutin Lillian triple-buckle pumps. Wait, did he know? Finally, his look was one of resignation. He sighed. Geez, did I look incompetent?

Marguerite turned to me as she introduced us. "Jairus, this is Merci. She will be helping you with the invitations for the big gala coming up for James."

"Hello," he greeted with saccharine cheerfulness. Looking elsewhere, he grabbed another chair.

"Hi, Jairus," I greeted.

He wrinkled his nose and said, "Just call me J.J. Only Marguerite can get away with that." Marguerite grinned at him and left.

"Okay, J.J." He looked at me and managed a fake smile.

"Okay, Merci, you can sit here and help me stuff these invites. I heard you were pretty fast and we have a lot of them, so let's get cracking."

I hurriedly sat down and started stuffing. They obviously didn't play around up here. How did they know I was fast? Was somebody watching me other than Jasmine and reporting back to James? I was actually a little creeped-out by this revelation.

J.J. and I worked silently but comfortably for about an hour. I noticed it was already after one. Teresa! I peeked around the office between stuffings and noticed another set of huge double doors across the room. Where did that lead? Just in that moment, the door opened and out stepped James.

"Ms. Townsend," he stated with an unreadable expression. Did I detect a twinkle?

At that moment, I could feel J.J. eyeing us back and forth. I guess he was wondering what the connection was.

"Hello, Mr. Jansen."

"James. You can call me James." From the corner of my eye I could see J.J.'s neck rolling in question. He wasn't discreet with his expressions at all.

"And please, call me Merci. Hello, James." I smiled brightly. His eyes narrowed and penetrated my soul. I forced myself not to look away. I wasn't going to be intimidated by all of that beauty and power. He was human like everyone else.

He had on a dark blue suit today, crisp white shirt - no tie. I don't think he liked ties very much. He was so handsome. His curly hair looked damp like he just got out of a shower. Not possible, right? His eyes looked slightly red but it didn't matter - he was ridiculously hot. For a second, James looked around like he wasn't sure why he came out of his office.

As if suddenly remembering, he snapped his finger and said, "Merci, may I see you in my office a moment?"

"Sure."

He walked back into his office. J.J. was looking at me in such perplexity I thought his head was going to explode. I got up and followed James through the double doors.

Now, this was nice. His office was furnished with what looked like state of the art everything. There was no walnut anywhere to be seen. Actually, I think his huge desk was some type of metal. His entire office looked like it was straight from *Architectural Digest* with a couple of white leather sofas accented with deep red pillows, a mounted flat screen, cool looking red chairs, glass end tables, a wood linear cabinet, and walls that were a warm pewter gold color which made the red subtly pop. Of course, one wall was nothing but window that was separated into panes, ceiling to floor. The view of Lake Michigan was spectacular. There was also another door. Could that be a bathroom? I liked this space because even though it was modern, it wasn't stark like a lot of other contemporary spaces could be with no warmth. He even had a huge potted tree in here. I couldn't help my admiration.

"Wow, this is really nice."

James turned around in casual surprise at my comment. With a raised brow, his gaze slowly traveled the length of me and back up to my face. I was determined not to squirm. He studied me for a moment and his eyes, usually passive, actually lit up a bit.

"I see you have an eye for taste. Glad you like it, I designed it."

Oh, that's right. He was looking to change the design of JWC when he takes over. Teresa said he hated the interior design. I was impressed.

"You did a good job, Mr. Jansen - I mean…James."

"Thank you." Did his eyes twinkle again? He sat down behind his desk and motioned for me to sit. The cold mask reappeared.

"I requested your assistance because I inquired into your job performance so far and the managers are impressed with your speed and efficiency. Of course they don't know of your disastrous, tardy lunch day like I do, but that's of no consequence."

Was that an attempt at a joke? I was about to give an awkward giggle, but he wasn't smiling.

He continued. "I've been here steadily now for about six months and we need good help. J.J., as you can see, is swamped. Please assist him or me with whatever tasks we need. You will report up here from now on. We are in the process of having a desk moved out there for you. I've already informed the managers you were assisting that you will be assigned here immediately. I know that won't be a problem, right?"

Was he really expecting me to disagree with him? I knew my mouth was slightly open in shock at the dramatic shift in my tectonic plates, so I quickly closed it. *Be cool, Merci.*

"No, it won't be a problem." I hesitated. "I have a question, though." He eyed me with a bit of surprise. What? I had the audacity to ask questions? I was thinking about Teresa now. "Will I still have the same lunch hour?"

He looked thrown off. "What is your lunch hour now?"

"From one to two."

"You will be taking lunch depending on your work flow - we have deadlines to meet so be prepared to be flexible."

I tried to hide my disappointment but I think he noticed. Was it just me or did he seem really irritated now? His eyes were back to frigid. He looked down at some papers.

"Alright, that will be all," he dismissed.

"Okay." I hopped up and was out of there quick. What was his problem?

CHAPTER FOUR

When I returned, J.J. was eyeing me dubiously with a small frown. I decided to get this settled once and for all. Since I was going to be up here, I didn't need the unwarranted tension. It would be bad enough dealing with James Jansen's mercurial moods.

I smiled. "J.J., is there a problem?"

Surprised at my direct question and tone, his ears turned pink as he stuttered, "Um, no - no. Why do you ask?"

"J.J., you're clearly not happy I'm up here, and I need to know what's going on. I'm not one to play guessing games and since I'm going to be up here with you for a while, let's get the truth out." He looked startled for a moment and then seemed to relax.

"Alright, you are way cooler than I thought. I'm not really upset you're here. I really need help, but I'm just wondering what's up with him," he eyed James's office, "since this has never happened before. I've needed help for the last six months, and now all of sudden he chooses you – no offense - an intern who will, most likely, be leaving. You're still in school, right?" I nodded. "Other assistants from downstairs have been trying to get up here for months. I'm just wondering why, that's all. No hard feelings, okay?"

"Yeah, I find it strange just as much as you, so let me know what you find out." I giggled and J.J. laughed along with me. Maybe we might be able to get along, after all. He looked at his designer watch.

"Merci, you can go to lunch now and we can finish when you get back. Also, make sure to stop by your floor and get your stuff. You may even have a desk by then." He laughed.

"Okay, great." I smiled and left.

Once outside, I went right around the corner to a 7-Eleven convenience store to grab a sandwich. I thought about texting Teresa, but I didn't want to take the chance of getting her busted if her phone wasn't on vibrate. We hadn't discussed texting etiquette for work, yet.

While I was looking in the fridge to pick a sandwich, out of the window I could see a sleek, black limo facing Michigan Avenue. Was it the same limo from this morning? A driver popped out to quickly open the door for a man arriving. The man was James. He straightened his jacket lapels before climbing in the back. The driver closed the door. Wow, he was really big time. Since I didn't think I could be seen, I stood there waiting for it to pull off. It didn't.

After a moment, the back door abruptly opened and James stepped back out. He looked a bit ruffled and impatient. As he tried to close the door, a small but shapely leg with *real* Louboutin shoes kicked out to stop it. A very angry blonde woman climbed out. She was short, even in her heels, dressed in what I believed was a pink Chanel dress suit with a fur stole - in the summer? Her hair was piled into some elaborate style reminiscent of the eighties, she had on tons of makeup and her red lips were in a tight, straight line. Boy, was she pissed. I guess she was attractive, but her scowl wasn't helping me detect a trace of beauty. She was repeatedly pushing her finger into James's chest while he stood there like a marble statue, absolutely unmoved. Feeling real nosy, I moved closer to the window to see what

I could hear. These windows were tinted, right? I could hear her shouting but couldn't make out what she was saying. Darn.

After another minute, James continued looking down at her angry, red, blotchy face with his now infamous blank stare. I chuckled. I was pretty sure that infuriated her more. I was glued to the window when suddenly, James's head swiveled sharply in my direction like the zombie from the horror movie that suddenly spots you. Yikes! Could he see me? I backed away as quickly as I could. His gaze turned back to her and I thought I was safe. I really needed to get out of here just in case he saw me.

I turned back to the fridge and grabbed any sandwich and a diet soda. When I snuck a peek back out the window, James, the tiny woman and the limo were gone. Did he get back in? I wasn't going to worry about it. I decided I would return to the building to eat in the cafeteria on my old floor and then I could get my stuff. As I exited the store, James was waiting right outside with his arms folded, leaning against a light pole. Dangit, I was busted.

He was staring at me in expectation. Apparently, I needed to speak first?

"Hi, James."

I didn't know what else to say. With his tall frame and tightened jaw, he made quite the imposing figure. His eyes were especially frosty now. Well, that was his problem. I didn't do anything wrong. I couldn't help it if his crazy woman went off on him. This was a public area. I was getting upset now. This wasn't some silly romance novel and I wasn't going to be intimidated by this blood and flesh man.

"So, I guess you got a little show?" he asked.

I tried to keep my face blank. "I don't know what you're

talking about," I deadpanned.

"Merci, I know you saw what transpired. Let me explain-"

"Oh, you don't need to - none of my business, sir." I gave him a cheerful smile and turned to walk towards our building. Once I was facing away, I let out a huge grin. My first name sounded so lovely coming from his lips...

"Wait," he commanded. I halted and looked back at him. Was his cool actually broken? He looked exasperated and his eyes were a stormy brown. I wasn't sure what this look was, but it was a new one. Why did he want to explain to me? Who was I? I waited.

His eyes implored. "What you saw, please don't spread it around."

Oh, that's what he was worried about?

"I'm not like that, Mr. Jansen...James. I didn't really see anything anyway," I lied. Well, that was partially the truth. I certainly couldn't hear anything...

He smirked doubtfully but then seemed to be satisfied with my reply. "Good. I need my assistants to be discreet and keep our upstairs matters confidential."

"No problem."

I wanted to ask him so badly to verify who she was but I'm not supposed to have seen anything, right? He was staring again and I felt a bit uncomfortable. Did he want to say something else?

"That was my fiancée', Lorelei Sampson. Just so you know." His eyes were intently searching as if he was trying to gauge my reaction. I didn't get it.

I feigned friendly indifference. "Oh, okay."

The mask was back up and he turned to walk towards the doors of the building. I wasn't about to look like a fool trying to catch up with him, so I let him go through the doors first. As I entered a moment later, he was inside walking slowly.

He looked my way and motioned for me to catch up. He was all business, so I walked swiftly.

"After you finish lunch, make sure you bring your belongings. You won't be returning."

Why did that sound so ominous?

"Alright."

He stared again as we entered the elevator.

Before I was able, he pushed buttons thirty-one and forty. I smiled in thanks. Silence was a bit awkward again, but I wasn't as bothered this time. I never could tell which way he was coming from. James was looking straight ahead as if in deep thought. I decided to check out his profile on the sly. He reminded me of the profile of Michelangelo's *David*. Curly dark hair scattered every which way, but still in place. How did he achieve that? His strong nose, pouty lips, strong chin and prominent cheekbones were a work of art. As always, he smelled good. And he looked like he had a fantastic body. Did he workout? Good lord, he was sexy. As they said nowadays, he was *making me feel some type of way*. I shook my head hard internally, looked away and tried to get a hold of myself. I refused to be affected by this other woman's man. Although, I revisited, she didn't deserve him...

I questioned myself again. *Who are you kidding, Merci, he is not interested in you.* Well, why was he explaining himself? *You are now one of his assistants and must keep matters on the hush- hush. Did you not hear him?* Yes, that's right. Back to reality.

I exited thirty-one and like before, he didn't say a word. Well, neither was I. Rude jerk.

§

Heading to my desk, I saw a surly Jasmine giving me the eye. I gave her my best smile while she rolled her eyes and looked away. Pshh, whatever - I was leaving. As I gathered my belongings, Lance leaned over into my cubicle.

"Hey, I heard you're going up to the executive offices."

"Yep, how did you know?"

"That's all anyone's been talking about since you left. I guess somebody up there informed one of the managers down here. Are you going to be working with James?"

I continued gathering my things, not really looking at him. I knew this was leading to something.

"Looks that way," I said noncommittally.

"I should've known after he paid special attention to you at CPK, that something was up. By the way, this has Jasmine hot. I heard she's been trying to get up there, in any capacity, for the last six months. She's so pissed that an 'intern,'" he finger quoted, "is going up there to help his assistant out. I heard her ranting and asking Jessica, just what does he see in you."

I shrugged. "Well, I was told it was my efficiency with the invoices *she* gave me, so it's her fault. You can tell her that, too." I snickered. "She can go up there after I'm gone. It's not like I'm going to be here that long. She needs to chill."

He laughed and turned to leave. "Alright, Merci, call me if you need anything. You have my extension. Don't be a stranger when it comes to lunch either."

I smiled sincerely. He was really cool. "Okay, thanks Lance. Whenever I get a chance, we can definitely still do lunch."

As I was leaving, Darren, who was leaning back in his chair, grabbed my free hand. Looking at his sorry, puppy dog face, I laughed and snatched it back.

"I'm gonna miss you, girl. Don't get into nothing you're

not supposed to," he warned.

I giggled some more and kept walking.

"I'll see you around, Darren."

§

Back upstairs, as promised, I had a new desk that was situated on the adjacent wall of J.J.'s. After I stored my belongings and got settled, J.J. happily provided me with three more boxes of invitations to stuff.

He smiled genuinely. "It's so nice to have help! I'm glad you're here, Merc."

Oh no, he was already using my nickname?

"Glad to help, J.J."

We worked silently for the next few hours until five o'clock. I expected to see James again, but according to J.J., he'd been holed up in his office since he returned from lunch. Oh well, fine with me. I was out of there.

§

On the train, I apologized to Teresa for not being able to notify her about lunch. I told her about my staff change, the episode at lunch, and the reaction from my old area, including Jasmine. She listened raptly with mouth and eyes wide open.

Afterwards she said, "Wow, you've had some day. I was wondering where you were for lunch."

"I figured you would be. Sorry."

"No, that's no problem. I know if you went up there, it was hard to do anything except what they told you to do. You're up there with the big dogs. I'm sure it was scary."

"Yeah, a little, but after a while his assistant, J.J., was

cool."

"What about James?"

"The jury is still out on him." I laughed evasively.

Teresa smirked. "You know what I think? Even though it's not cool since he's engaged - I think he likes you."

"No way. I saw his fiancée'- she's all glamorous. Why would he like me? I'm probably too young for him anyway."

Frowning, she contemplated this. "You don't look nineteen, more like twenty-two or twenty-three. Maybe he doesn't know."

I chuckled, thinking about how he found out I was efficient, my email, etc.

"Um…he seems like the type who knows everything."

§

As the next week went by, I quickly got accustomed to my new surroundings. Marguerite warmly greeted me each morning, and I found out that J.J. and I had a few things in common since he also originated from the New England area. We worked well in companionable silence most of the time. I didn't see James, though. According to J. J., he was away on a business trip and wouldn't be returning until next week.

That following Monday, as I settled in at my desk, I received an email.

To: Merci Townsend
From: James Jansen III
Subject: Lunch
Please plan on having a business lunch at 12:30 today. We will meet downstairs in the lobby.

He could at least greet me instead of just barking out orders, right?

To: James Jansen III
From: Merci Townsend
Subject: RE: Lunch
Hello, James. Alright, I'll be there.

I didn't hear back. About an hour later and before I could look up, James whisked out of the office so quick I didn't get a glimpse, leaving only a waft of his expensive cologne. I loved that scent. I continued with my work, which included more envelope stuffing, until it was time to get ready for lunch. I assumed J.J. was coming along, but he wasn't moving.

"J.J., are you coming to the business lunch?"

He raised his eyebrows high. "What business lunch?"

"James said that we were having a business lunch at twelve thirty."

J.J. smirked and waved a hand. "I know nothing about it. There is nothing about it on his calendar and I don't think I'm invited. You go ahead." Then, looking me up and down, gave me a knowing smile.

I shrugged since I didn't know what was going on, nor did I want to play into whatever J.J. was suggesting.

Nonchalantly, I said, "Well, I'll see you later."

CHAPTER FIVE

In the elevator, I thought about the fact that obviously, this was a lunch between only James and myself. What did he want to discuss? I was just an intern. Now anxious, I checked my appearance in the reflection of the elevator. I had on a beige, sleeveless peplum blouse that cinched at the waist and black, pleated cuffed pants with black four-inch pumps. I straightened out my hair which was down again today and quickly reapplied lipstick. Barely finished before the elevator opened, I quickly stuffed my compact back into my purse. He said to meet him in the lobby, so he could be right outside these doors. Why was I worried about this?

I didn't see him until I rounded the corner from the elevator corridor. He was leaning against a marble pillar, checking his phone, and he hadn't spotted me yet. He had on a grey, double breasted tweed suit with matching vest and a scarlet tie. There was not a curly hair out of place. Man, he looked good. I smiled and tried to walk confidently in his direction. As I approached, he finally looked up. For some reason, I expected his look to be…welcoming at least, since I knew he really didn't do *nice*. It wasn't. His eyes were as remote as ever when they assessed me. Did I foolishly think he would be pleased to see me, like I was him? I came to my senses and reminded myself that this was a business lunch like he said, nothing more. I was relieved I had the foresight to stuff a writing pad into my bag. *No more fantasies, Merci.* He looked all business.

Once I reached him, he turned to walk towards the exit.

"Ready?" James asked in a detached voice, not bothering to look at me as he strode purposely towards the outside doors. I really didn't think he cared for a response as I attempted to catch up.

"Ready," I replied in a voice to match his. I could be just as funky as him.

We hopped in a taxi which sped us through the downtown streets. No driver today? While ignoring me and checking his phone, I was turned towards the windows trying to enjoy scenery I hadn't seen before. I tried to look up to see how high some of the skyscrapers reached, yet I couldn't see the top of most of them. They were huge. We arrived at a beautiful restaurant on LaSalle Avenue called Fogo de Chão, which I remembered was a Brazilian steakhouse I wanted to check out with Teresa.

Once seated inside the warm, comfortable ambiance, I took out my pad and pen. Across from me, James was still checking his phone. Two could play this game. I took out my phone and started going through it, not really looking at anything in particular. A server arrived and asked us if we wanted something to drink. I ordered a lemonade as James waved his hand dismissively while still preoccupied with his phone. Picking up on his attitude, the server turned to me and asked if we needed a few more minutes. I smiled apologetically and told her yes. After she left, I decided I was very hungry, but was slightly disconcerted to see that the two black books to the side were drink menus that contained an extensive list of wines and Brazilian cocktails.

"Get whatever you want," he said, not looking at me.

"Thank you, but I don't want anything to drink." My stomach quietly rumbled. "I am hungry though," I mused aloud, smiling at the aroma in the air in anticipation. "What about you?" I asked, since he didn't seem interested in anything but his phone.

He gazed at me for a moment before answering. "I already know what I want." He stared a few more seconds and looked back at his phone. *Huh?*

"Okay."

Determined not to consider that his words may have had a double meaning, I resumed blindly staring at the menu. At this point, I was done trying to figure out James Jansen.

I eyed the salad bar, which was humongous and I couldn't wait to dig in. After a few minutes, the server came back with my drink and explained the dining experience at Fogo de Chão. James was still busy with his phone while she informed *me* about all of the different selections at the salad bar. She gave us cute little round green cards to turn up after we were done so that tableside service could begin with a choice of fine meats. I was uncomfortable with his behavior, although the server seemed to take it in stride. She was probably used to rude business people. After she left, I wheeled on James who was still casually looking at his phone. What was his problem?

"Excuse me, sir," his eyes jumped up, no doubt prompted by my curtness and form of address," is everything okay?"

He looked at me closely as if trying to discern my mood. "Yes, everything is fine. I've been here countless times and my mind is on other things. Please, don't mind me. I'm not that hungry." He dismissed and continued with his phone.

"Alright."

Happy with an explanation at least, I went to the salad bar and filled up my plate. Out of curiosity, I decided to look around to see what he was doing. When my eyes fell on him, to my surprise, he was looking directly at me. Our eyes locked and I quickly turned away, but not before I spotted the way his eyes smoldered.

What was that?

Still determined not to read into anything, I came back to the table where the server had returned to ask if James wanted a drink now. He ordered a scotch on ice. Drinking during the work day? I wasn't going to acknowledge anything, so I dug into my salad. Soon, I became accustomed to his stony silence and was very much enjoying my food. James continued to check his phone and sip his drink. After my salad was done, I flipped over the card as instructed and pretty soon another server came over and showed us a selection of meats. My stomach protested. Deciding I was stuffed from the enormous salad bar, I politely declined and turned my card back over to red.

"Are you sure, this is the best part of the dining experience," James murmured after the server left, still checking his phone. Was he a bit tipsy?

"No, thanks, I can't eat another drop. What about you?"

"No, I'm satisfied." I didn't bother to figure out what he meant.

"Ok, let's get down to business," he said. Surprised, I quickly grabbed my pen to begin taking notes.

"As you may have heard, I'm taking over my father, Jim Jansen's position in a few months. He rarely comes in these days, so I've been very busy. What I would like to concentrate on is redesigning the office space where you and J.J. work. Eventually, the entire space up on forty will be remodeled, and soon, the entire firm."

As I furiously scribbled, I couldn't help but be amazed that this was what our "business lunch" was about. For some reason, I thought he'd be asking me to take notes regarding some small company JWC wanted to fund, or something like that. I was still learning what, exactly, the company did. So far, I knew they were a business development company or a (BDC), **that** were special investment vehicles designed to facilitate capital formation for small and middle-market companies.

"So what I would like for you to do, Merci, is correspond with the design firms listed on the contact list I'll be emailing you soon. I'll need us to start ordering materials and I want you to be in charge of making sure we get the samples. Once the orders are made, you'll be making certain they arrive in our warehouse expediently and be a liaison between me and the design firms."

Wow, I was flabbergasted. This seemed pretty important. I was still confused as to why J.J. wasn't entrusted with this duty. Apparently, J.J. handled all of the other duties that actually dealt with company business.

Picking up on my confusion, he added, "I chose you for this since you seemed to appreciate interior design."

"That's true, I do. Thank you." I beamed and looked at him expectantly, waiting for him to continue. He gazed back at me, not saying anything. He began studying my hair, my face, and then down to my blouse.

After an uncomfortable minute, I cleared my throat. "Alright, is there anything else?"

He leaned back some and draped his arm over the back of the booth. He was still staring. He looked very relaxed now and I knew the alcohol had something to do with it.

"Nope. That's it for now." His chestnut eyes were way too intense, so I looked away.

"Okay." I started rifling through my bag to escape his powerful magnetism.

"So, Merci," he took a languid sip, "how have your lunches been going since you moved upstairs? I remember you were very concerned about your lunch hour. Did you coordinate with your...boyfriend?"

What? I was stunned how he went from business to personal in zero to sixty. I stopped what I was doing and looked pointedly at him. His eyes were intently curious.

"Boyfriend? I don't have a boyfriend." His eyes lost a bit of its intensity. "Oh, you're thinking about Lance or Darren. No, they are just my fellow interns," I explained.

It just occurred to me that with Lance sitting next to me and Darren next to Samantha at CPK, we might've appeared "coupled up." I hoped I didn't sound too eager to correct him, either. Taking another swig, he seemed to loosen up even more. Glass in one hand, his eyes continued to openly assess me. Boldly, I stared back. This time, he was the first to look away. He shook his head infinitesimally and I thought I heard him mutter *too young*. I could've been wrong, but now, the mask was back.

"Alright - sounds good." He thumped the empty tumbler on the table in finality. "Please be prepared to have these lunches with me periodically, so that we can discuss materials, progress, etc."

I hesitated. Did we really need these lunches to discuss this? But since I wasn't really sure how the business world worked, I quickly nodded my assent before he picked up on my wariness.

"No problem."

We were getting up to leave and as I was gathering my bag, he leaned closer.

"Merci, please keep in mind that sometimes our lunches may run over."

Although my heart skipped a beat, I looked back at him, attempting to keep my face strictly business.

"Okay, I will." He was the boss, right? No one could

reprimand him for keeping me out.

Back at JWC, James repeated his patented elevator behavior by ignoring me completely. I was game. However, from my point of view, we made the foolish mistake of returning at the same time, because J.J.'s eyes looked at us in high suspicion. James made a beeline straight for his office and closed the door while J.J. just sat there, gaping at me.

"What's the problem, J.J.?" I asked smoothly.

"You were gone so long and boss looked a bit stranger than usual. What in the world did you two discuss?"

I hadn't bothered to look at my phone but he was right, we had been gone at least two hours.

"He wants me to help with corresponding with the design firms for the remodeling job up here."

J.J. was slow to respond and his look was one of disbelief. "Oh."

I grew a little anxious. "Was that something you were going to do, or had been taking care of?" I didn't want to step on any toes.

"No, not at all," J.J. responded breezily. "This is the first I'm hearing of it. I didn't have that responsibility, nor do I have time for it in the first place. He had his office remodeled before he joined permanently, and I had nothing to do with it. Interesting that he's entrusting you, though, seeing as though it has nothing to do with company business which should be the focus of your internship - and, you'll be leaving in a few months. I don't get him, but whatever," he waved his hand dismissively. "Sounds exciting, though - so have fun." He smiled happily and went back to work.

§

That night, I thought about James's puzzling behavior. I

didn't really mention our business lunch to Teresa because I didn't want to go into it. First, I needed to figure out some things for myself. For sure, even though he could be indifferent, he acted like he was interested in me. I knew I wasn't imagining things. I went over his questions regarding having a boyfriend and remembered his perusals of me. I admitted I was also very interested, but I had morals. If he was single, I would date him in a New York minute, but he was engaged and off limits.

Although he wasn't in the office the next day, I received the email with the contact list and instructions on who to call first and what samples to request. James also recommended that I give him my cell phone number so that he could contact me if he ever needed to send me out to inspect materials. He said he would need my feedback right away. His explanation seemed a little bogus. I didn't really see him entrusting my extremely limited design knowledge for something so vital, but I acquiesced because he was the boss. Who knows, it may have very well been necessary. After all, I wasn't really sure how all of this worked. Plus, I was determined not to let his mild interest in me manipulate my thoughts into fantasizing about the possibility of a relationship. He was just flirting - I told myself - nothing more.

I heard nothing back after I responded with my number, and I didn't see James for the rest of the week. That made it easier for me to accept that there wasn't and would never be anything between us. I was resolute in erasing any and all thoughts of it from my mind.

I found my new responsibilities very interesting. In addition to helping J.J. with filing and stuffing envelopes, most of my time was concentrated on the remodeling project. James had me ordering samples from quite a few places and instructed for them to come directly to my attention. I received boxes of mosaic tile samples from China, Indian marble samples, wood samples including beech, pine, cherry (never walnut), maple and basswood. Apparently, he was planning on brightening things up at JWC.

CHAPTER SIX

Teresa went home again for the weekend. On Saturday, while I was reading a book, I received a text from an unknown number.

What are you doing tonight?

Who was this? I debated whether I should delete it or respond. My mind involuntarily went straight to James. Darn, I was weak. Curious, I texted back.

Um - who is this?

Hi, Merci, it's James.

OMG, OMG, it's him - it's him. I foolishly sat straight up and smoothed down my hair in the mirror across from the bed. *Calm down, Merci, he can't see you,* I thought. I considered what I should say for a full two minutes. That was good, though - he needed to be kept waiting. What business did he have texting me on a Saturday night anyway?

James who...?

I was letting him know it could've been another James I

knew, even though I didn't. But he didn't know that. It was also good for him to believe I hadn't been thinking about him. I didn't hear anything back for a few minutes. Now, I was constantly checking the phone and wondering if I chased him off. So what if I did? Of course, I didn't really mean that...

James Jansen, he texted back.

Of course it was. My heart pounded in my chest. I appropriately paused like I was letting it sink in - and it was. James Jansen III was texting me!

Oh, James. Hi, how are you? I waited. That was okay, right?

Fine. Are you busy tonight? There is a design showcase that I would like for you to see. May I call you?

Oh, it *was* business. I felt stupid. Then I thought about the fact that it was Saturday night. I was instantly suspicious again.

Sure.

Ten seconds later, my phone rang. I didn't pretend to not know who it was.

"Hi, James."

"Hello, Merci," his deep, smooth voice vibrated through my phone and reverberated throughout my entire body. I shivered. Even if it was business, my accelerated heart rate didn't know the difference.

"As I was saying, there is a designer showcase at the Merchandise Mart where they have the best selection of commercial furnishings. I know its short notice, but it just occurred to me that you should definitely come along to get a better idea of what we'll be doing at JWC. They have a lot of the materials showcased that I've had you order and more. What time is it-" he murmured, and I assumed he was looking at a clock of some sort, "six fifty. Can you be ready by eight? I can be there to get you."

Geez, this was a lot to take in. My head was spinning not only at his text, his call, and his request out of nowhere to go to some function - but what in the world was I going to wear?

"Uh, okay. I'll be ready." I hesitated. A bit nervously I asked, "How should I be dressed?"

He was quiet for a moment. "It's not really formal, but you shouldn't wear jeans either. I'm sure you will do fine," then his voice got even lower, "you always do."

Goodness. I took a deep breath. "Okay. I'll figure something out."

"Good. Which dormitory do you reside in?" I couldn't even be surprised that he knew where I stayed. James Jansen seemed to know everything.

"I stay in Wick House, in Broadview Hall. Do you know how to find it?"

He seemed a bit wistful as he answered, "Yeah, I had quite a few buddies that stayed in Wick House at UChicago. Be ready at eight o'clock sharp." Then he hung up.

He was too much.

I took a quick shower and gave my small closet a thorough inspection. Not formal but no jeans. I picked a burgundy, ruffled chevron top and my faux leather paneled pants paired with my four-inch fake Louboutins. I pinned my hair away from my face and let it fall down in soft waves. I paid special attention to my makeup selection, making sure it matched my shirt, but subtly. I didn't want to look like a clown, but I made sure to put on more than usual since, not only was it Saturday night, but we might be around a lot of stylish people. I inspected myself in the cheap, full length mirror for more than twenty minutes, making updates and edits. It was nice out, but I slung my fringed shawl over my arm just in case. Oh well, I thought as I checked the mirror once last time - I did the best I could. He obviously knew I was a poor college student, so he shouldn't expect much.

At eight, I walked out of Broadview Hall down the steps and I looked around for James. I didn't even think to ask what he would be driving. Along with two other empty cars, there was a black stretch limo in front. Could it be? No way! A driver came out of the front, nodded at me directly and opened the back door. Reminded that James was probably watching me through the dark tinted windows, I quickly closed my open mouth. A few students were loitering around the steps, curiously watching to see if the limo was meant for me. Embarrassed, I walked towards it and smiled at the driver who looked like he was in his fifties. As I scooted in, I could see James slightly reclining far in the other corner of the limo opposite me. He was twirling a drink in his hand while appraising me with dark, inscrutable eyes. Not again. We all knew how he could act when he was drinking. I kept my composure as the limousine took off.

"Hi, James."

He looked at what I was wearing, slowly assessing from my hair down to my feet. I clutched my little purse on my lap. He finally spoke, his deep voice going straight to the pit of my stomach.

"Hello, Merci. You look very nice. I knew you would."

"Thank you. So do you."

James had on a flint grey, mock turtle-neck cashmere

sweater and black slacks. I hadn't seen him in anything but a suit, and if I thought he was fine then, he was super gorgeous now. His hair was loose curls all over the place, but perfect. Wafts of his cologne mixed with whatever strong drink he had came my way. It definitely wasn't unpleasant.

"Anyone ever tell you, you have a very sultry, sexy voice?"

I blushed. Oh my goodness, that was so out of left field and I didn't know how to answer. I'd heard I had a deep voice for a girl, but never described like that.

"No, I've heard deep, but not-not-" I stuttered, "sultry." I couldn't bring myself to say sexy. He continued studying me a moment and then seemed to break out of his spell and sat up a bit. I wondered if my stuttering changed his mind. I felt like an idiot.

The mask somewhat reappeared. He cleared his throat.

"Just so you understand. Today, I realized how helpful and important it would be for you to attend. This remodeling project is extremely important to me and I'm almost single minded about it. Unfortunately," he shook his head with what looked like frustration, "I have tons of work to do specific to the company, so I'm truly relying on your help. I don't want to work in an environment that isn't conducive to my tastes which would undoubtedly hinder my work performance," he justified. "So right now, I'm focusing on getting the ball rolling and I am pleased that you seem to be taking care of what I've asked so far. From what J.J. has told me, you received plenty of samples this week. Seeing some of the samples and fabrics tonight should give you a better idea of what direction I want to head in."

I was flattered that he was sharing so much of his aesthetic vision, but I couldn't help but wonder if his alcohol consumption had anything to do with him speaking so freely.

"No problem, I'm happy to learn more about it." I smiled. I decided to ask a few questions that had been weighing heavily. "While I'm flattered to be a part of it, I was just wondering if J.J. will be taking over once I'm gone. I only have about two months before school starts back up."

He looked taken aback as if he either hadn't thought of that - or that far ahead. He was quiet for a moment, swishing his drink. Then, with stony eyes, he gave a solemn, half-smile.

"We'll worry about that when the time comes," he said with finality. I believed this subject was closed for now.

James turned detachedly toward the windows for the rest of the ride. I did the same.

Merchandise Mart was a huge, wide square edifice off the Chicago River. Although old, this fact didn't diminish its sheer magnificence. It was colossal. Over the years, I'd heard about it being owned by the Kennedy family and that it was the world's largest commercial building. The driver came to open my door. I felt I had been rude, especially since he was opening my door and all.

"Thank you. I'm sorry, I'm Merci," I said, stretching forth my hand. He shook it and gave me a brilliant smile.

He was very elegant, yet seemed very affable.

"I am Bernard, Merci. Pleased to meet you." In a manner of which I was becoming used to, James ignored our exchange while looking at his phone and walking ahead. We entered the elevator much in the same manner.

After we reached the eleventh floor, we approached a table where a woman appeared to be waiting to check us in. She saw James and smiled with delight.

"James, it's great to see you. How are you?" She eyed me

politely. He gave a rare smile - well, at least rare to me, and kissed her on the cheek.

"Hi, Leslie, I'm fine. It's been a while. Good to see you, too." He had a badge out that she waved away.

"Go right in. Enjoy yourselves." She smiled and attended to the guests behind us.

We crossed into a room that had warm recessed lighting, white walls and samples everywhere. There were several people milling about looking at materials with goblets in their hands. I could see that along with the examination of materials, they would be serving wine and hors d'oeuvres. I snuck a peek at James - and his eyes were lit up like a Christmas tree! I didn't think he was capable of looking so excited. I was stunned. Where was the cold, intense dude? He spoke animatedly.

"The Merchandise Mart is the largest wholesale design center and is the epicenter for high design and luxury products. Originally designed as a market center for trade professionals, The Mart is catering to a core audience tonight. Many showroom floors of The Mart are accessible only to interior designers, architects, wholesale buyers and escorted visitors. Tonight's showcase is called NeoCon, which provides access to the latest and most innovative products." His voice sounded in awe. He obviously loved being here. His excitement was contagious and I indulged him and myself.

"Wow, they have the coolest stuff." I knew I sounded juvenile, but I didn't know what else to say and I didn't know the standard designer's lingo. He didn't seem to notice.

"Yes, they do. I can always find what I need here." He walked hurriedly over to the textiles rack and found a teal fabric and felt it, rubbing his hands over it as if determining something due to the texture. He looked up at me as I came closer.

"Feel this," I did. It felt okay. "This would be suitable for the new guest chairs I want in the manager offices."

"I like it." He looked at me in satisfaction. I looked over to a grey colored fabric. It was called 'Theater Velvet Graphite. "And this is nice too. I'm not sure for what, though."

He seemed thoughtful as he looked at my selection and felt it. "Hmm, I like this even more. I believe this would be perfect for the manager offices. Good pick, Merci." He looked at me with an impressive glint in his eye. I grinned in delight. Wow, he liked my pick and it was actually going to be used for all of the manager's guest chairs in JWC. I decided I liked my assignment a lot.

I was provided a pad and pen from Leslie and for the rest of the evening, followed James to and fro as he explained his vision and picked out materials to carry it forth. At one point, a server came around to offer us wine in which James grabbed a glass. Not wanting to be busted out by James because he knew my age, I politely declined. He intercepted.

"Yes, she'll have some." The server smiled, put the wine in my hand and took off. I looked at the wine and then at James in bewilderment.

"James, I don't like wine that much anyway." Plus, he should've remembered I wasn't legal.

"They have some good tasting wine here, not that nasty, over expensive crap they try to shove down our throats because of the price. Take a sip," he demanded.

Hesitantly, I did. It was fantastic. Most of the wine I'd tasted either wasn't sweet enough or I didn't like the flavor.

He smiled knowingly. "Good, huh? They usually serve Frankenmuth wines here - that's Frankenmuth Rose,' and their White is just as delicious. Their wine isn't ridiculously expensive and it's tasty as hell."

I smiled and took another sip. He regarded me for a moment, his brown eyes warmer than I'd ever seen and more expressive. I also caught a glimpse of discontentment.

"I know you're not twenty-one - *believe me*, I know," I flushed, "but one little glass can't hurt. Especially when you're really helping me make some good picks tonight."

I gave a toothy grin in response, ready to explode with happiness of his acknowledgment. He seemed startled and stared at me with some unnamed emotion. I stared back – too joyful to have the usual urges to squirm from his glares. After a few moments, he looked away and seemed to relax again.

"So, Merci," he said, leaning back against a column, "tell me about yourself."

"Well, what do you want to know that you don't know already? I'm sure you have secret files on all of your employees," I joked.

He sipped his drink, smiling as if I was right. "That's true, I do check up on employees, especially the ones who I work in close proximity with. Tell me something I don't know."

"Alright." I mulled over this for a moment. "My middle name is Lynn. I can put my hands together behind my back and bring them over my head and to the front." He flinched. "I love to read and write songs in my spare time." His eyebrows rose at this. "I won the spelling bee every year in grammar school except fifth grade and I was valedictorian at my graduation."

He nodded. "Impressive."

I couldn't tell if he was sincere or not but I didn't care – the wine was taking effect.

"Now, you tell me something I don't know-" I thought about what I asked and grimaced at my idiocy, "which is basically everything."

Not seeming to pay attention to my embarrassment, he too, seemed to be seriously giving thought to my question.

"My middle name is Thelonious."

He paused to view my reaction with a hint of a smile as I tried to keep a neutral face. I think I was successful as I took into account that since he was the III, it wasn't his parent's fault that the old school name was passed down.

"Like the jazz musician, Thelonious Monk."

His eyes lit up with surprise. "That's right. I didn't think you were old enough to know who he was."

"I told you I dabble in songwriting, and since I love music, I've at least heard of him."

He nodded again as if my explanation sufficed and continued.

"I never went above a C grade in grammar school, except for art. Conversely, I was among the top of my class in college and...I can do the Moonwalk like Michael Jackson."

That one was so unexpected, I nearly spat out my drink in laughter and sputtered as it tried to go up my nose instead. Just imagining cool, composed, aloof James doing the iconic dance almost sent me to the floor. He laughed along for a moment but soon looked offended by my display.

"Okay, Merci, it's not that funny."

I was still crying. "Yes, it is. I'm sorry - I just can't imagine..."

He gave me a serious look and I abruptly straightened up. Was he getting mad for real? No, because the humorous glint never left his eye. He was having fun, too.

CHAPTER SEVEN

I only had one glass but it was pretty potent, so I carefully attempted to walk back to the limo with a bit of finesse. Overall, I was so thrilled with my night that I wanted to dance. Bernard was outside waiting for us. He smiled politely as he opened the door. Once inside, I continued to take advantage of this newfound liquid courage while James was in a good mood.

"James, thank you for bringing me here tonight. I enjoyed it very much."

Pleased by my gratitude, he smiled. "You're welcome." He had another glass in his hand by this time. He sure liked to drink.

"How do you know the lady from the front table?"

His eyes seemed to revisit some fond, distant memory. "Leslie is an old college friend. She was my buddy, Mark's girl, and we had a lot of the same classes."

"Where did you go to college?"

He stiffened and looked off in a daze.

"I went to the Illinois Institute of Technology College of Architecture or IIT College of Architecture for short. That's where I received my bachelor's degree. Then afterwards, because I loved interiors as well as exteriors, I went to Harrington College of Design to get my master's in interior design." His look became grim as he took another swig. "I didn't finish."

I waited a moment for him to continue, but being too curious to let him off the hook when he didn't, I prodded.

"Why not?"

"I dropped out to attend your school for my MBA."

No wonder he knew where my dorm was. "Did you finish?"

"Yes," he said matter-of-factly. "I received a master's in business." He gulped down the rest of drink and looked pensively at his lap. Because it appeared he was going to shut down when he didn't expound, I got in one more.

"What was that badge that Leslie didn't need to see?"

"The design shows are only opened to the trade and that's my state issued license badge. I am a certified architect."

§

Bernard arrived at Wick House too fast for my liking. It was just as well because James was no longer chatty and was in some kind of stupor. Now, not only was I down because of whatever his problem was, but because I was parting with him as well.

I tried to linger as Bernard held the door open for me but James only mumbled incoherently.

"Goodbye - see you Monday."

I bid him and Bernard goodbye and went into the dorm.

Once washed up and in bed, I thought over my night out. My boss's strange mood swings were beginning to make sense. Obviously, from the way his eyes lit up in The Mart, he loved all things designer when it came to exteriors and interiors. I should've known by his cool office. Poor James. He obviously wanted a career in architecture or interior design but had to quit working on his masters in design to get an MBA for the family business. No wonder he was so cold at work, he hated his job.

I felt so sorry for him that I debated sending a text message to check up on him. I knew we weren't like that, but since he was drinking and we had been together tonight, I thought it would be responsible to see if he was okay. It shouldn't look too presumptuous. This deliberation went on for fifteen minutes. Finally, I went for it.

Hi, James. I was just wondering if everything was okay.

Almost instantaneously, I received a reply.

Who in the hell is this??

I jumped up out of the bed. My blood ran cold and I began pacing the room. Oh no, oh no! I knew it wasn't James who responded. I had an idea of who it was. I believed it was his fiancée,' Lorelei Sampson, who responded on his phone. Darn it. I was so glad I wasn't stupid enough to say who I was. Obviously, my name wasn't programmed into his phone, since they didn't know who I was, right? I nervously waited to see if I would get another text - but I didn't.

After ten minutes of pacing I got back in the bed to try to sleep. I definitely didn't want to get him into trouble with his fiancée. Why did I forget all about her? I thought they weren't intimate - at least that was the rumor. They could've been living together for all I knew. Stupid, stupid Merci. From the looks of it, they were obviously together right now. Why did I feel strong pangs of jealousy? Get yourself together, Merci.

Drifting off to sleep as I made yet another pledge to discard my misplaced notions, my phone vibrated. Scared to look at first, it took me a moment to gather resolve.

Merci, sorry about that…before. That wasn't me. Thanks for asking, I'm much better now. I'll see you on Monday.

So I was right. If possible, my heart sank lower. He said he was much better now - probably due to being with Lorelei, I thought. I sighed. Ok, this was the way it was. I responded briefly just in case Lorelei jacked his phone again. That way it would look innocent - as it was.

Okay, see you Monday.

§

Teresa returned early Sunday evening, gushing about the great message she heard at church on truly seeking God first and everything else will fall into place. I half listened because I was so eager to tell her about James. I pretended to listen respectfully - I'd heard it all before - and waited until she finished. About to burst, I told her all about my Saturday evening with James. She seemed suspicious at first but shared my excitement of the actual experience at Merchandise Mart.

"That sounds so cool, Merci. Not everybody can get access to their design showrooms. So you two did actual work, like picking samples and documenting materials?"

"Yeah, I even picked out a material that I liked, and James ended up deciding to use it for all of the guest chairs in the manager offices throughout the entire company." Her eyes bugged out and she was silent for a moment. I looked at her in puzzlement. "What?"

"Merci, that's really great. Be careful, though. While I

think it's great that you're getting some extra experience you hadn't counted on, his intentions seem a little suspect. Interns don't normally get these kinds of privileges."

No longer wanting to beat around the bush and play coy, I relented.

"Yeah, I know he digs me a little, but I think he just likes to flirt. So, no worries. I know he's engaged," I dismissed.

"Okay…if you say so. I'm just worried you'll be lured in by all of that beauty and power. Remember, he's off limits."

"I know." I sighed, but just a little. She would've really freaked if I told her about the texting incident. I debated whether I needed her input and after deciding I did, spilled all. After I told her about the exchange, abruptly she stood up and began pacing around the room with her arms crossed, her long black ponytail swinging disapprovingly.

"Okay, Merc - that doesn't sound good. While Lorelei was truly out of order for that, you can't really blame her since he's her man. You do *not* want to get involved in anything like that - a lot of these wealthy socialites can be ruthless if they believe something is getting in the way of their money. Believe me - I've heard plenty of tales from that circle. Promise me you'll be adamant about keeping things exclusively on a business level when it comes to him. I don't want to see you get hurt."

I actually thought she was tripping at this point. Didn't Lorelei Sampson have her own money? Why was she jumping the gun?

"Sit down, T. I'm not doing or going to do anything. Why are you so upset? He's just flirting, and while I admit that I think he's gorgeous, I would never mess around with someone else's fiancé."

"Okay," she relented. "I know you're not like that, but please stay on your Ps and Qs around him and remember - it always starts with a little flirting." She sat back down and looked at me gravely. "Promise?"

I smiled. "I promise."

§

Keeping my promise in mind, I went to work Monday less focused on my looks – hair in a bun and glasses instead of contacts - and more determined to take care of business only. But apparently, due to our weekend and the way we seemed to bond, James was having none of that. He emailed me less than twelve minutes after work began.

To: Merci Townsend
From: James Jansen III
Subject: Saturday
I enjoyed our visit to The Mart. Please bring in the notes you took. I'd like to go over them.

To: James Jansen III
From: Merci Townsend
Subject: Re: Saturday
I enjoyed it as well. Thank you for revealing a whole new world to me. I'll bring them in right away.

Not bothering to check my face, clothes or anything superficial, I grabbed my notes and went right into his office. I sat down in one of the chairs and waited. James, who was faced away from his desk, swiveled around to look in my direction. He was dressed casually in a celadon green long sleeved shirt, and from what I could see behind the desk, black trousers. The green really made his bronze skin look fantastic. *Chill out, Merci.* He had a small smile on his face while he regarded me inquisitively. Ah, I guess he wasn't too pleased with how I looked. I smiled triumphantly. Too bad.

"Hi, James."

"Merci, you look like a naughty librarian. I like it."

I looked back at him in disbelief. This was not what I was going for. Although deep down I was pleased that even like this, he found me attractive.

"Umm, thank you?" I cleared my throat to refocus. "Here are the notes you requested." I tried to hand them to him across the desk but he brushed them away. He was still looking intently.

"That's okay, you read them to me," he demanded quietly.

I locked eyes with him, and then quickly looked down. Today, I was really nervous. I read off the design notes and when I got halfway through, he interrupted.

"Merci, about that text message Saturday night - I apologize. My fiancée' grabbed my phone while I was in the shower-"

Oh no, too much information. I blanched and sputtered quickly to cut him off.

"No, James. You don't have to explain." I tried to focus back on the notes hoping he got the message.

"Yes, Merci, I want to," he added softly.

I couldn't bring myself to look up right away but he seemed to be waiting for me to.

What I saw almost took the fight out of me. His jaw was set with a steely resolve, but his eyes were tinged with profound misery.

"I went home and there she was, waiting. Don't misunderstand - we do not live together. Of course I was a bit drunk and needed a shower. Obviously, that's when you texted and she responded back to you on my phone. When I got out, she was yelling and going off, and I was so furious when I found out what she had done that I put her out."

His eyes were stormy as he explained. I was bewildered. I couldn't believe he felt I was due such an in depth explanation. Teresa's voice was now ringing in my brain repeatedly, *stay on your Ps and Qs*. This really did seem like something more.

I absorbed this information but remained quiet.

"I just wanted to let you know, because her rude behavior was unjustified."

"No problem. I was just glad that you were okay."

His eyes lightened.

"Thank you for checking on me." He smiled gratefully and my heart melted.

Then the mask reappeared and I was safe. We continued with the notes and once I returned to my desk, I didn't see James for the rest of the day.

§

On the train ride home, I proudly told Teresa of how strong I'd been and how well I handled James's flirting. She laughed and was very pleased I had triumphed.

"That's great, girl. I'm glad you handled it but don't let down your guard."

"I won't. I'm not thinking about him anymore."

She raised an eyebrow but smiled anyway. "Okay."

She started talking about a guy named Jonathan from her department that had been flirting with her a lot. We laughed all the way to our stop.

The next day, I was all set to continue my off limits act, but J.J., who kept James's schedule, informed me that he would be out until the end of the week. I couldn't lie - the news made me miserable.

CHAPTER EIGHT

On Friday, James scheduled us to have another business lunch and I was positively gleeful because I had truly missed him. I guess I missed our interactions, whether it was business related or not. All of the vigilant admonitions to myself seemed to fly out the window.

Although he was back, I hadn't seen him as he had been in his office all morning. His email told me to wait at the restaurant which was reserved under his name. He would be there after he wrapped up an important conference call that had run over.

The location wasn't too far up on Michigan Avenue, so I set out on foot. Heaven on Seven was a seafood restaurant hailed as having the best Louisiana cooking outside of New Orleans in which Teresa and I had visited before. Their crab cakes were divine, so I ordered them as an appetizer while I waited for James. I knew I was growing weak due to the attention and detail I paid to my appearance this morning anticipating James's return. I had on a dark grey and blue Baroque chenille dress and four inch booties I'd purchased recently. My hair was down and wavy – my makeup soft, pink and romantic. I looked cute today and I wanted him to notice. Just to be sure, my pad and pen were prominently visible on the table, just in case he was in his no nonsense business mode. If so, he would know I was on the same page. *Wink.*

Once James arrived, I got to see what he had on today. He had on a white sport jacket, jeans, a pink shirt, and sneakers. As usual, he looked good in anything. This man was *fine*. He ordered calamari and we went right into discussing new materials he wanted after seeing them at NeoCon. After twenty minutes of notes and details, he sat back in the booth and stared intently. I stared back - a direct query on my face. When were we going to stop playing? I was tired of pretending. He seemed to sense it.

"You obviously know I'm attracted to you, and I believe you are to me, as well. I would like for us to start seeing each other." My stomach somersaulted at his directness. Excited, I needed to know some things first.

"There are dozens of other beautiful women who would love to be with you. Why me?"

"I find you very fascinating and very sexy. I like everything about you. From your soft, exotic eyes to the color and texture of your hair." He looked at each attribute. "Your brilliant smile, your sexy voice, your rockin' body and your intelligent, witty brain. You don't fall all over me like most women, so that's refreshing and a bit humbling, I must admit. I also find myself sharing things with you I've never shared with others because you're easy to talk to - to be with. That's unusual for me. You're very mature - a lot more mature than women much older are supposed to be." With the way his eyes narrowed, he seemed to be indicating someone in particular. "I know you're young and believe me, I've tried to fight it – but I can't anymore. I won't anymore. I want you."

Furiously blushing, my stomach was doing flips at his bold, lengthy declaration. I was elated, internally bouncing up and down on my seat. I wanted him too - so badly.

Thrilled that he had obviously broken up with Lorelei, I checked to be sure.

"What about Lorelei?"

"What about her?"

Dubiously, I asked, "You're still engaged to her?"

"Yes, and that shouldn't be a problem, right? I'm talking about you and me."

My heart sank. He was obviously crazy - and with no morals.

"No way, I'm not that way," my voice rose. "You've got me twisted, James. I don't mess around with somebody else's man. I'm flattered that you would consider me, but - no."

I rifled through my purse that was down at my side just to keep from looking in his persuasive eyes. When I ventured a peek due to his silence, he looked mildly astonished. Apparently, none of his other conquests had refused him before.

"Merci, we could be so good together," he purred softly.

I considered his statement. "Maybe - then break up with her," I said directly.

He was quiet for a moment. "This usually isn't a problem," he said, looking mystified.

I looked at him like he was nuts. "Oh, in other words, your side-pieces don't usually care if you're engaged?"

He looked as if he had been struck a blow at my bluntness. "Merci -"

"Break - up - with - her," I insisted.

His turbulent eyes went flat. "I can't."

I looked back at him with haughty insolence and rolled my neck. "Oh well."

I turned to look out the window. I was amazed at how our exchange shifted in this direction. It started out so good.

When I glanced back, his expression was unreadable and I prepared to gather the pad and pen. I figured we would be leaving soon. Then he unexpectedly reached for my hand and began caressing it. Tingles ran up through my arm and my stomach dropped. His touch was electrifying. I gasped. He smiled knowingly at my reaction to him.

He murmured seductively, "Feel that? That's how good it could be and even more-"

"Stop it, James," I tried to snatch my hand back but he had a firm grip, "you heard me, right? Don't think because I'm young, I'm stupid-"

"Merci," he interrupted, "I surely don't think that." His eyes sobered and he dropped my hand. I returned it to safety underneath the table.

"I tell you what," he said. "Think about it. Can you do that for me?" His eyes implored mine and I knew right then and there, they were specifically designed to put a girl under a spell. I couldn't look away and he knew it.

I said nothing because I could hardly catch my breath.

He repeated slowly, "Can you do that for me?"

I blinked and looked away, refusing to show defeat.

"Yes," I answered glancing back at him guardedly.

He leaned back in the booth with immense satisfaction on his face.

As if he already knew my answer.

§

I tried to walk ahead of him with some new found resolve as we made our way back to the office. He insisted we catch a cab for the four block walk, but I wasn't anxious to be in close proximity with him anytime soon.

"No, I don't mind walking. You go ahead," I said.

"Merci," he called as I took off, "are you alright?"

I responded as breezily as I could. "Sure, I'm fine."

I continued to walk and I could feel his eyes blazing my backside all of the way there. Admittedly, I was swaying my hips a little more than usual for his benefit. He said it was rockin' and if he wanted *this*, he needed to drop *her*. I knew that his eyes were specifically trained on my curvaceous behind. I could've sworn I heard a low chuckle or two but I couldn't be sure. I thought I could out walk him but his long legs easily kept up right behind me.

As we entered the building, I actually felt relieved that we would be in the elevator because I anticipated his standard "elevator" mode of operation. Once in JWC, James usually put on his business mask. But as soon as the doors closed, he was two inches from my face and had me backed into the corner. I almost shrieked in surprise but my breath was caught in my throat. *Oh my goodness.* His nose was almost touching mine.

"Merci, I want an answer. Very soon," he murmured in a deep, sensuous voice.

I closed my eyes under his full-on intensity. His smell and everything about him was making me feel faint. His nose left a fiery trail as it skimmed up and down my cheek. I weakly tried to open my eyes and was caught like a butterfly in his stormy brown ones. They were almost hazel with fervor. He gazed down at my nose and then my lips. I gasped at what could possibly come next. At this point, I knew I looked like a wanton hussy with my heaving full bosom, but I couldn't help it. His full, pouty lips grazed mine softly, but it was enough to almost make my knees buckle. Feeling I was about to collapse, he got even closer. He gave me a full smooch on my lips and stepped back. I gasped and my eyelids fluttered in surprise. I tried to compose myself to look unaffected but I knew I was unsuccessful.

"There is more from where that came from." He smirked and turned back around while I continued gathering my wits.

Just as I seemed to get my bearings, the doors opened to the fortieth floor. James's relaxed demeanor abruptly shifted once we exited. More so than usual because there was an older man that looked to be in his sixties standing outside of the middle set of the walnut doors.

Standing casually with his left hand in his pocket, it appeared as if he was waiting for someone. He was as tall as James, dressed impeccably in a dark grey, three-piece pin striped suit with a distinguished full head of black and silver hair. His lined face was still quite handsome but his grey eyes were stern and cool as they assessed us. The older man didn't move a muscle while James's back straightened and stiffened. Was it from fright?

"Hello, sir, how are you?" James asked, actually sounding intimidated. This was new. The man didn't answer right away and looked at me. I tried not to flinch under his powerful scrutiny.

"James?"

James turned to me and seemed to understand what the older man was inquiring.

"This is one of our new interns, Merci Townsend, who has been assisting J.J. and I for the last few weeks. Merci, this is the President and founder of JWC, Jim Jansen."

His dad - OMG!

Refusing to be daunted, I gave a bright smile and held out my hand to shake his.

"Hello, sir, a pleasure to meet you."

He took it in his and gave a small smile that didn't quite reach his chilly eyes. Now, I could really see the resemblance.

"Hello, Merci, the pleasure is mine." He glanced over at James and back. "So, Merci, are you learning anything about what we do here at Jansen Worldwide? I assume James is showing you how we help fledgling businesses grow into lucrative ones." He said it with a tone of doubt and from what I could detect - mild sarcasm.

James seemed to scramble to interject before I was put on the spot. I was grateful because I didn't have words.

"Yes, sir, she's learning all of the facets of the business." Jim raised a doubtful eyebrow. "She's fast and efficient, and that is why she was chosen."

"I'm wondering why she would be up here instead of down with the other interns learning from our account managers," he said with what I sensed, a hint of suspicion. He looked at me for a moment, let out a sigh and seemed to relax. In turn, I could see James visibly doing the same. Was the interrogation over?

"Alright, it was a pleasure to meet you, Merci." Jim smiled genuinely this time, jostling the hand that was still in his and finally letting go. It seemed he had decided to stop embarrassing his son. He turned to James.

"May I speak with you in my office?"

"Yes, sir." James turned back and eyed me to go ahead to our offices. Picking up on it, I flew by Marguerite who had a gleam of amusement in her eyes, and darted into the office.

As I was stuffing envelopes, I thought about James's interaction with his father. From what I sensed, they didn't have a warm and fuzzy relationship. It seemed more like military interaction between general and private. It figured that the one person who could reduce someone as confident and self-assured as James would be his father. Not once did James introduce him as his dad or allude to them being related. It could be because they were in a business atmosphere. I doubted it, though. It would've taken one second to interject "my father." Was it possible that their relationship was strained due to James's previous aspirations as an architect and not the family business? I was guessing now, since it hadn't been confirmed. Something told me I was on the right track.

I didn't hear from James for the rest of the afternoon. That was fine since I had a lot of information to process. My lips were still on fire from that elevator kiss. What a day.

On the train, I didn't dare tell Teresa about his proposition. She would accuse me of not definitively saying "no" and probably fuss that he wasn't ever going to break up with Lorelei. I just didn't want to hear any preaching, so instead, we discussed her playful interactions with Jonathan. I sighed as I listened. Things seemed so uncomplicated and peachy keen in her world. Jon, as she called him, was only a few years older, he wasn't married or engaged and he seemed straight-forward with honorable intentions. I decided that from now on, I would be mum on anything related to James. If I was honest, it was because I was seriously considering his proposal.

§

Teresa went home again that weekend and I secretly harbored hope that James would contact me like he did last Saturday. I had already made him a contact in my phone and he was one of my favorites. I know - I was pathetic.

Saturday night passed uneventfully, and I was down in the dumps again. *You told him that you weren't down with being the side chick, so what did you expect?* I admitted to myself that I at least wanted him to try.

Sunday night, after deciding what to wear to look cute for work, I went to sleep. About an hour later, I received a text from my vibrated phone, still in my hand under the pillow. I knew who it was but my heart leapt anyway.

Merci, you up? Can I call you?

I sat up quietly trying not to wake up Teresa. She would freak out if she knew James Jansen was texting me at eleven thirty on a Sunday night. I crept quietly to the bathroom and shut the door before responding. I took a deep breath to relax.

Yes, I'm up. You may call.

My phone vibrated almost right away.

I spoke quietly, "Hi, James."

"Girl, you sound so sexy," he slurred in his smooth, deep voice. Oh no, James was drunk. Was this the only way he could confide in me?

I responded with an ambiguous chuckle.

"Merci, you saw that display at the office Friday. My father is such an ass. I couldn't believe he tried to humiliate me in front of you…Merci, you still there?"

I wasn't sure what to say so I empathized.

"Yes, I'm here. James, what he said wasn't that bad. I don't think he was trying to humiliate you," I lied.

"But you picked up on it, didn't you? You knew he was trying to be slimy with his words - but you're a lot sharper than most so I'm not surprised."

"Have you been drinking?"

He chuckled and slurred, "See what I mean?" Then he seemed to sober up a little. "Yes, I have. Merci, I'm going through a lot right now."

My ears perked up due to being extremely desperate for details. Would he spill? I didn't want to mess this up.

"Talk to me, James," I asked softly.

He was silent for a moment. I panicked. Did I mess up already?

"James?"

"Merci, I'll tell you all about it tomorrow. I know a nice place where we can talk. We can go during lunch."

Alarm bells went off but I ignored them. We were probably going to another restaurant so it was no big deal. Plus, if this was my opportunity to find out more about him, I wasn't going to pass it up.

"Okay, tomorrow then."

"Good." He had a satisfied smile in his voice. "I'll see you tomorrow." He hung up.

I went back to bed and dreamed of James earnestly pouring his heart out to me over dinner at Fogo de Chão.

CHAPTER NINE

Refreshed and excited about the big reveal, I wore a Theory houndstooth dress with sheer black thigh-highs and three and a half-inch pumps. Wearing my hair down since he seemed to like it like that, I carried a black wrap shawl since it was always a little nippier downtown.

Not able to concentrate well on work at all today, I operated in a daze until noon. I got a text.

Go downstairs and get in the black limo out front. Bernard is inside.

That was weird. We were taking the limo today? Maybe the restaurant was far.

Okay, I texted back.

I got up casually, told J.J. I was going to lunch, grabbed my purse and left. Once out front, I saw only one limo parked, so I looked around to make sure no one I knew was watching, opened the back door and slid in. I nearly jumped to the ceiling when I saw James sitting in the opposite corner gazing at me. I thought he was still upstairs.

"How did you get down-"

"I've been down here for a while. I didn't want to draw attention to us leaving together."

Oh, that made sense. I guess he had left when I went for a bathroom break about half an hour ago. He had to come past me to leave the office. He was dressed casually in a pomegranate crew neck sweater that fit snugly over his muscled chest. His long, muscled legs were clad in dark grey trousers and he had on some really nice black shoes. There was also the familiar smell of his cologne mixed with alcohol. Because, of course, James had a drink in his hand. Did he have a bit of a problem? It was probably due to stress about the job. Maybe he'll tell me today. He had an amused look at my assessment.

"See something you like?"

Quickly averting my eyes to the window, I blushed and laughed. "No, I was just thinking."

"About what?"

Deciding to be vague since everything was coming to the light today, I responded, "About you."

He gazed at me quizzically, and from the front, Bernard piped up. "Where to, sir?"

James looked at me with smoldering eyes for a moment. "To The Fairmont."

I had never heard of that restaurant but I was looking forward to it. James looked at me as if he was waiting for me to say something but I just looked back and smiled. Later, I found out what that look was for.

It was a short trip as we made our way down Lower Wacker Drive, a street that was partially built underground, and went into an underground parking lot that led to big glass doors that in large script read, *Fairmont*. Wait, was this a hotel? Bernard came back to open the door for us with an unreadable expression on his face. I refused to assume the worst. Surely, James wouldn't be bringing me to a hotel. Maybe they had a nice restaurant inside. I convinced my brain that this was the reason - meanwhile my heart was beating out of my chest.

James grabbed my hand as we made our way past the elaborate lobby and front desk to a group of elevators. After all, we were down on a lower level, so maybe the restaurant was upstairs. James was still looking at me intently as if expecting me to say something. I was saving all of my questions for when we were seated, so I simply smiled. He seemed pleased by my behavior. The elevator continued going to the top floor. Wow, maybe it was one of those rotating top floor restaurants. I bet it had a great view. I was getting keyed up now. The elevator stopped and James motioned for me to get off first. When the doors opened, it wasn't to a restaurant but an elaborate, huge hotel suite. I gaped in horror - we were in a penthouse suite in a hotel!

I quickly tried to bolt back on the elevator but James held me until it closed.

"Uh un, you didn't tell me we were going to a hotel," I raged, "you said we were going to eat!"

He grabbed me with both arms. "Calm down, Merci, I said we were going someplace to talk. I thought you would figure it out once I said 'The Fairmont', but it just dawned on me that you might not have heard of it since you're not from here."

"Take me back, James, I don't want to be in a hotel room with you. You're engaged."

He tried to console me. "I know, I know, I just wanted to go somewhere really private to talk. This is my suite. My family owns it and I stay here from time to time. I thought we could order room service and just talk."

I looked at him disbelievingly. I may have been naïve to let him lure me here under false intentions, but I wasn't a fool.

"I don't care, James, this doesn't look good." I thought about Bernard and my cheeks flamed in embarrassment. "No wonder Bernard was looking at me like I was crazy," I lied, "he thinks I've just become another one of your side chicks," I spat, standing ramrod straight with balled fists.

James looked exhausted and plopped down on a sofa and sighed, putting his head in his hands.

"Merci, I know you don't believe me right now, but my intentions aren't bad. Yes, I'm attracted to you but I really did bring you here to talk. I'm sorry if I misled you." He gestured towards the adjacent chair. "Please Merci, sit down. The bedroom is way on the other side," he gestured backwards, "and we don't have to go back there at all. Just sit down and relax a moment."

My arms were crossed in defiance but I huffily plopped down on the opposite, oversized chair.

After a moment of silence I began to feel better. The chair was exceptionally comfy and I really didn't want to miss our talk. After sensing a shift in my mood, James pushed a menu my way.

"The food here is pretty good, so order whatever you like - I'm going to the restroom." I looked up at him as he got up to go.

"What about you?"

"Order me whatever you get." And he was gone.

I called and ordered two burgers and fries which sounded good once I realized I was starving. James came out of the bathroom with slightly red eyes, sleeves rolled up and without shoes. I guess he was comfortable since he practically lived here. I wondered if this was where the episode with Lorelei and his phone took place. For the first time, I really looked around.

The huge suite was decorated a lot like James's office.

Lots of light colors: creams, oranges, reds and light greens. There was also plenty of leather, velvet and clean lines. I got up to look at the view out of the massive double corner windows that faced both east and south. On the other side of the glass was a large balcony. The view was absolutely stunning. We were almost right off the water and facing Navy Pier. I looked down and watched the cars on Lake Shore Drive. In the southern direction, I could see *The Bean*, Millennium Park, Buckingham Fountain and way down to the Shedd Aquarium. This place was boss.

"Beautiful, isn't it?" his low voice murmured. I tried not to jump in surprise that he was right behind me.

"Yes, it's very beautiful."

"And the view, too."

Ignoring his cheesy joke, I turned around, side stepped him and walked about the place. He chuckled.

"I really like the way it's furnished. It reminds me of your office."

"I actually had this place redecorated according to my tastes. Some of the other rooms were just too ornate for my liking but I couldn't beat the view."

"Wow. That's cool. How often do you come here?"

"Just about every day, after work. I actually live further north in Bucktown, but sometimes in the summer I like to walk here, just to enjoy the fantastic view and the sounds of summer in Chicago. There really isn't a better city to enjoy the summer. Everything you want to enjoy happens here."

"I'm finding that out."

A signal coming from the elevator indicated that our food was here. James opened it up and gave the server a tip. I never got to see his face as James wheeled in our food.

"What did you order," he asked as he lifted the silver top, "burgers?" He laughed. I told you to get what you wanted, they have better food."

"James, I'm just a small-town girl from Stevensville, New Hampshire. A burger is always a good idea." He laughed heartily and sat down to eat.

James agreed that the burger was a good choice after we were done eating. I looked at my phone and saw that we had already been gone forty five minutes. For some reason, lunch running over here as opposed to a restaurant felt just plain wrong. Probably because I felt guilty about being in hotel room with an engaged man who was my boss in the first place. We definitely weren't having a business lunch. Suddenly uneasy again, I fidgeted.

"James, we don't have much time. Maybe we should leave and talk tonight on the phone," I offered hopefully.

He looked at his Tag Heuer watch and seemed to consider what I said.

"How about this? After work, we can come back here and have that talk with no interruptions, and then I'll have Bernard take you home."

I thought about it and it wasn't such a bad idea. I only needed to make excuses to Teresa. It really seemed like I would be more relaxed if we were to talk after work hours.

"Okay, I don't have a problem with that."

He grinned. "Okay, let's go."

We left and returned to the office. As instructed, I got out of the limo around the corner and James was to get out later. Although it felt somewhat illicit, we didn't need any gossiping eyes to spot us and grind up the rumor mill again. Back at the office on time, I breathed a sigh of relief. J.J. eyed me with an unsuspecting expression.

"Good lunch?"

I smiled at the hilarity of the past hour. "Yes, it was pretty good, thanks."

James came in ten minutes later and went straight into his office, resoundingly shutting his door. While J.J. looked up with a bit of a annoyance at the noise, I secretly smiled down at my work. No one was the wiser.

§

At four thirty, I still hadn't thought of a believable excuse to give Teresa about my whereabouts with James. Then I received a text from him.

Just to avoid scrutiny, Bernard will now be picking you up on the corner of Michigan and Illinois. That's one block north. Okay?

I giggled, feeling like I was a part of some covert ops mission.

That's fine.

Teresa and I had established our texting rules for work: Always, no matter what, phone on vibrate. I sent her a message.

Hey T. Got research I want to do for the design project. You know I've been wanting to chk out H. Wash Library, so going after work. Don't worry, won't be out too late. I'll keep you posted.

K Merc, that's fine. Kinda glad you didn't ask me to come, really beat & can't wait to go back to the dorm and crash lol. TTYL

Positively exuberant that this was all working out, I left at five o'clock sharp trying not to beam. I got to Illinois Avenue in no time. Guessing that I should just climb in the back, I did. I knew for a fact that James wasn't in here yet.

"Hi, Bernard," I greeted shyly because I was still embarrassed about this afternoon.

"Hello, Merci," he spoke politely and looked at me through the rearview mirror without an ounce of judgment. I felt much more comfortable since I decided that James and I were just friends and we were just going to talk.

I was a little confused when Bernard took off, but soon I realized he was just circling the block to park in his standard spot on the corner of JWC to pick up James.

As soon as we stopped, James climbed into the back over to his usual corner. He quickly poured himself a drink. He looked over at me with a small smile. I smiled in return.

"How are you doing?" he asked.

"Fine, how was your afternoon? Were you really busy?"

"Yes, as usual. Can't wait to kick back and really relax."

I still wasn't sure how much I could say to James since we were in new territory as friends, so I just smiled. I wanted him to lead our conversations when we had our big talk. So I made small talk.

"What do you usually do once you get back to your place?"

"Most of the time I'm still working when I get home. I'm pretty busy all of the time now. Tonight, I don't plan to do anything but gaze into your beautiful eyes." My heart rate picked up. He was always crossing the line, wasn't he? I ignored the last statement.

"What are you drinking now? Scotch again?" I asked a bit accusingly. He twirled his glass casually.

"No, this time, it's cognac - Hennessey. Have you ever tried hard liquor?"

I smirked. "Of course I've tasted it, my dad used to let me try his when I was little. I thought it was the nastiest thing I ever tasted. I guess he was using child psychology on me and it worked. I never asked again. He stopped drinking years ago anyway. Besides that wine, I haven't really enjoyed alcohol. I've tried a couple of mixed drinks and they tasted a little better, but not much."

"Merci, I think that's the most you've ever talked. I'm glad you seem to be getting more comfortable around me. Tell me about your folks."

I started to tell him about my parents but before we knew it, we were at The Fairmont. We jumped out of the back and Bernard sped off. I raised an eyebrow but James understood my silent query.

"He'll be back."

CHAPTER TEN

As we were in the elevator, James stood next to me very close. I felt his right pinky slightly touching my left hand. I discreetly moved it away. What was he playing at? He just chuckled under his breath.

Once in the suite, I set down my bag and shawl and plopped in the same comfy, oversized chair.

"You can take off your shoes."

"Okay." No harm in that, I guess. I kicked them off and curled up in the chair.

James went to a bar area and looked like he was fixing another drink. Me and him were going to have to have a talk about his alcoholic tendencies.

Surprisingly, he walked over with two tumblers.

"James, I told you I don't like hard liquor," I protested.

He sat down across from me and made me take the glass in my hand.

"Just take a sip and tell me what you think. If you don't like it, you don't have to drink it."

I hesitated and took a sip. It tasted pretty good. I barely tasted the alcohol. It was fruity and sour at the same time. Yum.

"Mmm, what is this?"

He smiled in approval and sat back to enjoy his own drink. "It's called an Apricot Stone Sour." I took another sip and decided I really liked it. I looked at him suspiciously.

"James, is it your intention to ply me with strong drink and seduce me?"

His perfectly sculpted eyebrows shot up to his hairline and he laughed uproariously.

"Merci, you are hilarious." Why was that so funny to him? Did I guess right? "You're here because you want me to pour my heart out to you, right?"

I nodded and smiled bashfully. "Right."

I watched him closely as his smile dissolved.

"Well, we'll need a few drinks before I can do that," he said bitterly. Wow, that mood change was swift. I thought I'd better take it easy. Loosened up a bit due to my new favorite drink, I relaxed and changed the subject.

"What music do you like?" His face relaxed at my question.

"I have a wide range of eclectic tastes. You sure you want to hear the list?" I sat up straighter and nodded eagerly. "I'll go in chronological order." He leaned his head back on the sofa and looked straight up at the ceiling, swishing his drink. "I like Beethoven, Chopin's Nocturnes, Tchaikovsky, big band classics with Benny Goodman, Duke Ellington, Cole Porter, jazz classics like Ella Fitzgerald, Coltrane, Byrd, Thelonious Monk, of course," he lifted his head and winked, "Sarah Vaughn, Frank Sinatra, Dean Martin, Nat King Cole, Stevie Wonder, The Beatles, Burt Bacharach, Marvin Gaye, Led Zeppelin, Paul McCartney & Wings, The Stones, Sly and the Family Stone, The Eagles, The Carpenters, Earth Wind & Fire, James Taylor, The Ohio Players, Simon & Garfunkel, Queen, Kiss, Paul Simon, Chicago, Billy Joel, Steely Dan, Toto, Michael Jackson of course," he lifted his head and smirked at me while I giggled remembering Saturday night. He continued, "Aerosmith, Duran Duran, Prince, The Boss,

John Cougar Mellancamp, The Cars, Culture Club, Wham, A Tribe Called Quest -"

"Stop, James, I get it. You like them all."

I'd had enough. My head was spinning from my drink and trying to visualize each artist before he moved on to the next. He looked up with an exaggerated pout on his handsome face.

"You didn't even let me get to the nineties." His head plopped back down on the sofa. "That's probably just as well, music started to go to shit with some notable exceptions like Nirvana and Jamiroquai. I don't even listen to most of the crap they play today." He lifted his head back up. "And you're wrong, Merci. I don't like everyone, just good, quality music."

I nodded understandably. "I've listened to a handful of them and you're right, they're amazing, but I disagree. There is still some good music out there today."

"Like who?"

"Adele, Katy Perry… I like Maroon 5, Dwele and a few others, like..."

Now buzzed, I was having a hard time coming up with more names. He waited patiently with an amused look. I cracked up as he'd obviously made his point. He laughed along.

"My point exactly. They're cool, I guess – but quality artists are few and far between. Back in the day, you *had* to have good music to get on the radio. Now, anybody can get a deal it seems. And the music is so simplistic."

"I have to agree with you, there. Complex chord progressions seem to be a thing of the past. I could probably learn a song today in five minutes."

He snickered.

"Good for you. I told you I believe you have good taste.

You like *me*, don't you?" he said smugly.

Ignoring the question, I felt things were getting out of hand due to our drinking. He got up to fix us more but I refused.

"No, James, that's enough for me." Getting back on track I said, "Tell me what you were going to tell me last night."

Sitting back on the couch with his drink, he was quiet for a moment.

"My father." He took a huge swig. "He's the problem."

"What do you mean?"

"He doesn't care about what I think, what I want, nothing. My mom isn't much better since she backs him up on everything. My dad has been grooming me for this position since before I could walk. Before he started the company back in '79, we were a modestly wealthy family due to an architectural firm my grandfather started back in the fifties. His company, Jansen, Probst & Welling built several historical landmarks down here. I'll show them to you one day. My father started off working there but was never interested in anything related to design, so once my grandfather got sick, he sold off the company and started JWC."

"Were you close to your grandfather?"

"He was ill for most of the years I was a kid, but he was the only one I was really close too."

"When did he die?"

"He died when I was twelve. Everyone agreed I was the most like him. We both operated with the left side of our brain. We're creative, artistic individuals. And while I know I'm more than capable of taking the helm of JWC, I just don't have the same vision my father has for me. To be truthful, I don't really have the interest."

Whoa, that was a heavy statement in light that he was

about to become CEO.

"What happens when you tell him that?"

James turned sideways to recline on the sofa, putting his feet up. I felt like a psychiatrist. I also reclined in my seat getting more comfortable.

"He just looks at me like I'm crazy and then starts his pathetic spiel to play on my sympathy. 'Who else can I get to pass the company down to? You are JWC,' and all of that nonsense," James spat bitterly.

"Is there anyone else in family that could take over the business?"

"Yes! My younger brother, Andrew, is just like my father. Drew's interested in numbers and the whole nine, but my Dad is ready to retire now and doesn't think Andrew is quite ready. I, for one, believe he's ready. Drew's just finishing his MBA and he's itching to get his hands on JWC. And you know what? That's fine with me. After I received my MBA, instead of starting at Jansen as my father wished, I moved to Europe and worked at an Italian interior design firm. It was one of the happiest times of my life. I loved it." He laid his arm over his head.

I was astounded. James was really in a conundrum. I didn't know what I could say except something to encourage him to go after his dreams. It was never too late, right?

"I believe you should do what you love. That's the only way to be truly happy." He shrugged under his arm but was quiet. I felt so sorry for him. I changed tack and went for gold.

"Tell me about Lorelei." He groaned as if in pain.

"Oh no, please...do I have to?"

I laughed a little to lighten the oppressive mood in the room.

"Yes, I want to know about your relationship. Am I

wrong in sensing, it's not a good one?" I wanted to laugh out loud at my *Captain Obvious* question, but I wanted James to tell me in his own way.

Not surprisingly, he laughed out loud for me.

"Of course it's not a good one - it's horrible!"

I tried hard to keep from giggling. "Why?"

"My parents and her parents thought it would be great for us to get together to merge our companies. She's the heiress of Sampson Electronics. While in the beginning I was fond of her, she's just become this utterly horrible person over the years. She nags, scowls and isn't remotely attractive in any way. Her personality makes my skin crawl."

"Why can't you two break up?" I asked, bewildered.

"We've broken up several times. Our families have a deal in place so that when we marry, our two entities will merge in which they've invested millions already. Mostly, it's my mother along with my father guilting me back with her. It's really hard to say no to my mother. It's basically greed, which is what my family is all about."

"Rebel and leave her."

"I can't. I promised them both I was straightening up once and for all and I wouldn't let them down this time."

Astonished, I said, "But you two don't love each other."

"What's that?"

I was sure I heard him wrong. "What's what?"

"Love?"

"Do you seriously need a definition?"

"Yes, because I don't think it matters much these days. That's why I didn't care about marrying her at first. She claims she loves me, but if that's what it is, I don't need it."

I looked at him like he had grown two heads. "I take it you've never been in love before?"

He pondered this for a moment. "No, I don't think so.

Have you?" Truthfully, I was falling now but I couldn't tell him that yet.

"No," I lied.

"So, you don't have any insight on it, either."

"I haven't felt it but I can imagine what it's like." He didn't seem satisfied with my answer but I went on.

"Is that why you don't mind cheating on her?"

"Actually, Lorelei doesn't…fulfill my needs in bed." Oh, that's right - the frigid rumor!

"Sorry to hear that," I awkwardly responded. I wasn't sure what to say so I asked, "Doesn't or won't?"

"Neither."

Hmm, now I didn't think that was fair. A young, virile, handsome man like James obviously had needs and if she was holding back... He just needed to break up with her some type of way. I needed to help him with that so I could be the one to fulfill his needs.

"If she supposedly loves you, why is she withholding sex?"

"She says she doesn't want sloppy seconds, but truthfully, we both grew apart in that way, years ago."

"Sounds complicated and doomed."

"That, it is."

Not knowing what else to say, I checked my phone and saw that an hour had passed. James sat back up on the sofa and motioned for me.

"Come sit by me, Merci. I'm not going to bite." I got up and went to sit by him.

"So, we're friends, right?" he asked somberly.

At his question, I nodded.

"Well, this 'friend' needs a hug."

I could do that. If I was being honest, I wanted to feel him in my arms. I wrapped my arms around his strong lithe body and guided his curly head to my shoulder. With his head comfortably in the crook of my neck, he held on tightly. He smelled so good and felt so wonderful. I knew I could stay here in his arms for the rest of my life. After a minute I tried to pull away but James wasn't having it and held on tighter. This was innocent enough, I figured. Then I felt liquid drops on my neck. Was he crying? James's body started quaking with sobs. Get out! James Jansen III was crying in my arms. Shocked and not knowing what else to do, I patted his head and shushed him.

"It's okay, James, let it all out." His sobs got even more violent. Two minutes passed of me patting his curly hair and soothing him. He took his head off my shoulder and laid it down towards my chest so he could talk. He wiped furiously at his eyes as he tried to speak normally.

"Sorry about that, I'm so embarrassed. See, Merci, I could never talk to Lorelei like that. You just have something that's so calming to me. I feel like I've known you for a long time."

Filled with warmth, I patted his head again. "I feel the same way."

He reached up to put his head back in my neck. I felt something wet again. Was he crying again? Wait, was that his tongue? I stiffened when I realized it was. He was giving my neck open mouthed kisses. Although it felt sublime, I valiantly tried to push him away. He held on tight.

"Merci, please, just let me…" he murmured in my neck.

I panicked - feeling myself slipping. "No, it's not right."

"I need you, Merci. I promise to find a way to break up with her."

"No, James, you just told me you promised your dad that you two would marry. How dare you insult my intelligence? I'm not an idiot."

"I know I said that earlier, but after holding you like this and talking to you like this…I really want us to be together," he pleaded. "I've got to find a way for us to be together. This feels so right. I've made a firm decision now to break up with her, because…I need you, Merci."

My eyes rolled back in my head. That sounded so good. I was growing weaker by the second. I knew I was falling for his lines, crap or not. He was too smooth.

He continued kissing and licking my neck and taking me into delirium. Between his kisses and the alcohol, somewhere in my brain I made myself believe he would break up with her and I decided I would help him. Apparently, I wanted James just that much. Deep down, I knew I was a fool. My body went limp as I let go. He felt my surrender and began to kiss and nibble more fervently.

"Is that a yes?"

He kissed up my jaw to my mouth and paused for an answer. I couldn't answer, but instead, turned my mouth toward his in response. He gasped and took my lips in his, opening my mouth and invading mine with his alcohol tinged tongue. He tasted so good. Our tongues dueled and licked. Tasting, sucking and biting. I was being taken under on a cloud of ecstasy I'd never felt before. The pit of my stomach had butterflies that didn't seem like they would abate anytime soon. I was caught in his spell and I was done for. Somewhere along the way, James stood up and guided me back towards the bedroom. He sat me on the bed, kneeled on the floor and began undressing me. I complied like a wanton ragdoll. I was completely powerless under his ministrations. He still had a wary look as if he expected me to run screaming.

"Merci…is this what you want? I need to know, now."

"Yes, James. I want you."

That was all he needed. He slipped my dress over my

head and left me sitting on the bed in my *VS* garnet colored underwear and thigh highs. He stood up, stepped back and let out a low whistle.

"Merci, you are so beautiful. One of the most beautiful women I've ever laid eyes on." His darkened eyes looked sincere.

I smiled bashfully. He pulled my legs towards him and I fell back on the soft downy comforter. James climbed over me fully clothed and began kissing my face. He placed small pecks all over my forehead, my cheeks, my neck and lips. I grabbed his hair, which is something I've wanted to do since I laid eyes on him, and held his face to mine to kiss him back with as much ardor as he was giving me. He groaned at my boldness and fell over onto the bed, pulling me on top of him. I felt powerful as I looked down at James Jansen's blazing beauty. His gorgeous chestnut eyes that looked like they were only for me and his handsome, strong face. With an appreciative gleam, he gazed up at my face and my chest that was spilling out of my bra. I watched as his eyes darkened even more in hunger. I kissed him like he kissed me - his broad forehead, his strong nose, his high cheekbones, under his strong jaw, his thick neck, his ear lobes, and back to his beautiful, full lips. His eyes were closed and he groaned as I had my fill kissing and tasting his stunning face.

If nothing else happened, this was enough to carry me for the rest of my life. I reveled in having the most beautiful, powerful man I had ever laid eyes on let me kiss him like this. James rolled us back over and got off the bed. I sat up on my elbows and watched him through hazy eyes. He slowly began removing his sweater. His glorious, olive skin was stretched taut over his bunched muscles. He was muscular without being bulky, no doubt due to his height as well. They rolled and ripped as he pulled the sweater over his head. He dropped it to the floor, never taking his heavy lidded eyes off of me. He unbuttoned his pants. This time I laid back and put an arm over my eyes. I wasn't ready to see what was next.

"Merci, look at me," he demanded.

"I can't. Please don't make me," I pleaded from under my arm.

A moment later, I felt the bed dip down with his weight as he dislodged my arm from my face. He looked incredulous.

"Merci, are you a virgin?"

I gave a nervous giggle.

"No." He relaxed at my answer. "But I've only been with one guy and that was a while ago and only a few times. So, I'm not very experienced."

He seemed pleased by my reply. "I knew you were special. Don't worry, your innocence is a turn on."

I didn't need to look down to know he was naked as he pressed against me. *My goodness.* He started kissing me again in earnest and my stomach did somersaults, flips - you name it. My heart was beating so hard I thought it would hammer out of my chest. One by one, my bra, panties and thigh-highs were discarded and then, we were nothing but a big mass of writhing flesh. I felt like I was in another dimension. Pleasurable turmoil lurched in the pit of my belly as I trembled at every single touch he gave me. It was unbelievable to me that this was really happening.

The thick curtains were drawn and as the sun went down, I couldn't see much. All I could do was feel. Touching, tasting, caressing, squeezing. We were ravenous for each other. James kissed every inch of me, even places where I should've been embarrassed, but he let me know I was sweet all over.

At one point, he reached over me to grab something, I assumed protection. He backed away as he applied it while I impatiently reached for him. Addicted, I was missing his touch already. I caressed his beautiful chest while I waited. Once he was done, our passion reignited.

James slid over me and at once, I felt the pang of being stretched uncomfortably. I winced and he paused to ask if I was okay. After a moment, I adjusted and nodded. Then we took off to Wonderland, moving in a rhythm as old as time.

I was consumed by him, utterly and totally. I surrendered and allowed James to take me to heights I had never imagined. How did stars get inside the room? We were floating so high I could've sworn that we were soaring. I mewled and cried out repeatedly as he made sweet, sweet love to me. He whispered that I sounded so sexy. Pretty soon I felt myself building to a pleasure I hadn't ever felt being joined with someone.

James moved more rapidly as if anticipating my impending rapture. We were building, building, rolling and rocking. We cried out together in ecstasy as our bodies jolted and convulsed in bliss. I reared up off the bed, and he with me, as my muscles violently tensed. I was wide-eyed and astounded of such pleasure. It took a hold of me and didn't let my body go for what seemed an eternity. I faintly heard James telling me how beautiful I looked at that moment. I drifted away. I knew for sure I blacked out for a moment.

As I regained awareness, James's head was in my neck, his body still joined with mine, releasing and stilling. Soon, his weight settled more on mine. Though he was heavier, I gripped his strong, broad back tightly. I never wanted to let him go. I never thought it could be like this.

I was in love.

The Clouds Come Crashing: Part II

CHAPTER ELEVEN

"Merci?"

"Merci?" James jostled me. I didn't know how much time had passed. I must've fallen asleep. I was in La La Land. My head was on his shoulder and I was wrapped in his arms.

I looked up at him with what I'm sure was love in my eyes and slowly grinned.

"Yes, James," I answered languidly like a star struck fool. He had a relaxed but amused look on his beautiful face.

"We need to get you back to the dorm. Bernard is downstairs waiting." I looked at him in puzzlement. I had just experienced the best moment in my life and he was already putting me out? I whined and kicked a bit. He chuckled.

"Can't I stay just a little bit longer? It's not even that late."

"You're so cute. It's seven thirty. And I actually have work to do." His eyes crinkled with mirth as he looked down at me, kissing me on my eyelids and cheeks. I melted.

"Okay. Then I need a shower first." He motioned to his right.

"Right through that door." We were covered with a sheet from the waist down but I suddenly got shy again.

"Don't look, James," I pleaded as I tried to get up with the sheet. He quickly pulled it back and I squealed.

"Merci, I've already seen, tasted and loved everything

you have to offer."

I blushed. "I know but – please," I begged.

"Okay, I'll close my eyes for now, but you'd better get used to it," he warned.

I took off to the bathroom and got in the huge marble shower. The enormous bathroom was masculine with grey, black, and white decor. The water was hot and relaxing. Just as I was soaping up, James opened the shower door and in all of his male glory, stepped in. I shrieked and vainly tried to cover up.

"James! I meant a shower for me, not both of us." Standing behind me as the water cascaded on us both, he wrapped his arms around my waist.

"Merci, you are much too shy for me. I see I'm going to have to break you of that habit sooner, rather than later."

He began kissing my shoulder blades, neck and ears. I was falling under again. I placed my hands against the glass to keep from collapsing, although I'm sure he wouldn't have let me.

If possible, it was getting even steamier in here.

"James," I murmured as he took in an ear lobe, "I have to go…you said he's waiting downstairs…" I weakly protested.

He turned me around, moved my hands away from my chest, replaced them with his, and kissed me thoroughly.

"Later," he responded against my lips.

§

I traveled back to the dorm in a daze. I looked out of the window but saw nothing. I was remembering his kisses, his touch, our passion and the heights he took me to with his powerful lovemaking. I wasn't expecting the bonus shower sex, but we'd had it and it was fantastic. I'd never done that before. I'm sure James would show me plenty of things I had never done before. I shivered and trembled in remembrance of our intense physical connection and of more to come.

Once in the dorm, to my pleasant surprise, Teresa was still napping. Grateful that she wouldn't be able to read my face like the open book it was, I took all of the design books I'd taken from the office, sat at the computer and pretended to do some work just in case she woke up. Meanwhile, I stared at the screen, day dreaming of my evening with James, and getting worked up remembering our glorious passion.

Teresa woke up not long after that and it seemed my plan had worked.

She yawned sleepily. "Did you get a lot of work done today?"

I kept my eyes on the monitor and smiled. "Yes, I got a lot of work done." I smirked at the screen.

I was *so* bad.

§

Once in bed, I revisited our evening over and over as my body still twinged pleasantly from his amorous affections. Even though I was heavily affected, I believed he was too. I thought about our long talk and how he broke down in my arms. I felt like we were both falling in love. Before we went outside for him to put me in the limo, he gave me another passionate, thorough kiss. His eyes seemed to reflect what I was sure was in mine. Next on the agenda was for him to break up with Lorelei for good. From the way things turned out today, I didn't see this as a problem. He had to know that we were meant for each other. I expected they would be broken up by tomorrow, at least.

In the middle of the night, I woke up with a start. Oh no! James hadn't brought protection into the shower and I hadn't remembered until now. Apparently, he didn't remember either. Although I was pretty sure I was safe according to my last cycle, I couldn't make that mistake again. I had to be cautious from now on because apparently, James made me stupid. I also decided to check out that Plan B "morning after" pill tomorrow.

§

The next day, I was ecstatic about going to work. I dressed as cute as possible and tried to tamper down my glee so that Teresa wouldn't be suspicious. I deflected by asking her about Jonathan instead. She happily gushed about their latest exchanges all the way to work.

At work, I opened my email to see a message from James. Obviously, he couldn't stay away either.

To: Merci Townsend
From: James Jansen III
Subject:
Please come into my office when you get here, ASAP.

With a secret smile and not bothering to reply back, I got up and knocked lightly on his door for J.J's sake. I opened his door and went in. His chair was swiveled around to the back. I had a huge grin waiting for him when he turned around.

When he did, what I saw made my stomach plummet. He looked downright angry.

"Close the door." I complied and turned back towards him in confusion.

"Sit down."

Once I sat down, he continued.

"Yesterday, we got carried away, and while I don't regret it, we carelessly went into things without discussing our history first. I apologize. I know you said you only had one partner and I believe that, but I failed to tell you about my history and you didn't ask, nor did you tell me if you're on any birth control or when you were last tested. It's not your fault, but while we were protected the first time, in the shower - we were careless. I am so angry at myself about this." He looked down in aggravation.

I relaxed a bit since I knew the anger wasn't directed at me.

"Are you on birth control?"

This all felt so clinical - where had the romance gone?

"No." He blanched a bit but retained his composure. I continued. "I wasn't planning on being involved with anyone so I didn't feel a need for it. I got tested a year ago and there hasn't been anyone else. I just realized about our mistake in the middle of the night, too. I'm sure from my cycle schedule that I'm safe."

He looked at me doubtfully. "Okay. Well...?"

"Well what?" Confused, I waited. He looked incredulous.

"Why didn't you ask if I was safe? Why *aren't* you asking me if I'm safe? Merci, I could have a disease or something and you didn't even ask."

"I know, James, but I didn't think about-"

"See, that's the attitude that reminds me of how young you are."

What the hell? So now, this was directed at me?

Heatedly, I retorted, "You didn't have to go there. Yes, I made a mistake but so did you! I was going to say I didn't think about it, like you didn't - because we got caught up.

How dare you try to make me feel stupid by bringing up my age. If that's the case, what's your excuse?"

He looked at me a second in amazement. I had him there.

He deflated. "You're right, Merci, I don't have an excuse." He sat up in his chair. "Just so you know, I haven't had a partner in five months and I've tested clean."

Hmmm, I'd heard he was a player so I didn't even want to know who that was. I'm pretty sure it wasn't Lorelei…well I couldn't be sure. He reached in his drawer and pushed two fifty dollar bills across the desk.

"Just to be sure, here's enough for that morning after pill or whatever it's called. At lunch, go buy it and take it. Just in case."

I hesitated, feeling dirty for some reason. I ignored the money.

"No, thank you. I was going to buy it myself anyway. I have enough for it."

Angry and about to cry at how our beautiful night turned sordid, I got up to walk out. James was from behind the desk, grabbing my arm before I made it to the door. He wrapped his arms around me from behind.

"Baby, I'm sorry if I made you feel bad, but these are things we need to talk about, should've talked about before. I'm the adult here-"

I stiffened. "What??" I said, offended.

"Sorry, babe. Let me rephrase that. I'm the older one here with more experience and I should've been more careful, for the both us. So please, take it." I let him fold the bills in my hand. I still felt disgusting.

"James, I'm not a child. I was an adult at eighteen and you know I'm mature for my age. I am a woman."

He chuckled and moved my hair to the side to kiss down my neck. I softened like melted butter.

"Oh, I know that, baby." He turned me around and I let myself surrender into his strong arms. He felt so good - smelled so good. He took my face in his hands and began his butterfly kisses that I loved so much.

"You're definitely not a child, you're my woman." I giggled and thrilled at his words and thought that might mean he was finally free. I'd ask him for details on that conversation later.

He kissed me so completely I thought I would faint. My hands went into his glorious hair, giving back as much as I could. He seemed to like it as he moaned low in his throat. Would I ever get used to his overwhelming kisses, his touch?

"Now get back to work," -kiss- "before J.J.," -smooch- "becomes suspicious." I laughed knowingly and went back to my desk.

I was the future CEO, James Jansen's woman. How awesome was that?

§

Later that day, I received a text from James.

Did you take care of that?

I knew what he was talking about.

Yes, I did and I have change.

Lol, keep it. Same time and place as yesterday. Be ready.

I balked. I didn't really have an excuse for Teresa today. She would definitely get suspicious two days in a row.

James, I can't. I don't have an excuse for Teresa and she could get suspicious.

What? I don't give a damn what she thinks, I want you.

James, I care what she thinks. I'm not going today.

I valiantly tried to put my foot down. After waiting two minutes and growing anxious, he responded.

But I miss you and I need you. Please, baby. I would love nothing more than to love you again like yesterday. It was so beautiful.

He sure knew how to get to a girl.

What about our mishap yesterday? I'm sure he knew I was ready to break.

I've got it under control. Be ready.

I got excited by his words and had to keep myself from visibly squirming. He was so sexy. I couldn't believe this powerful and beautiful man was mine.

With no new options, I left Teresa the same, lame excuse. She seemed to be disappointed but said she understood. She didn't mention napping today, so I was relieved she didn't invite herself along. Did she suspect?

At the hotel, we were hardly inside the penthouse when James attacked me. We had already been heavily making out in the elevator.

He led me right to the bedroom and began undressing

me. There was no preamble as we got busy. As promised, he didn't forget protection. Through a haze, I remembered that I was supposed to ask him about Lorelei. That thought came and left almost instantaneously. James was taking me on his rollercoaster of love - say what?

Just as I imagined, he showed me more and more about the pleasures to be had between a man and a woman. Ways I'd never dreamed. I loved every moment of his aggression because he made me feel so feminine. Slowly but surely, he was bringing me out of my shyness, even putting me in charge, so to speak.

After pleasures beyond compare, we laid together in bed, relishing in our afterglow. I decided this was as good a time as any. I shouldn't have been so nervous, right?

"James, what happened between you and Lorelei?"

He stiffened. "What do you mean?"

I sat up clutching the sheet to my chest. I couldn't believe him.

"What do you mean, what do I mean? I assumed because you said I was your woman, you broke up with her."

He shifted and looked at me directly.

"I haven't had a chance to talk to her yet."

Not waiting to hear a response, he got up out the bed and went to the bathroom. Incredible. I was such a fool. I wasn't dealing with this a second longer. Yes, I was already in love with him, but it was obvious he didn't feel the same. I took advantage of his bathroom visit to get up, get dressed and wait in the other room on the sofa. I could've left and got on the train but since it was already getting dark, I thought Bernard could drop me off. The truth is, if I had any dignity, I would've left. But deep down, I didn't want to leave James without him knowing. I was a shameless coward. A few minutes later he came to find me. He had on black sweats with no shirt. His eyes were red and he smelled a little like…marijuana? I was too pissed to ask. He looked a little panicked like he thought I might've left but his eyes relaxed once he saw me.

"Why are you dressed? We still have more time."

"Are you crazy? You didn't break up with her. You led me to believe that you and she were over. Otherwise I would NOT have had sex with you today," I shouted. Tears were streaming down my face.

"Shh, shh, baby. I told you I haven't had a chance to talk to her yet-"

"If it meant that much to you like it means to me," I bellowed, "you would've gotten it over with already. I'm not doing this. Please have Bernard take me back to campus."

I could hardly see through my tears as I picked up my bag and marched to the elevator. I pressed the down button and waited. I could hear James on the phone instructing Bernard to take me back to the dorm. He obviously wasn't going to try to stop me. That made me even more miserable.

Once downstairs, I tried to wipe my tears to keep my pitiful face from Bernard's. If he noticed, he was too polite to acknowledge it as he opened the door for me. Once inside the limo, I noticed the screen that separated us was closed. How kind of him. All the way back to the dorm, I bawled like a baby.

CHAPTER TWELVE

There was no hiding from Teresa. I came in the dorm slinging my bag on the bed. She was instantly on alert when she saw my face. That cat was on its way out of the bag.

"What's wrong?"

I stared at her as a fresh wave of tears contorted my face. She came over grabbing my shoulders in panic.

"What's wrong, Merci? Tell me!"

I sniffled trying to get my words out between sobs. "James..."

"What did he do? What did that jerk do?"

"He didn't break up with Lorelei."

She looked bewildered. "What are you talking about?" Her face was disbelieving as she realized what was going on. "Merci! You've been seeing James Jansen?"

I looked down and nodded. I plopped down on the bed in shame as Teresa began her infamous pacing.

"Merci, how could you get involved with him? I told you that he wasn't someone you needed to be involved with since he is engaged. I could've told you that he wasn't going to break up with her. It goes deeper than just a relationship. Millions of dollars are probably at stake."

I couldn't say anything as I continued to cry.

"Did you sleep with him?" I nodded. "Merci, oh no. When?"

"Yesterday and today," I replied, sniffling.

Her mouth was wide open in shock. "So that's the 'library visits.'" She shook her head. "Is this something that just happened out of the blue or have you and he been more involved than you let on recently?"

"For a few weeks we've been talking at our lunches," I rambled between tears, "and he let me know he was interested in me," I hiccupped, "and we were just going to be friends at first because I was adamant about not messing around with him while he was engaged. And then…"

"Then what?" She prodded.

"Then, I went to his place yesterday – just to talk - and he poured out his heart to me…" Teresa was looking at me like I was an idiot. I guess I was.

"Go on."

"So then, things got carried away after he cried-"

"You've got to be kidding me." She plopped down on the bed. "James Jansen III was crying?" She laughed. "Boy, is he smooth. That's a new tactic. I heard he was good," she mumbled.

"No, no. He was really sincere." She smirked. "So after he broke down, I comforted him and that's when he promised," I looked at her, pleading for understanding, "that he would break up with Lorelei since we both get along so well and we needed to be together."

"Okay, then what happened?" Teresa was regarding me stoically with what appeared to be great patience.

"We made love. I know it was stupid to do but I wanted to believe his promise and he was just so irresistible. It's James Jansen for goodness sake! And then I came back here. I thought he would call her and break up with her right away. Seriously T, we had a real connection."

Teresa was quiet for a moment as she thought about what I said.

"Did you use protection? Because from what you told me, you're not even on birth control."

"He used it – the first time."

Her eyes almost bugged out of her head.

"James Jansen is not only engaged, but a player. He could have all types of diseases not to mention you could be pregnant! Merci!"

Looking at it from her perspective made me feel really dumb. I still tried to shut it down.

"I know, but we talked about our one mistake yesterday, our history and how we couldn't get carried away again, and today we were safe. He told me he's clean and hasn't been with anyone for five months. He was the one who brought it up. I believe him. He also gave me money for the morning after pill which I took today, just to be sure about our slip-up."

She looked at me like I had grown two heads and scrunched up her face in disgust.

"Merci, this sounds...I don't know...'hoochiesque' - if there was such a word. Him giving you money to take care of a 'potential problem'? It just sounds...so wrong."

"I know, I know. The last straw was when I found out he hadn't broken up with her. I marched out and left. I told him I wasn't doing it anymore, so don't worry - I'm not dealing with James again. It was a mistake, I know."

Seeming a little satisfied with this, Teresa's face softened.

"Please come home with me this weekend and come to church. Getting into God's Word will help you walk in the spirit and not fulfill the lusts of the flesh. It's the only thing that will help what you're going through. You also have your Bible here to help you."

I knew she was trying to help but that was the last thing on my mind. "I said I'm done with James. I'll be okay - I promise." She shook her head doubtfully and threw up her hands.

"Okay, Merci, I'm praying for you. Let me know if you change your mind." Happy the subject of church wasn't going to be shoved down my throat - I reached over and gave her a hug.

"Thanks T, I will."

§

That night I received a text from James.

Baby, please talk to me. I'm sorry I hadn't gotten around to talking to her.

Hearing him call me baby sounded so good. I couldn't break, though. Determined, I responded.

James, I don't want to hear it. We're done.

What? Can't you be patient?

Why wasn't it important enough to take care of right away?

It is. The timing needs to be right. You just don't understand all of the logistics involved.

Then, why even promise me if you knew you weren't?

I am. It's just that I need more time. I miss you already.

I didn't respond and another text quickly followed.

We are so good together. I love how your body feels in my arms, how luscious you are. I want you so bad.

I knew what he was trying to do and it was working. It brought on a fresh wave of memories, making my nerve endings tingle, betraying me.

I still didn't respond.

Baby, you there? I know you're imagining what we did this evening. We fit together like a puzzle. You are so soft, so perfect for me. Please don't give up on us. I'm going to break up with her. Just give me time.

I contemplated what he was saying. Truthfully, I didn't want to mess up and lose him if he was really going to end it with her. He was like a dream come true to me.

I tell you what, James. Check back with me when you've ended it with Lorelei. I'll wait.

There. I wasn't giving in but I wasn't totally letting him go, either. The ball was in his court. I waited for his response. After five minutes I began to worry.

James?

My ringer vibrated after two minutes. I quietly ran to the bathroom to answer.

"Hi," I answered.

His deep voice was slightly off as if he'd been drinking again. No surprise there.

"I like you a lot, Merci, but there are plenty of other women who could easily take your place. While I can't deny

I'm growing feelings for you like I've never experienced before, I *will* get over you."

Wow, he sounded so cold. Admittedly, I was worried.

"James, I just want you to be mine, totally and completely. Can't you understand that? You wouldn't like it if I had a fiancé and you were the side-piece."

He sighed at my usage. I knew he hated to hear that term come out of my mouth.

"That would never happen in the first place. Look, I don't have time for this. I told you I would get around to Lorelei. In the meantime, are we going to waste time over something that's going to be taken care of eventually or are we going to spend every moment we can, together? Time is precious."

I agreed, time *was* precious. "Yes, you're right. Okay."

"Good, baby. I'm glad we can move along." He gave a loud smooch through the phone. "I'll see you tomorrow."

"Okay -" He hung up before I could add *James*.

While in the back of my mind, I marveled at how smooth he was to turn it around in his favor, he made some great points. Plus, he implied he was falling for me! Let's face it - James Jansen III was too fine, too precious, too good in bed and too dynamic for me to give up. I may never meet anyone like him for the rest of my life. Literally and figuratively, I was screwed.

§

The next day, I received another email summoning me to his office. This time I shut the door automatically. He had a big smile on his face. Today he had on a blue, long sleeved shirt rolled up to his forearms and black slacks. He looked great as usual. I had on my black pencil skirt and a bright coral blouse. I opted to put my hair back in a bun and wore my glasses. Mistakenly, Teresa thought I was demonstrating my dowdy look to ward James away, but little did she know it had the opposite effect. He said he liked my librarian look.

"Hey, babe, lookin' sexy in those glasses. Come here." He motioned for me to come and I timidly went behind his desk. I had never been back here. He abruptly pulled me down onto his lap. I gasped in surprise.

"James!"

He shut me up by covering my mouth with his. He gave a long three minute exploration of my mouth. I was in heaven. He tasted so good and he kissed me so well. When he finally released my lips with small sensual pecks, I gave him my brightest smile. He looked at my eyes and mouth intensely. I could really tell that his feelings for me were growing. I was determined to make him feel like I felt. And I was in love.

"Mmm, good morning," I breathed.

He smiled back. "And what a good morning it is." He gave me another kiss and gently pushed me off his lap. I let him since I'd already been in his office too long.

"Don't leave yet. Sit down, we need to talk." Had he talked to Lorelei? I eagerly went to the seat across from his desk and waited to hear what he had to say.

"Since we're going to keep seeing each other, I think it's important for you to get birth control."

Surprised, I second guessed myself. That should've been on my mind too but everything was happening so fast. I tried to straighten my face into one of serious consideration instead of disappointment that it wasn't about a breakup with *her*.

"You're right, that's important."

"I think you could get one of those patches or a shot and you could probably get it quickly. I have several places listed here where you can get it done." He pushed a piece of paper containing a list of doctors and clinics. "Don't worry about the cost." Then he pushed a black credit card my way. "I want you to have this. This is for paying for medical costs and anything else you need."

What? He was giving me a credit card? Carte blanche? I felt like this was heading into dangerous territory.

"No, James, I don't need your credit card. While helping with birth - um - medical costs is okay, I don't need your help with anything else. It just feels…wrong." I pushed the card back his way.

He sat back in his seat in confusion. "Why? Aren't you my woman? Then it's my job to take care of you. I will be buying you things anyway and I have more than enough. Plus, while you look great, I know a new wardrobe would set you apart from everyone. You're beautiful, but James Jansen's woman is supposed to look absolutely stunning at all times." He was speaking in third person - really? "I want you to go to salons, get pampered at spas-"

"James, stop. This is overwhelming. While I appreciate the gesture, you have to let me get used to the idea. We are moving too fast, I think. Let's take care of… first things first, but can we slow down on the other stuff?"

My heart was beating so fast. I finally realized I was out of my depth with a man as powerful and charismatic as James Jansen. Now, instead of the fun, down to earth guy he had been at the hotel, naming his favorite music artists, he seemed like the wealthy, controlling CEO he would soon be. I was in over my head. I needed to dial it back a bit.

He looked at me curiously for a moment and then smiled in amazement. He slid his card back towards him.

"Merci, this wasn't a test but if it was, you passed with flying colors. Do you know how many women would've taken my card without blinking twice? You are truly special, baby. Now, I'm never letting you go."

If possible, I felt even more unsettled by his words and I wasn't sure why. Taking the list, I got up.

"James, I'll consider which one of these to go to. I need to go back to my desk now, if that's okay?"

He shrugged. "Okay, babe, I'll talk to you in a bit." Adding in his business tone, "I also have some more samples that need to be ordered."

"No problem - just let me know." And I was out. I couldn't get away fast enough.

As I went back to my desk, J.J. was eyeing me speculatively. I ignored him. Darn it, we had been in there too long and I only came out with a slip of paper. I think we were getting sloppy. I didn't even pretend to take design books in there anymore to talk to James. Too overwhelmed to really give J.J. any more thought, I pretended to work on my computer while thinking about James.

What was I getting myself into? This was turning serious and he still had Lorelei. He was acting like both of us were going to be his women. I was so confused.

Too bewildered to face Teresa, I told her I was working through my lunch when in reality, I went at twelve so that I could eat alone and think. While I was in Popeye's having a small meal, I received a text from James.

Hi, Baby. Bad news. I have to fly out to Boston right away. I'll probably be gone by the time you return from lunch but I just wanted you to know. Btw, I left the credit card in your top drawer so you can get that taken care of while I'm gone. I'll only be gone a few days so be ready lol. I'll miss you.

I didn't know how I felt about his news. In a way I was sad that he was leaving but also relieved that I would have time to process what direction we were heading in. Resigned, I texted back.

Okay James, I understand. I'll take care of it. Have a safe trip - I'll miss you too.

He texted back after a minute.

Wow, you don't sound too disappointed.

Panicking, I tried to smooth it over.

What? I am! I just want you to know I understand your obligations, and I do. Of course I can't wait for you to get back.

Mmm, can't wait either. I'll call you tonight, baby.

Okay, looking forward to it, baby. I piled on to make up for his doubt.

You called me baby - so sweet…

Lol

TTYL babe.

Okay.

CHAPTER THIRTEEN

On the train, I was subdued by everything that was going on which was just as well whereas Teresa was concerned. Of course she thought I was still upset over our "breakup." Even though she was reluctant due to not wanting to hurt my feelings, I encouraged her to tell me about Jonathan. It worked out well. She would've never guessed that I was down because of my fast growing, train wreck of a relationship with James.

§

That night, as promised, James called. Already in the bathroom, I answered.

"Hello, James. Did you make it in okay?"

"Yep, everything's fine," he slurred.

Let me guess...

"James, do you drink every night?"

"Yes. I have to have a drink to wind down from this stressful job."

Thinking about the marijuana smell I detected, I asked, "Do you smoke weed, too?"

He was quiet for a moment. "Occasionally, how did you know?"

"I smelled it on you yesterday right before I left. You do it in the bathroom?"

"Yes, it calms me down. You were asking me way too many questions yesterday."

Oh no, he wouldn't. "What? You're going to blame it on me? Don't I have a right to know what's going on with us?"

He sighed and I thought I heard him grumble, *here we go.*

"Babe, are you *trying* to start an argument? We just got together and we're already having big blow-ups."

"No, I'm not trying to start an argument but I don't see anything wrong with asking a few questions. You are not going to turn it around and make me feel like the guilty one. I can tell you're real good at that."

He chuckled as if I was right. "You sure are sharp, Merci. That's why you're my girl."

He was incredible. So he was basically admitting to be a master of pointing the finger?

I was speechless.

He sighed and relented. "Yes, I know you have a right to know what's going on. It's just that things are so complicated."

"They don't have to be complicated. Your solution is right in front of your face. Break up with her."

"That's easier said than done."

"Why?"

"Because I told you, there are a lot of things that have to be dealt with first. Things I don't want to get into right now."

"James, try to understand how I feel. When you're talking about me being your woman and all that you want to do for me, it sounds so good. But at the same time, I know that I'm not really your woman. You have two women!"

"No, no, it's not like that. She is not my woman. She's my fiancée in name only and not for long. I have only one woman and that's you, Merci."

I melted at his words, but I was cautious.

"All I'm asking is do you understand how I feel?"

"I do. Please, Merci, just be mine. I'm going through a lot right now and I don't feel like I have anybody but you to talk to. So when you berate me, I feel so dejected and lonely. I guess I turn to drink and stuff to help me out. I know it's a cop-out but I'm working on it." Saddened at his words, I could feel myself giving in.

"I am yours, James. But please, communicate with me more. You told me I was easy to talk to, so talk to me."

"I want to, but I feel like you're judging me harshly because I haven't broken up with her yet."

I thought about that. I didn't want him to close up if he felt that was a barrier between us. I wanted to help him in any way I could.

"I don't want you to feel like that. Please talk to me."

"I will if you promise not to bring her name up again. Know that you're my only woman and I'm working on ending it with her. Just stop pressuring me." He sounded so gloomy that I couldn't resist.

"Okay, I'll trust that you're taking care of it and I won't bring her up again."

Satisfied with my answer, his voice was buoyant in an instant.

"Good, baby. Let's just concentrate on me and you." Somehow I felt like I had been bamboozled. I'd think about that later. "So did you make an appointment?"

"I did. I'm scheduled to go tomorrow on lunch."

"Good girl. Don't forget the card." His voice smoldered, "I should be back by Friday."

I gave a small laugh. "Okay."

"Well, baby, I'm going to let you go to sleep. I have some work to do before I turn in." His tone changed. "By the way,

I emailed the new sample list for you to order. Please take care of that tomorrow."

"Yes, sir."

"Ooh, that sounded so sexy," he said, his sultry voice back.

I laughed. "Good Night, James."

"Good Night, Merc."

We hung up. Smiling, I tiptoed out of the bathroom. To my utter horror, Teresa was sitting up in her bed and the lights were on. I froze. Oh no – busted?

"You got some splainin' to do. I know that was James. You were giggling way too loud. What's up?"

I decided to lay it all out there. "We're working it out."

"Did he break up with Lorelei?" She asked pointedly. Not able to continue looking her in the face, I got back into bed.

"He's working on it. It's not as simple as you think."

"Didn't I tell you that? And he isn't going to break up with her, either."

"He said he was and I believe him. I think he's falling in love with me, Teresa. I'm going to give him another chance and time to take care of his dealings with her. I don't want to lose him."

"So you believe you *have* him? Girl, bye." She turned off the lamp, plopped down on her back and pulled the covers up to her head. "Don't worry, Merci, I won't say anything else to you about James. I see you're not going to listen anyway. I'll be praying for you." She turned over away from me.

Upset and defiant, I mumbled, "No, thanks."

I was done too. From her point of view, I could see how bad it looked, but I couldn't explain everything from my perspective where she could understand. It was more complicated than that. This was cool anyway, maybe now she could stay out of my business.

The next morning, I left for work earlier than usual to keep from riding with Teresa. She tried to smooth things over, but I didn't want to hear it.

"Merci, I'm sorry I was snappy last night but I'm not perfect. It's just that I care about you and don't want to see you get hurt." Not looking her way, I continued dressing so I could get out of there. "Please forgive me?"

"No problem." I grabbed a sweater and left without a backwards glance.

As I was trying to fall asleep last night, I kept getting mad over her attitude. I got tired of her acting like she was right all of the time, and all I did was wrong.

§

At lunch, I went to my appointment. They gave me a pap smear, took blood and administered the shot. I opted for the shot as opposed to the patch since the doctor said it would be effective for three months, and I didn't need to be worried about changing a patch every week. Also, it cost more but I had James's card. She made sure to warn me that I wouldn't be protected for a week, so my partner and I needed to continue using condoms. James wouldn't be happy about that, but too bad.

I actually felt good that the burden of trying to keep things a secret from Teresa was over. Now, I didn't have to explain anything. We weren't really speaking as far as I was concerned so I didn't have to make up an excuse for going to get birth control on lunch. I didn't need to tell her anything. I didn't need her or her opinions - not right now. James would be back soon, I justified. I'll be spending most of my lunches with him.

Purposely missing the train that Teresa and I were usually on, I lingered around my desk and left to catch the one afterwards. Deciding I didn't want to go to the dorm, I went to the campus library instead. I missed him so much already. Nervously, I decided to text him.

Hey, baby. I just wanted to see how you were doing today.

He responded back in five.

Merci, I'm on a conference call right now, can I call you later?

A conference call this late?

Yeah, sure. No rush, though, I was just checking.

No response. Feeling a bit depressed and alone, I picked a book off the shelf and mindlessly skimmed it. It was hard to concentrate on anything but James.

§

At the dorm, Teresa was at her desk on the computer. She gave me a friendly smile. Feeling a bit sorry for her because I wasn't raised to be rude, I decided to bend.

"Hi," I said.

Her eyes lit up. "Hi, Merc, where were you?"

Immediately my hackles went up. "I wasn't with him," I said defensively, "I was at the library for real."

Teresa looked taken aback. Slowly, she said, "I really wasn't thinking about him or that you were with him, I was just asking. Sorry." She gave me a look like I was loony and turned back to her PC.

Now I felt stupid, but I said nothing. I think it would be better if we didn't say much to each other. Then I wouldn't have to explain anything.

§

By the end of the week, it seemed our routine was set. Teresa, probably tired of futilely reaching out to me, accepted my remote behavior and remained silent. I left early and came back late, usually spending time in the library or the bathroom waiting for James to have time to call. I was also miserable that he hadn't been calling me back like he promised. With only a few brief texts, I hadn't even had a chance to tell him about the shot. I had no communication with him at all on Thursday. I chalked it up to him being a very busy man and I needed to discipline myself to accept this if I was to be the future wife of a CEO. That thought encouraged me.

I needed to find other things to do with my time except getting caught up in James and the idea of James. It was so hard because everything I did, I related it back to him. I love this show - I wonder if James likes this show? This sandwich is good - I wonder what kind of sandwiches James likes? I should take the cheese off of this burger – would James agree? This guy has on a purple suit in this book, what would James think of that? And it went on and on. I was completely obsessed already.

But today was Friday and my man would be back. Enough day-dreaming, I was going to see him in the flesh. I pulled out a wine colored wrap dress I hadn't had the guts to wear because it accentuated all of my curves – but today I didn't care. I also put on the foreboding five-inch heels. It was just the dire situation that called for them. I needed him to really see me. I made sure I brought my shawl just in case I felt shy all of a sudden.

§

I got to work and was disappointed there was no email. Since J.J. wasn't here yet, I decided to see if James was in since the door was slightly ajar. He wasn't. Feeling deflated again, I worked on ordering samples for an hour. J.J. had finally arrived and we were working in comfortable silence. At eleven thirty, James whisked through the outside doors and into our quarters with a flourish. He had on his black Armani suit and briefcase. He looked so distinguished. J.J. and I stared.

"Hello, guys, how's it been going?" James asked.

"Oh, it's been pretty busy but we've managed," J.J. answered.

James turned my way. From my vantage point, J.J. couldn't see his face since he was behind him. James winked and quickly looked me up and down, his lips formed in a silent whistle. He couldn't really see anything under the desk but there was more cleavage visible than usual. I tried my best not to blush because J.J. could see my face. I answered before J.J. got suspicious.

"It's been fine. How were things in Boston?"

"Busy - very busy." He continued to his office. I went back to work, satisfied that he thought I looked good and I had his attention again.

Five minutes later I received an email notification.

To: Merci Townsend
From: James Jansen III
Subject:
Please bring your sample books and come to my office, ASAP.

Inside, I was doing the samba. With a secret smile, I grabbed my books and went into his office, closing the door lightly behind me. As soon as it was closed, James, who was standing by the window, came over and pushed me up against the wall. His head went into the crook of my neck, kissing and nibbling. I moaned in pleasure. This was all worth the wait.

"Merci, I've missed you so much and you look and smell so good. I don't ever want to be away from you that long again." He didn't give me a chance to respond before he took my mouth in his. I gave just as good as I got since I missed him too. Boldly, I grabbed his hair to hold his face still while I plundered his mouth. I reached up and began kissing his ear, neck or whatever I could find. He groaned in delight.

"James, I missed you so much, too. I felt like you didn't want to talk to me," to my dismay, my eyes watered, "please don't make me feel that way again."

He pushed my head up to look at him, cupping my face. "Oh, sweet baby, don't cry. I've been so busy I haven't had time for anything. After our meetings, I'm so beat, I fall asleep before my head hits the pillow. Please don't think I didn't want to talk to you. I couldn't wait to get back to you."

He kissed me again and placed me away so he could see the length of me. "And you're looking so sexy in that dress and those heels - too sexy. I don't want anyone to see you like this but me. I want you now."

I panicked with J.J. in the next room. "No...no, not here, James," I pleaded. His eyes, now dark with passion challenged me.

"Then where? Because I need you now. I'm not going to wait until later." He had me back in his arms, his hands roaming and groping everywhere on my body, beginning to peel away my dress. I was on fire. I tried to think quickly through my hazy mind.

"Okay, okay - how about we get together during lunch?" That seemed to placate him as he slowed down his greedy kisses to my neck and face.

He stood back and began to straighten up my clothes, pulling my dress back up a shoulder and shaping my hair.

"Okay, lunch is in fifteen. Meet me in the limo on Illinois," he commanded.

"Okay."

He stood back looking like an unsatisfied caveman - hair wild, jaw taut, clothes disheveled. He was so *hot*.

"Go on, now - before I change my mind." His deep voice growled.

I put the finishing touches on fixing myself back up and swiftly exited back to my desk with the design books that were never opened.

CHAPTER FOURTEEN

Once in the limo, James and I picked up where we left off in his office. We kissed nonstop until we made it to the hotel. Not caring what Bernard thought anymore, I hopped out with James and ran hand in hand inside the hotel, continuing our make out session in the elevator.

That afternoon, James took me like his life depended on it. I made sure he knew that we still needed protection. He wasn't happy but he cooperated because nothing could stop his mission. He was aggressive and forceful as if he was angry about something. Beneath him while he ravaged me, I gladly let him take out his frustrations and I loved it. That's what I was here for. I was his woman.

We returned to work separately and James sent me a text for us to go back to the hotel after work. Happily, I consented. I had no excuses to give anyone.

That night, our lovemaking was much slower, less intense. His mind seemed finally at ease. His languid ministrations were in stark contrast from this afternoon. I trembled with the tenderness he showed me as he took his time attending to my every desire. Strangely, I didn't know which method I liked better. Maybe both?

§

Once we were done, he went into bathroom. When he came

back out in sweatpants, he had a joint in his hand, smoking it freely. I stared in amazement. He looked like a pro.

"James, should you be smoking that up here? Isn't it against hotel policy?"

"I wish they would say something about it. My family invests too much money in this franchise - they wouldn't dare."

Duly chastened, I continued to stare as he sucked it in, held it and let it out slowly. I had never tried it, but I wasn't unaware of it. Kids in my high school smoked it around me at parties. Still, it was so up close and personal here. My man was smoking it like it was a regular cigarette. Quickly, before I knew it, he was on the bed next to me.

"Open your mouth and suck in when I blow. Then hold it."

"No, James, I don't want any."

"Open your mouth, now," he fiercely commanded with feral, bloodshot eyes.

I weakly complied and opened. He took a long pull, got up close and blew a stream of steady smoke in my mouth. "Now close it and hold it." I did and the smoke burned my throat. I began coughing uncontrollably.

"That - was - horrible," I exclaimed, still coughing.

He laughed uproariously. "Haven't you ever tried weed before?"

"No. Thanks a lot, James."

He looked surprised but didn't stop laughing.

"Well just wait a few - I think you'll like it."

At the time I didn't feel anything but a scorched throat. After a moment of just staring at each other, I began to feel...different. I felt light, like I was floating a little. I tugged his arm.

"James, what's happening?"

"You're getting high, that's what happening," he said, chuckling. "Take some more." He handed me the joint and I tried to take a strong pull. I coughed violently and shoved the joint back in his fingers, my eyes watering.

"Easy, easy. You've got to pull it in easy. Try again."

I hadn't stopped coughing and he wanted me to try again?

"Here," he insisted. I reluctantly took it from him and took a slow pull as instructed. "Now hold it." I did until my throat couldn't take it. "Now blow it out." I did without any coughing, but my throat was on fire.

"Good girl." He took the rest of the joint and stubbed it out in the ashtray, got back in the bed with me and gathered me in his arms. The room started changing shapes a bit. I was frightened.

"James?" I panicked, clutching his arm. He chuckled softly.

"Calm down, you're fine. Just relax - I'm with you. You're just being a bit paranoid right now."

"James," I called again. This time he cracked up.

"Merci, you are so funny. You're going to be fine. Let's talk about something. Watch anything good on TV lately?"

I tried to think. I had hardly watched TV in a week, I'd been so consumed with him. I made up something.

"Yeah, I saw a show about a girl who's crazy about a guy who's engaged to someone else and won't break up with her. Sound familiar?"

He laughed and looked down at me. I looked back up at him defiantly since I was high now, and didn't care.

"Yes, it sounds familiar. Let me tell you the end of the story. The guy dumps his fiancée' and gets engaged to the girl instead."

I got so happy, I stood up on the bed and jumped up and

down. Then I tripped and landed face flat on James.

"Oomph," he grunted, but continued laughing heartily. "Lord, have Merci on me," he exclaimed, laughing. He lifted his head and looked at me. "See what I did there? That was pretty good, huh?"

"James, that was so coorrnny," I bellowed, dragging the word out until I lost breath.

"Girl, I shouldn't have given you any weed. You are trippin.' "

"I'm not - I'm just happy." I got up and started jumping up and down again. He pulled me back down and rolled me underneath him.

"I know how to calm your ass down." He kissed me soundly and I could taste the marijuana in our mouths. It was strange, but exhilarating, too. I don't remember much about the lovemaking that followed, except that I felt a bit disjointed from my body. It was like it was happening, but not really happening. Everything was more intense and magnified. When James brought me to that special place, I screamed like a banshee.

Afterwards, we came down from both highs.

"I don't know whether giving you that was a good thing or a bad thing. You were like a crazy, uninhibited, wild woman in bed. I liked it, but I also like it when you have some sense, too. I'll have to think this through," he said, amused.

I just looked at him in with a hazy smile. Suddenly, all I could think of was food.

"James, I'm hungry."

"Oh, you've got the munchies. Go order room service - anything you want."

I ran out the room, butt naked, to where the menu was. Uninhibited, indeed. I was dissatisfied with the choices, but was assured over the phone that I could get anything I wanted.

I ordered Doritos, Cheetos and fruity soda. James laughed at my selections.

"Yeah, that's usually what you want the first time."

§

Instead of going home that night, James insisted I spend the night. He reasoned that it was the weekend and we didn't have to go to work. After already showering and putting back on my clothes, I wasn't too comfortable with that idea.

"I don't have any clothes with me."

"Then let's go shopping."

"What - now?"

"Aren't we close to the shops? Some of them are still open."

"We don't have to do that. Maybe I could just go back and get some clothes." I didn't have a problem with going to the dorm to get clothes, especially since I knew Teresa should've already left for the weekend.

"Why? I told you I wanted you to have new clothes. Let's go."

I wasn't one to keep refusing new gear, especially when he kept insisting.

Sure enough, Water Tower Place was still open when we got there. Just inside the promenade, James's business cell began buzzing with messages. He looked irritated.

"Babe, I need to respond to these. You still have my card, right?"

I checked my purse. "Yes."

"Good, go get whatever you want. New underwear, shoes - the works. I'll be right down here." He indicated a nearby bench.

Disappointed he wasn't coming with me, I reluctantly started to walk away.

"Okay, I understand." Then, making sure he knew I was grateful, I gave him a big smile. "Thank you."

He grabbed my arm to pull me back into his chest. He cupped my face tenderly and gave me a slow, sensual kiss on the lips. I swooned, ready to fall under his spell again. It didn't take much.

"You're welcome, baby. Have fun. Remember, there is no limit. You can text me if you need me."

Overjoyed to have such a beautiful man and his glorious credit card, I took off. I felt like a kid in a candy factory.

The first place I went to was my beloved Victoria's Secret. I bought ten pairs of fancy panties and bras, some negligees for James's viewing pleasure and a few comfy sleep shirts and shorts. Then I hit a place I'd always wanted to go, Free People. Their clothes were just my style, but I'd never been able to afford them. I bought some tunics and henleys, and a few jeans. I hit Forever 21, White House Black Market for a few dresses and was headed to Banana Republic but then I remembered that I didn't have him to help me carry all of these bags, so I decided I was through. Although as I was returning to James, I saw the shoe store and I couldn't resist. I actually bought a real pair of Louboutins! My new violet, five and one half-inch Lady Peep patent leather pumps cost nine hundred seventy-five dollars. He said there was no limit, right?

I think the weed was still having an effect on me because I didn't feel bad about spending his money anymore. So far, today was one of the happiest days of my life. I was so over the moon with joy that I no longer cared. I was too far gone.

I was done after getting the shoes because the stores were

about to close. I heard a buzz in my purse. It took a balancing act for me to retrieve it with all of my purchases.

Are you done? Place is about to close.

Yes, coming down right now.

Once I got to James, his eyebrows shot up. He seemed to be wrapping up a phone call as he stood up to take a few bags off my hands, his eyes darting around as if looking for someone.

"Alright, Stuart, I'll touch base with you on Monday." He hung up and looked at me in surprise.

"Look at you. You had a good time, didn't you?" He smiled as I looked at him a bit shamefaced.

"Yes, I did. Thank you so much, James!" I jumped up and gave him a big kiss on the cheek.

He turned to face me and said, "You're going to have to do better than that." I complied and gave him a deep, thorough kiss, showing him my gratitude.

Boldly, I declared, "I'll thank you even better later on."

He groaned. "Oh, look at my Merci. Not so shy anymore. I'm looking forward to it," he whispered.

Later that night, James taught me many new ways to show my gratitude. Moving into erotic dimensions I never thought I'd go to with anyone, I showed James that I was eager to learn. I had to admit, drinking and smoking seemed to help me do whatever I needed to do to please him and be adventurous. It was already a high to be with such a powerful and sexy man like James. I couldn't believe that out of all of the women he could be with, he chose me. Because of this distinguished honor, I knew it was my mission to do whatever it took to keep him satisfied. Also, so that he could eventually end it with *her*…

§

I spent the whole weekend with James at the hotel. We ate, made love, drank, smoked weed and lazed around in bed watching television. Today, I wanted to walk around downtown, but he wanted to stay in.

"It's such a nice day and there are a few fests going on. I see a lot of people at Buckingham Fountain," I said, nose smushed to the window like a grounded kid. It was already one o' clock on Sunday afternoon and we still had on our bathrobes. James hadn't seen fit for us to get dressed yet. Right now he was rolling up another joint.

He shrugged. "We can go another day. Come back to bed."

Tired of just eating and laying around, I pressed. "Why can't we go out, James? I have clothes I can wear now."

He looked at me grimly. "Come sit down, Merci." He sounded so serious. Uneasily, I sat down next to him.

"What's wrong?"

"Friday, we took a bad risk going shopping. While I was waiting for you, a so-called friend of *hers* saw me. I had to make up some excuse that I had just left The Drake for a business dinner, and being close by, decided to browse and make a few phone calls. Miki is nosy and a gossip. If we had been seen together, it would've gotten back to her and she can be vicious."

Stunned by his confession, I felt like a bucket of ice water had been dumped on my head. I hadn't seen this one coming.

"Oh. Why didn't you tell me?"

"Because you were so happy, and I told you I don't like

talking about her or anything related. When it's me and you, it's just *me and you*."

Sufficed only a little at his answer, I needed more clarification.

"Are you saying that we'll be sneaking around, not able to go out in public together or anything?"

He looked at me like I was an idiot for asking the obvious.

"Yes, Merci, for the most part. Until I can get things handled - that's the way it has to be."

I got up to leave the room before he could see the tears that were coming.

"Merci?"

I turned around abruptly.

"James, I'm not dumb. Yes, I understand what you're saying, but that doesn't mean I have to like it. Leave me alone to think right now."

I turned away from his puzzled face and went to the sitting room and plopped in my favorite chair. I drew my knees up under my chin and thought seriously. I had been so high on cloud nine - and other stuff - that I stopped being rational. I was also a bit nervous. He said Lorelei could be vicious. Even though I felt that what James and I had was special, she was still his fiancée and from what he indicated, still loved him. I kept having to remind myself that I was actually sleeping with someone else's man.

Again, I asked myself the question. Why did I feel the need to risk being with him? Because I was obsessed and I might never meet anyone like James again? The fun we had yesterday could never happen with anyone else, I reasoned. He was powerful and the most gorgeous man on earth and he wanted *me*. Plus, the biggest reason was that he was breaking up with her soon. I justified all of this in my mind and again, it sounded good enough. I wasn't going to leave him, it was settled.

From now on, I was just going to go with it. Deep down, I could sense we were on borrowed time, so I would relish every moment together. I went back into the bedroom where he welcomed me with open arms.

CHAPTER FIFTEEN

On Monday, I went to work in one of my new dresses - a slinky, stretch print wrap dress that showed off my legs and my new violet Louboutins. I knew I looked very sexy today - Layla would've been proud.

J.J.'s mouth was open and he gave an appreciative smile. I found out that he really could detect whether my shoes were real or not.

"Wow, you look great," he looked down, "those are nice! I bet they set you back a pretty penny."

"Thank you. Yep, but I love them and they're worth it."

At the behest of James, I apprehensively combined the two items together. It was breaking my rule a bit but James wanted it. Last night, I never bothered to return to the dorm since James insisted I had everything I needed at the hotel. He even made me hang up my stuff and store them. I felt at peace with that decision since I could only conclude that Lorelei did not come to the penthouse.

This morning, it took two times for me to get ready. After the first fitting of my ensemble, James got horny and attacked me, even insisting that I leave my shoes on. He really seemed to enjoy that and I did too. Whatever he liked...

After showering and getting dressed again, James instructed me to wear my hair down and told me he loved my smoky eye effect, which I promptly tried to apply. He stepped back and whistled appreciatively at the finished result. I spun around for his perusal. In these heels, I was almost as tall as he was.

"Now you look like the woman of James Jansen III. You're beautiful, baby."

"Thanks to you."

"No, you were always gorgeous, it's just enhanced."

I beamed in response.

"So beautiful." He gathered me in his arms, kissing my forehead and looking down at my body. "I don't want to let you out of my sight. You're for my eyes only but since you have to go out into the world, you might as well look your best."

I smiled thankfully and we headed down the elevator towards Bernard, who was waiting outside.

I wasn't embarrassed anymore and greeted Bernard like an old friend. James seemed to approve of my new, confident demeanor.

He reached over and gave me a kiss before I was dropped off at the corner of Michigan and Illinois. I got out, trying my best not to teeter on my extremely high heels when a thought occurred to me. High heels and getting dropped off on the corner - that sounded a bit sleazy. Was I sleazy now?

§

Not wanting to think too deeply about that question, I worked dutifully that day. Subconsciously, I knew I was trying to make up for all of the dirt that was performed over the weekend. I knew what I was doing was wrong, so I felt my good works should make up for it in some way…

I continuously asked J.J. if he needed help and performed the tasks with lightening speed. I called all of the design firms on the new list James sent me and had all of the samples ordered from The Mart before lunch time. In between tasks, I checked my phone constantly for a word from James, but I hadn't heard a peep since he strode into his office fifteen minutes after me and closed the door. Obviously, he was very busy today.

Since I was still getting adjusted to my shoes, I leisurely walked over to Subway for lunch. I got a few whistles, stares and catcalls on my way, more so than usual. James made me feel sexy, and now - I really was. I ignored them and made my way inside to the ordering line. I halted when I saw Teresa already in line giving instructions on her sandwich. Not wanting her to see me, I started to turn around, but suddenly her eyes locked on mine. There was no avoiding this now. She had stopped mid sentence with her order as her wide eyes scrutinized me from head to toe, no doubt checking out my upgraded appearance. I could tell she was trying not to show judgment, but either it wasn't working or I was paranoid. I decided to be the bigger person - or was it that I was defensive?

"Hello, Teresa. How was your weekend?" I asked boldly, getting in line.

Surprised, she answered slowly, "It was fine, how was yours?" Distractedly, she turned back around to the server who was impatiently waiting for further instructions. "I'll take a little lettuce, tomatoes and double mayo." She turned back to me as the server commenced fixing her sandwich.

I gave her a smile as confidently as I could. "It was fantastic, thanks."

Teresa looked towards the new server putting on gloves to start my order.

"Can we eat together here?" she asked hurriedly.

Internally groaning because I didn't want to stick around

to hear her inevitable preaching, I shrugged reluctantly.

"I really don't have time, I have to get back up-"

"It will just be for a moment. Please."

Looking at me, the new server asked, "What can I get you?"

Teresa's eyes pleaded with mine as she moved down the counter towards the cashier. I gave in and nodded at her with a sigh, turning back to place my order.

I slinked over to where she was seated once I had my sandwich and soda. I had no choice but to "slink" in these heels if I wanted to look cool and not fall on my face. Teresa was sipping through a straw, watching my every move as I made my way over. Her eyes were gigantic behind her glasses as I femininely sat down. I knew I was overdoing it a bit but my defenses were up. I had to show her I wasn't concerned with what she thought or what she was going to say.

Obviously, seeing me "doing the most" turned her look of wonder into pity in two seconds flat. She tilted her head to the side and studied my face.

"Merci, are you okay?"

"Don't you see I'm okay?" I snapped, and took a defiant bite out of my sandwich. She straightened up and changed tack.

"Yes, you look great, actually. Really...sexy. Are those new?" she asked, indicating my dress and shoes.

"Yes. *James* bought them for me this weekend, along with a lot of other clothes."

Her eyes enlarged again.

"Wow, I figured. Were you with him all weekend? I was surprised - well not really - that you weren't at the dorm last night. I was a bit worried but I figured you were probably with him."

I took a noisy sip through my straw.

"Yes, we were together all weekend. We had a *great* weekend."

"Okay, that's...good." We ate in awkward silence for a few minutes. She seemed to be gathering courage to say something. Here it comes in 3-2-1...

"Merci, has he broken up with his...fiancée' yet?"

I slammed my cup down because I'd already had enough.

"No, he hasn't - but he will," I gritted out. She looked at me pitifully. I was done. "Teresa, do me a favor. Don't mention me and James anymore like you promised. We are together. Accept it."

I got up to leave. Apparently deciding that she had nothing left to lose, she grabbed my arm.

"Merci, forgive me if I seem to be giving you a hard time. It's just that it's our duty as believers to help one another if we see the other stumbling. Premarital sex is already wrong, but to covet someone else's-"

"They're not married!"

"Okay. Alright. Calm down. You're right, they aren't married, but I have to tell you something I found out this weekend. Sit down a sec." I hesitated. "Please, Merci."

Nervously, I sat down. She placed her hand on my forearm.

"My mom is friends with someone who is close to Mallory Sampson, Lorelei's mother," I cringed as she said her name, "and according to her, wedding announcements for her and James were sent out a few days ago. They're planning on getting married next spring." My heart sped up, my stomach dropped and my blood ran cold. I knew she could see the misery on my face, even though I valiantly attempted to hide it. Her eyes started to water.

"Oh, Merci, I'm so sorry. If you pray and get into your

Word, God can help you look at things clearly and break it off. He has the power to change your outlook towards a situation and get you out of it-"

Pissed enough as it was and horrified we were going in this direction, I snatched my arm away and got up.

"I won't believe anything you just told me until I hear it from James. And I really don't want to hear your preaching right now. I'm out."

Without a backwards glance, I stomped out of Subway, almost pathetically tripping as I remembered I had on these monstrous shoes. I tried not to think about what I'd just heard. I didn't want to start bawling in the middle of the street. I decided to be strong until I reached the office and demanded the truth from James.

§

On the elevator, I trained my face to be pleasant enough for Marguerite and J.J.'s sake. I passed the test with Marguerite who cheerfully spoke but never looked up from her computer. I stepped into the office, grateful to find out that J.J. was still at lunch.

I knocked boldly on James's closed door.

"Yes?"

"May I come in for a moment?"

No answer. Ready to knock again, he finally spoke up.

"Yes, you may." Why did he sound so formal?

What I saw when I opened the door could've knocked me over with a feather. Sitting in a guest seat was none other than Lorelei Sampson.

I stood at the door trying not to gape in shock. Lorelei's bleach blond hair was loose and in big curls. Her face was somewhat garish with makeup, and up close I could it see it contained sharp, hard angles. She had on an expensive looking black dress with a matching bag and sparkly, black Jimmy Choos. She looked me up and down with blatant curiosity. Her expensive perfume overpowered the office. I looked at James, whose face was cool and calm as ever, but in his eyes I saw wariness. I was getting better at reading them. *Get it together, Merci.* Play it off, for both of your sakes.

He read something in my expression which thankfully made him speak first.

"Yes, Merci, may I help you?" I was about to stutter something when he spoke up again. "Were you looking for the design list you had earlier? I took it off your desk. There it is."

He gestured towards the cherry wood linear cabinet where there was indeed, a list sitting on it. I don't think it was a design list but it didn't matter.

Lorelei, who was now staring at me with a suspicious expression, turned to James.

"James, who is this? Is this the new assistant? Introduce us." Her bright inquiry rang false.

"Pardon me for being rude. Merci, this is Lorelei Sampson. Lorelei, Merci Townsend."

Time had granted me some courage and composure. It was still extremely awkward but I stepped forward to shake her well manicured hand that was black with polish and cold as ice.

"Pleased to meet you, Ms. Sampson."

She gave a toothy grimace that I assumed was supposed to be a smile. She had lipstick on her teeth.

"He forgot to say, 'Lorelei Sampson, my *fiancée.'*"

I tried not to blanch and gave her a bright smile instead. Her fake smile fell as she continued to scrutinize me with a dangerous glint in her eye. Vicious, indeed.

"What do you do here, Merci?"

James's expression didn't change but I saw annoyance flash in his eyes.

"Merci is an intern who is helping J.J. and I. She's also assisting me by ordering design materials for the remodeling project."

In exasperation, Lorelei turned to James and snapped, "James, can't the girl speak on her own?"

His face darkened and I knew he was getting angry.

Not wanting to see anymore, I grabbed the list. "Sorry for interrupting, thanks," I mumbled, stepping back and shutting the door.

I turned around to see J.J. at his desk, putting his bag away.

He whispered conspiratorially, pointing. "Who's that in there with him? His fiancée?"

I attempted a neutral face. "Yep."

"Ugh, I can't stand her. She's so hard and would someone tell her that Lucy Ewing from *Dallas* in the eighties wants her face back? I mean, she dresses the bomb, but her hairstyle and makeup are so outdated and overdone. She could use some tips from you."

I tried not to laugh, but he was making me feel better, and I was depressed for so many reasons right now. I couldn't help but smile.

"Thanks, but J.J. - that's not nice," I scolded disingenuously.

"No, seriously. She has all of that money and not much taste. What's the point?" He airily dismissed with a hand wave and twirled back around in his seat to work.

My stomach grew even more troubled as the day wore on when Lorelei still hadn't come out of James's office. At three thirty, she finally breezed out with a flourish while making a grand exit, perfume descending on us like Agent Orange. She stopped at my desk, looking at me intently with a hint of derision. I stared at her heavily rouged cheeks and waited to hear what she was going to say. I had a few hours to get used to the idea that they were probably discussing their upcoming nuptials and I was numb. She could bring on whatever she wanted. I wasn't having it.

"Merci, James tells me you've been helping him order materials for the project."

I stared at her glacier blue eyes and drawn on eyebrows.

"Yes, and?" My eyebrows were up in challenge. I wasn't afraid of this chick. I got tired of skanks like her and Jasmine thinking they could punk me around. She looked shocked at my aggressive tone.

"Well, I have a project of my own coming up and I was wondering if you could help me order some materials?"

Oh. Remorseful that I may have misjudged her, I put on my kindest smile.

"Sure, just let me know."

She gave me a smile that was pleasant, but just barely.

"I have one more question. Did you, perhaps, go with James to the Merchandise Mart event a few Saturdays ago? I remember he said he took someone who was helping him with the project."

Well, I certainly wasn't going to lie. I really didn't care anymore.

"Yes, that was me. I learned a lot," I said innocently. She stared as if she was putting something together in her head. I gazed back, waiting.

"Okay, thanks for letting me know. I will definitely be in touch, Merci," she said in a stilted voice. Then she was gone. J.J. looked at me and snickered before returning back to his work.

I had a chance to think over our exchange. Why did she ask me about NeoCon? Oh damn. I just realized she probably figured out it was me who texted James that night. Did I just get us in trouble?

James came out of the office and adjusted the door so it was wide open, no doubt airing out her perfume funk. He winked at me. I looked down so he would get the message that I was not happy. I continued looking at the list he gave me, counting all of the amendments. The "list" was a legal document of some sort. I was done ordering materials before lunch and didn't really have anything left to do. I received an email.

To: Merci Townsend
From: James Jansen III
Subject:
Please come to my office with your design book in 10 minutes.

To: James Jansen III
From: Merci Townsend.
Subject: Re:
Sure thang, boss.

He didn't answer back. Because I wanted to keep him waiting, after fifteen minutes, I went into his office with my design book and closed the door. Not wanting any Lorelei cooties, I plopped down in the other guest seat and stared at the ceiling. He said nothing for a full minute.

"Merci, before we get into anything personal, remember this. You are still my employee. When I send you an email, it means I'm all business as far as correspondence. Emails can be investigated and hacked, so you need to be careful with your responses, am I clear? Look at me." Embarrassed, I looked at his stormy eyes and nodded as he continued. "That goes for time as well. When I say, be in my office in ten minutes, I mean *ten minutes*," he said as his voice rose. Geez.

Ashamed, I apologized. "Sorry."

I felt really immature today, despite my sexy, grown lady appearance. Today was turning out to be a bad day after all. I looked away, swinging my crossed leg around in impudence.

"Now for the 'personal.' What did you want when you came into my office while Lorelei was here?"

I sighed dramatically. "I came in to ask you a few questions, but I think I know the answer now. Will that be all, sir?" I got up to leave.

"Merci, sit down," he commanded through gritted teeth. I sat back down, waiting. "Tell me what you wanted to know."

I debated whether to let it out or forget it, but I decided I wanted to hear his explanation. No doubt it'll be a weak one.

"I heard that you and *she* have sent out wedding announcements to be married next spring." He looked taken aback as if that was the last thing he expected out of my mouth. He looked guarded.

"Where did you hear that?"

Figuring I had him in the corner, I lashed out. "Don't worry where I heard it, is it true?"

"I'm not discussing it until you tell me where you heard it from."

I smirked. "You know what, James? You just answered the question for me." I attempted to get up.

"Merci, sit your ass back down and tell me," he bellowed.

I sat down and rounded on him. "Teresa's mom knows

some people in your *fiancée's* inner circle," I said nastily. "She said wedding announcements just went out a few days ago." I lifted an eyebrow in challenge.

He sat back in fatigue. *Amazing.*

"Yes, it's true, but I'm still calling the whole thing off. I told you, the timing has to be right."

I stared out of the window, crossing my arms and rolling my eyes. "Whatever, James."

He came to sit in front of me on the desk. "Merci, I mean it, just give me some time."

His soothing tone got to me and unbelievably, I started getting weepy. I got up out of my chair to go stand at the window. He came up behind me to put his arms around my waist but I shoved him back with my shoulder.

"No, James, you don't know how humiliated I was today." He moved my hair out of the way and stealthily crept closer, placing small pecks on the back of my neck. "Do you know how embarrassing it is for your best friend to know more about your boyfriend's marital plans than you?" I chuckled bitterly at what I'd just said. "That doesn't even sound right. Here I am, trying to be confident of our relationship, trying to look good in the clothes you bought me, and then to find this out is just a cruel reminder of my actual status. It's a big slap in the face."

"I know, I know, baby." He was really kissing and nipping now, "Just give me time." I melted, as usual, and I let him turn me around into his arms. He hugged me tight, his hands rubbing up and down my back, squeezing when he got to my butt. I shoved him away a little.

"I'm not finished," I protested weakly. "And then, you're in here with *her* - that really made my day."

He looked at me compassionately and drew me back into his arms.

"I'm sorry you had to deal with that. Just know that you're the only one I want, sweetheart."

Involuntarily, I shivered at his words. Why did he affect me so much? He took my lips in his as he bent me back towards the window.

"Wait, James, one more thing," I said against his mouth. "I think she knows it was me who texted you a few weeks ago after NeoCon."

He stood up but didn't let me go. "Why do you say that?"

"Because when she left your office, she asked was I the one who went with you to NeoCon. I didn't think I should've lied so I told her the truth. She put two and two together, I think."

He contemplated this for a moment and then went back to hugging me tightly.

"Don't worry about it, babe."

That evening, I was back at James's place like the fool in love I was. He smoothed over and justified everything with the "I need more time" excuse. The truth was I just needed an excuse - any excuse to hold onto James Jansen. I was that weak and I knew it. I could never let him go.

CHAPTER SIXTEEN

The next few weeks remained the same. I rarely stayed in the dorm anymore. Most of my things were now at The Fairmont. James and I were having the time of our lives. We had lots of sex, ate good food, laughed and joked a lot, smoked and drank a lot, and enjoyed one another's company. He ordered me to go shopping once a week and to visit a trendy spa to get waxed and pampered. While we couldn't really go out anywhere, he was spoiling me in his own way and I loved it. He even had my favorite drinks stocked. I loved the Frankenmuth Rose' wine from NeoCon, so he had a whole case refrigerated. He also made sure the bar was stocked with the ingredients for my favorite cocktail, Apricot Stone Sour. He even taught me how to make it. James was an enigma. I thought back to how he had the nerve to be upset with me for not asking responsible questions sexually, but then he had no problem plying illegal drugs and drink to someone who wasn't even legal yet. Go figure.

Sometimes at work, James couldn't wait to have me, so... I gave in a few times. After all, I didn't want him to have any excuse for not breaking up with *her*. I wanted to please my man. Please note: I was only comfortable doing this when I knew that J.J. was on his lunch. So, after James took me on the desk, or over the desk, or against the windows a few times, I found out what was behind that door I wondered about the first day in his office. It was a bathroom with a full shower. *Mystery solved.*

Teresa and I were cordial when we saw each other at work, but I could see that she still wasn't happy with me. What she needed was a man. I truly hoped things were working out with her and Jonathan. Honestly, I was so consumed with James, James and more James, that I couldn't really be concerned with her love life.

I wanted to ask James about Lorelei but I decided to keep my promise to not mention her and to let him handle her himself. There were a few times when his phone buzzed at night where he would leave the bedroom to go talk. I assumed it was her but I tried to remain indifferent. Since she wasn't successful with getting his time, I figured they really were a couple in name only. I'd been basically living here with him for weeks and she hadn't showed up.

§

Our little bubble of bliss was about to be tested again. One afternoon, Jim Jansen showed up in our office. J.J. and I were concerned because the "old man," as he was referred to in the company, never came in here. He marched straight into James's office and shut the door. J.J. and I didn't move a muscle as we heard deep, raised voices. They were obviously arguing. I tried to concentrate on some new orders but was desperate to know what was going on. At night, James had been complaining about his father more and more. After fifteen minutes, Jim stormed out much in the same manner he came in.

After another twenty minutes, James came out, suit jacket and brief case in hand and rolling his travel bag. My eyes beseeched him to tell me what was going on when he passed by, but he was looking straight ahead. J.J. and I exchanged bewildered glances after he left.

"What was that all about?" I asked.

"I have an idea, but I'm not sure. Rumor is Prez is not happy with the job James is doing."

Well, I knew that already.

I feigned surprise. "Really? Is the rumor wide spread?"

"Yes. They even say some shareholders are catching wind of James's job performance. They're starting to get pissed off and it's starting to affect shares in the market."

Oh no! James hadn't mentioned that to me. Maybe he didn't know.

"That's terrible. I hope everything works out for him."

J.J. shrugged.

Inside, I was devastated. I took out my phone and texted James.

Baby, is everything ok?

Anxiously, I waited for a response and fidgeted for about an hour.

Finally, my phone vibrated.

Bernard will still be picking you up to take you home. You have the key card. I'll call you tonight.

Satisfied that he would call me, I left for the day. I smiled at his reference to "home."

That evening back at the hotel, I restlessly awaited his call. I made myself a drink, turned on the TV and waited. I texted him again.

James, call me when you get a chance.

I didn't hear back from him that night.

§

The next day was the same. I was blowing up his phone all day, just to get him to respond in any way possible. It was starting to get real miserable at the hotel. Drinking and sitting around such opulence and luxury was not as thrilling as when he was here. It also gave me time to really reflect on my situation. It was kind of pathetic but I still wasn't willing to give it up. Not hearing from James, though, was excruciating.

On the third evening without James, I got so drunk I almost passed out. The phone rang. *Finally*. I groggily grabbed for it, fumbling around before I could slide the answer button.

"James?" I whined.

"No, Merci, it's your mother." Oh shit. I tried to straighten up and make my voice regular. I knew I was too drunk so I needed to feign sleepiness.

"Oh, hi Mom," I slurred.

"Merci, who is James? Is he your new boyfriend?"

"Mom, I'm sorry. I can't really talk right now, I am so sleepy."

"Oh, okay. I was just checking on you, dear. I haven't heard from you in weeks and you were weighing heavily on my mind. Is everything alright? You sound...strange."

"Yes, Mom, everything's fine. I'm just sleepy."

"Alright, baby, I'll let you go back to sleep. Before I go, where is your roommate, Teresa? She's such a nice girl and always jumps on the phone to say hi. If you don't mind, I'd like to say hello to her before I go."

I panicked. Sobering, I sat up and tried to think fast. "Teresa's not here. I can tell her you called, though."

"Alright. Me and your dad miss you and are a little sad you didn't come home this summer and don't call as much anymore, but knowing you're okay, helps. Don't forget to read your Bible and pray. Talk to you later, love."

"Okay, bye Mom." She hung up and I face-planted into the bed.

§

It had been four days and I hadn't seen or heard a peep out of James. Was he still alive? I went into the bathroom and cried on my lunch. I must've texted him at least two hundred times. I was petrified that he was dead or something.

J.J. noticed my face when I came back from the bathroom. He looked at me closely.

"Are you okay? Sorry to say, but you've been looking a bit rough lately. Like you're not getting enough sleep."

I gave a weary smile. "I'm okay but you're right, I haven't been getting enough sleep. I don't know what it is."

That seemed to satisfy him as I went back to my desk.

§

That night, I blew up his phone again. I was through drinking so much since the after effects weren't worth it, especially if it was affecting my looks. I decided to try a joint that was in James's bed side drawer. I was just about to light it up when I heard a ding indicating someone was coming in from the elevator. I was terrified. I hugged my knees up in fear until I heard keys jangling.

"Merci!"

I ran full speed into the other room towards the elevator and into his arms, almost knocking him down.

"James!"

We hugged for a full minute before he gently pushed me away. I tried to hold on, getting my smell fix, although I had to admit he wasn't as fresh as usual.

"Hi, baby," he said tiredly, smiling.

"James, why didn't you call?" Leaning back to study his face, I saw that it was haggard and unshaved, his eyes bloodshot. "Are you okay, baby?"

He turned around and started taking off his suit jacket and already loosened tie.

"No, not really. I'm exhausted, mentally, physically and emotionally." He started moving towards the bedroom. I dutifully followed.

"What happened? Why'd you have to take off like that, why didn't you call?"

Already partially undressed and heading towards the bathroom, he paused.

"Merc, let me get a shower first. I'll tell you all about it when I get out."

"Alright, I understand."

As he was still undressing, I rushed around him into the bathroom to turn on the shower for him. He smiled wanly in thanks.

I waited patiently in the bedroom. I did a quick inspection of my face in the mirror. I didn't look so hot. I ran to the other bathroom and doused my face with cold water and fixed myself up a bit. Not hearing from him had taken its toll. Satisfied with the results, I returned to the bedroom just as James was exiting with a towel. He sat down on the bed, drying his hair.

"Merci, I don't know where to begin. I guess I'll start at the beginning but please, let me finish?" he asked wearily.

"Okay," I said innocently. I wondered why he thought I'd have a problem.

He sat back on the bed while I drew up my knees beside him. He ran his hands through his unruly, curly hair. He looked drained.

"First of all, the reason my father came to the office was to tell me that the board of directors have been very unhappy with my performance and I needed to immediately do some 'due diligence,' if you will. I haven't yet been chosen as the CEO, as you know. As I'm just the acting CEO, the board met to appoint a successor to my father and my name was not at the top of the list.

"This caused some shareholders to squirm because it showed instability and our stocks dropped. My father got wind of it and forced me to go to the board's executive director, Daniel Westin's home in Wisconsin, right away. My dad is petrified that someone else could be named his successor other than one of his sons. That's the risk you take when you sell off shares of your company and have a board. So basically, I went up there to kiss Westin's ass so that by the time the next board meeting takes place, he can push my name to the front. Since he's the head, I would be a shoo-in if I perform the right ass-kissing techniques," he said scathingly.

I nodded in understanding. His expression turned guarded as he continued.

"He has this estate located on a golf course and I was forced to stay in one of his luxury cabanas. I had to get up and play golf with him every morning – I hate golf. Here's the kicker, he has money invested in the merger between Sampson Electronics and JWC, so you know who was invited up there by my father? Lorelei. I couldn't believe it. Daniel even insisted that we stay in the same cabana." I squirmed in shock. "No, Merci, don't get upset – I slept on the couch but we had to put on the lovey dovey act for him, in which Lorelei was all too happy to perform."

I was stunned and my heart felt like it was disintegrating.

"All of this time, you were with Lorelei?"

"Yes, baby, but nothing happened."

Tears started slowly falling down my cheeks. "You didn't even call or text or anything. For all I knew, you were dead. And you were with her?" I started bawling like a complete fool. He tried to gather me in his arms.

"I'm sorry but this was the only way to appease the director. He's vested. Please understand that this is the way business is. I didn't call because I hid my personal phone away, just in case Lorelei got any bright ideas. I don't mean to hurt you but I'm trying to be honest here."

Truthfully, I appreciated that. Trying to be more understanding, I cleared my head and tried to look at it in a more mature manner. I wiped my tears.

"So what does this mean? What's going to happen next?"

"Well, because things are 'shaky,' Lorelei and I are going to have to pile on even more. There will be several events that we'll have to attend to show a united front so that the investors can see that I'm stable, that our merger is a done deal and-"

"Wait a minute. It sounds like you're going to have to go through with it. Like you're actually going to have to get married."

He tried to look resolute but I saw a hint of uneasiness in his eyes. "It may seem that way at first, but I'll never go through with it."

Disbelieving, I pushed away from him. "Yeah, right. You

know what, James? I don't think you know what to do."

His brown eyes grew stormy. "Merci, do you have any idea how hard these past few days have been? I thought about just getting on a plane and flying to Bora Bora or somewhere. I'm under so much pressure. The only thing that kept me going was thinking about getting back to you. I missed you so much."

He opened his arms pleadingly for me to let him in and I couldn't resist. He looked so pitiful right now. I opened my arms and his head fell on my chest while I rocked him. I soothed him by running my fingers through his thick curls from front to back. On my chest, I felt wetness and realized he was crying silently. He was more sensitive than anyone thought. I knew he wasn't faking it.

"Merc, please don't leave me. I need you, now more than ever. The world is crashing down around me and I don't have anyone in my corner but you," his voice broke, "please promise you'll stay by my side.

So depressed about the turn of events, I hugged him even tighter.

"I promise."

§

After an hour of just snuggling, James went in the closet to get his travel bag. He pulled out a small pouch and brought it to the bed. Curiously, I watched as he opened the black leather pouch and removed a flat mirror like surface, a razor blade and a small vial of something white. My mind clicked as I realized what it was.

"James! What are you doing? Isn't that cocaine?"

"Yes, it is. I'm not an addict or anything, but doing just a bit has been helping lately." He stopped his preparations and looked at me pointedly. "I have so much stress and a little of this won't hurt me. You see how small this is?" He held up the black topped vial.

Alarm bells went off and my heart raced. I've read stories about people who've said the same thing and they got hooked or even worse, overdosed. Somehow, I had to stop him.

"That's what they all start off saying. Please stop doing this, you could become hooked."

He ignored me while I helplessly watched as he separated the stuff into lines with the blade, used a finger to hold down a nostril and sniffed up the other. Ugh, I don't think I would ever be able to tolerate anything going up my nose.

He sat up, looking disgusting with the white substance under his nose. Revulsion ran through me.

"I'm going into the other room. That's one thing you are never going to get me to try," I said.

I made my way to the sitting area and turned on the television. I didn't see anything on the screen as I thought about what to do. This was serious. Job pressure was taking its toll on James and he wasn't able to handle it. Not without some type of help in the form of substances including weed, alcohol and now - cocaine. What would be next - crack? Was that crack cocaine? I didn't think so because I believe you had to smoke it. What should I do? The only thing I could think of was Teresa and her insisting that I pray. Was there a Bible in here somewhere?

Nah, with the way that I'd been acting - sleeping with an engaged man, drinking, smoking, etc., God would not want to hear from me. Deciding that I needed some solace of my own after the bombshells that had been delivered, I got up to fix my favorite drink.

After twenty minutes, I got worried because I didn't hear

any sounds from the bedroom and I wondered if James was okay after his cocaine binge. I nervously entered, worrying that he had OD'd or something.

James was in bed, leaning against the headboard, flipping channels with a glazed look in his eyes. Every now and then he would remit a goofy chuckle from low in his throat. I stood there watching him, waiting for him to notice me. After three whole minutes, he still hadn't seen me. I ran and jumped on the bed.

Startled, he backed up away from me like I was the boogie man. He looked at me and put his hands up, shielding me from him. Then he laughed.

"Whoa girl, you scared me. Where did you come from?" His glazed eyes looked at me in absolute wonder.

This James, I couldn't handle.

Strictly, I folded my arms. "I've been standing here watching you for the last five minutes. You didn't even notice I was right here."

He giggled and exclaimed, "Really?"

"James, I don't like how that stuff is making you act."

"Too bad, baby, I feel much better now. You should try- "

"No way. I know you've been successful at getting me to try new things but I draw the line at that stuff, buddy."

He started cracking up.

"I see what you did there, Merc, you said 'draw the line' - that was a good one."

I chuckled. I had to admit that was unintentionally funny and his manner was a bit comical. I still wasn't going to let him think I was okay with his new habit.

"Okay, James, that was kind of funny, but I mean it. I don't like this…indulgence - one bit."

He sobered a little.

"I understand, baby, you're right. I won't mess around

with this once it's gone. We can stick to the other stuff. Truthfully, it's no fun without you."

He turned to the TV and burst out laughing at something. It was a commercial about disabled, elderly people.

I smirked in disbelief. "Really, James?"

CHAPTER SEVENTEEN

For the next few days, I didn't see any sign of James using coke. Work was different now since the incident last week. We went to work together, yet were separated during the day. James, no longer focused on the design project, spent all of his time with J.J. who was helping him prepare for upcoming conference calls, presentations and meetings. James no longer called me into his office for our impromptu "sessions." I wasn't upset, though. I understood he had a commitment and he had to be dedicated so he wouldn't lose his job. Plus, I had him at night. After a stressful day at the office, I made it my business to be everything he needed so he wouldn't turn to that dreaded cocaine for comfort.

Today, before getting ready to go back to the hotel, I received a text.

Babe, I won't be coming home today. I have to go to Bucktown tonight. I have an event I need to go to and my tux and everything is there. I'll be back late tonight but I'm sure you'll be sleep.

Disappointed, I texted back.

Oh, that's right - the gala you and J.J. have been preparing for. Have fun and see you later, sweetheart.

Depressed that I couldn't attend with him, I went home,

drank some wine and watched TV. When was the last time I'd read a book? It had been a while. I took out my new iPad Air that James bought me and purchased a book. While I was downloading it, an app named *Your Porta-Bible* kept popping up asking if I wanted to download it. My heart beat faster in my chest as I wondered if God was trying to tell me something. Closing the app store window, I wrote it off as me being silly. I purchased a steamy romance novel, something I never did since I usually read classic literature. Since I was in love, I wanted to read something cheesy to make me feel better about my relationship. After an hour of reading the lame love story, I deleted it from my library and shut off the iPad. The story was about a girl who falls in love with a married man - and he doesn't leave his wife. Talk about depressing. Was God trying to tell me something?

After downing my wine, I must've fallen asleep. When I woke up in the middle of the night, James was in the bed next to me. Happily, I snuggled up to him. He obviously didn't take a shower because I couldn't smell his fragrant soap. Did I smell perfume? Too sleepy to think about it, I turned over and went to sleep. He snuggled up to me from behind.

The next morning, as we were getting ready for work, I asked him about last night.

"How was the affair?"

"It was okay, lots of shareholders there. I think it was successful," he said rather vaguely.

"Well, that's good." I detected that he didn't want to talk about it, so I didn't question any further.

§

At work, J.J. had the Chicago Sun-Times newspaper laid out

on his desk.

"Come here, Merci. Look at this."

"Alright."

Curious, I looked at the spread on his desk. On the society page, there was a huge, full color page of arrivals to the '34th Annual Jansen Foundation Gala.' Smack dab in the middle was a bigger than usual, full color picture of James and Lorelei. She had her arm in his and he had his hand around her waist. He towered over her diminutive frame and they looked like they were laughing, as if they had just shared some inside joke. My knees buckled as I tried not to lose my breakfast all over J.J.'s shoulder. Since I was behind him, thankfully he couldn't see my reaction. He started reading.

"'Arriving at the Gala was Chicago's Most Envied Power Couple, James Jansen III of Jansen Worldwide Capital and Lorelei Sampson, heiress to Sampson Electronics. Longtime couple, James and Lorelei, have scheduled their nuptials for May, 2013.'" J.J. smirked. "Aww isn't that special - not. Although you have to admit, they do look pretty good together here."

I tried to give a chuckle. "Yeah, hey – I'll be right back. I've got to run to the bathroom."

No longer able to hold it, I rushed out. I don't think he noticed since he nodded without ever looking up.

Once in the bathroom, I went in a stall, plied the toilet lid with protective toilet paper and sat down. I covered my mouth with my hand and sobbed. How could he? How could he? I knew this was a part of his obligations. But they looked so happy, even though I knew they really weren't. How much of this did he think I could take? The pain was agonizing. So, this was what they meant by "heartache" because the muscle in my chest actually ached. I stayed in the bathroom sobbing quietly for at least ten minutes. When

I thought I had pulled myself together, I got up, doused cold water on my swollen eyes and went back to my desk. All of my makeup was gone and I didn't have my purse with me to reapply it, but I didn't care. I didn't feel like I had a man anyway.

Not surprisingly, James wasn't in the office long after he showed up. He breezed in, spoke to J.J. about materials for a meeting he was headed to, and breezed back out with his brief case ten minutes later. Meanwhile, I don't think he even glanced in my direction. If he had, he would've noticed my pathetic face. After about five minutes, I received a text.

Babe, are you okay? I caught a glimpse of you and I'm worried.

Amazed that he even noticed, I texted back.

Yeah, I'm okay, thanks for asking. Will I see you at home tonight?

Of course. I'm sure you have some questions for me, right?

How did he know?

I leaned up a bit and saw that J.J. still had the full spread of the gala open on his desk. James must've figured out that I'd seen it. He was one sharp cookie. I feigned ignorance.

I don't know what you're talking about. I'll see you at home.

Lol, okay Merc. See you tonight.

§

That night, James came in about seven. I had plenty of time to rehearse my nonchalant act. I planned on waiting for him to mention it to me. I had on one of my casual, Free People tunics, shorts, and my face made up to look naturally pretty. I was curled up on the couch in the sitting room, watching TV.

Undoing his tie, he came over and bent down to give me a kiss on the lips. I artfully dodged it, pretending to reach down to pick up the remote. I didn't look him in the face as I snacked on Garrett's Chicago Mix Popcorn that I'd picked up on the way home.

Not one to be totally rude, I spoke. "Hi, James, how was your day?" I asked breezily.

He chuckled as if he was on to me. "It was alright. Let's talk, Merci."

He sat down next to me, kicked off his expensive, Herring James loafers and stretched his long legs forward. I still looked straight ahead at the TV. *Big Bang Theory* was playing, and although I really wasn't paying attention, he knew it was one of my favorite shows.

"Talk about what?" I asked as I stuffed a handful of kernels into my mouth.

He turned my face towards his as I continued chewing, cheeks bulging.

"I know you saw the paper about the function last night. I know you saw the picture of me and Lorelei." I cringed at the way he put the two of them together. Now, I really felt like an outsider.

I forced my face away from his hand and continued watching TV.

"What is there to talk about? I know it's just business."

He sighed. "I know you do, but that picture they snapped could look deceiving to anyone who didn't know us."

"What do you mean? Because you looked...in love?" I turned my face pointedly at him.

He smiled uncomfortably. "Yes, we did look...cozy. But that's not how it was at all."

"Look, James, you don't have to explain it to me. I know you and she have been together on and off for years. It would be stupid for me to assume that all of the times you had were bad."

He looked impressed by my assessment.

"Merci, that's why you're my girl. You are so perceptive. That's exactly how it is, even though we don't really get along. But because we've been acquainted for a while, there are things that we just know about each other."

Not wanting to hear anymore, I flinched. "Okay, James, you don't have to go into how close you guys were and all of that. Truthfully, it still makes me want to puke."

He wrinkled his nose but nodded in understanding. "Alright, that makes sense."

"Thank you. So, I'm not as upset as you think. I admit that this morning was hard, but I've had all day to process and make sense of it."

His eyes warmed and he reached over and gave me a kiss on the cheek. "Good girl."

"I do have a question, though." His eyebrows rose in interest. "Why did I smell her perfume on you last night?"

Looking caught, he seemed to grapple for an excuse.

"You know how strong her perfume is! That day in the office, I thought she was going to kill us all," he sputtered.

I couldn't help but laugh.

"We had to formally dance, that's all."

My face fell at this new information. We had never danced together, except when we were blitzed out of our minds here at the hotel. What was finally revealed as an appalling Michael Jackson impersonation, did not count.

He turned my chin back to face him.

"Merci, please don't be worried about her. I am not attracted to her in any way. Especially when I've got my beautiful, juicy, voluptuous baby right here waiting for me. Why would I want anyone but you? She can't compare to you."

He started kissing me deeply and pushed me back onto the couch. I knew where this was headed but I wasn't ready to give in just yet. I pulled away from his lips, pushing my hands against his chest.

"James, James, I have one more question." He groaned in frustration. "I just have to know. What were you two talking about when they snapped the picture?"

"Aw babe, I don't remember," he whined.

I sat up totally. "Yes, you do." He grabbed his head as if he was in agony and groaned loudly.

"Alright, but you may not like it."

"I will - I promise. I mean, after all, what could possibly surprise me now? If you told me you had to have sex with her, you'd probably insist that it was for business and like I fool - I'd probably go with it."

He laughed heartily. "Merci, you are hilarious. No, it was nothing like that."

"Well, what was it?"

"Lorelei is able to do a really good impression of the lady who voices Howard's mom on *Big Bang Theory* since she's originally from Brooklyn. She had just finished imitating her when they asked us to pose. It was so funny. That's why we looked so happy."

My heart sank. "Oh, okay."

I tried to smile but I'm sure it didn't reach my eyes. He was right, I definitely didn't like it. This was probably worse than him having to have sex with her. It meant they were still connecting emotionally and about one of my favorite characters, no less. Sensing my disposition, James took me in his arms again.

"Baby, you know who my best friend is, right?"

"Who?" I mumbled sadly against his chest.

"You. There is nobody I can talk to or confide in, more than you. It's amazing to me how much I can open up to you. You think I ever cried on her or anyone's shoulder? Never. I've always been somewhat of a loner and I have an image to uphold. But you - you've broken down all of my defenses and barriers. I feel liberated with you. You are the most important person in my life, right now. Please don't feel threatened by that rare moment with her - it meant nothing."

Positively a puddle of butter at his words, I squeezed him.

"Okay, I believe you."

Really. I had no choice but to accept any and everything that was going on, good or bad. I wasn't going anywhere.

James took me to bed and tried to erase any insecure feelings I might've had. We made slow, substance-free, passionate love. It had been a while. This was the best kind, I decided.

CHAPTER EIGHTEEN

The next week was much the same with James being busier than ever. I tried to find things to do since I was so bored and it looked like the remodeling project was on hiatus for now. J.J. didn't have much extra for me to do, so most of the time I was on my computer reading a story or inconspicuously playing a game. I wasn't really apprehensive about James catching me. I had my excuse ready - boredom. But I never got that chance since he was in and out of the office like a whirlwind.

Still wearing my new, sexy outfits and shoes, I went to lunch by myself, hearing the same cat calls and whistles along the way. I was used to it now. This was what I had to contend with, if one day I was to be the future wife of CEO, James Jansen III. As I was making my way out of CPK after picking up my take-out, I saw Lance eating alone at a table by the window. Happy to see a familiar face I hadn't seen in a while, I waved when he looked up. He waved me over. Deciding I could eat my barbequed chopped chicken salad here, I joined him.

"Hey, Merci, you're looking really good. I haven't seen you in a while. How's it going?" he asked, eyeing me closely.

Brightly, I replied, "Thanks, I'm fine. How have you been?"

"I've been good. So how's it going upstairs?"

I hesitated, trying to keep my face unreadable. "It's been going fine," I said noncommittally.

"That's good. Look, I've got something to discuss with you. First of all, what do you do up there exactly?"

I opened my mouth to answer but nothing came out as I was actually at a loss for what I did, since it had been nothing, lately.

After a moment, my mouth started working. "I'm helping James with the remodeling project for JWC. Eventually, he's planning on redoing the whole company, so I'm in charge of ordering samples and stuff like that. Why?"

He nodded and accepted my answer as if something had just been confirmed in his mind.

"Merci, there is a rumor on our floor that's just starting to float around that James Jansen has a new jump off - and some are saying that it's you. That you've been seen getting into James's limo every day after work."

Mortified, my head started to spin and my mouth went dry.

Swallowing hard, I asked apprehensively, "What's a jump...off?"

He smirked and laughed. "You never heard of that? A 'jump off' is a side chick or dude - somebody who is messing around with a married man or messing with someone that's in a committed relationship, like an engagement." I didn't miss how he stressed the last word.

Dumbfounded, I could only gape. I couldn't believe what I was hearing. Word had gotten around that I was his....jump off?

Lance continued, "Now, if it's true, it's not right - but what you do is your business, and because I think you're cool, I'm giving you the heads up. Somebody's been watching you. If his fiancée finds out you two are messing around, be careful. I heard she is straight-up looney toon."

My heart was thumping erratically in my chest. Gathering my wits, I tried to think of something fast. Denial was a good start, though a little late at this point.

Feigning insult, I huffed, "I never said it's true."

Smirking, he shook his head. "Whatever, Merci, I'm just letting you know what's going around."

Not bothering to deny it, I stuffed my salad back in the bag and left. Lance seemed to understand my hasty departure and didn't attempt to stop me. I walked back to work with my head in a daze. The bad news just kept coming. Not only was I found out to be sleeping with an engaged man who was also the boss of the company, there was a revolting term going around with my name on it. Who was watching me and who was spreading the word around? My mind immediately went to Teresa because she was the only one I'd told, but I dismissed that thought as soon as it came. She wasn't like that and would never do that to me – no matter how upset she was at my decision.

Totally self conscious, I cautiously went back to work, avoiding all eye contact just in case somebody was looking at me like they knew what I had been doing. Upstairs, I apprehensively looked at J.J. to gauge whether he knew my dirty secret. He smiled and greeted me as usual, so unless he was a classically trained actor, I was okay. At my desk, I googled the term "Jump Off" and clicked the first entry.

Urban Dictionary: *Jump off: A casual sex partner. A mistress or a person that is usually only being used for sex while in marriage or serious relationship; The chick (or man) on the side. See also (Booty Call).*

Oh no. Now, completely miserable, I reluctantly looked at

the other results.

Jumpoff

A sexual partner who is more than a one-night stand but with whom one does not intend to form a long-term romantic relationship

Jump off

1.A casual sexual partner or girlfriend
2. A woman of dubious sexual practices

20 Words Related to jump off
Slut, hoe, whore, booty call, mistress, skank…

I couldn't read anymore.

My stomach continued to drop. Was that me? How dare they sully my relationship with James into something so filthy? We were in love. Or at least I was and I was pretty sure that he was on his way.

There were plenty of other entries on the site that made my skin crawl. The fact that a lot of them were grammatically incorrect made me feel a little better. Apparently, any fool could just enter something so vile.

I saw some lyrics from a song by rapper, Joe Budden. I pulled out my ear buds, put them in the computer and pushed play as I read along. I curled up my lip in distaste at the raunchy lyrics but my ears perked up at these lines.

My jump off doesn't run off at the mouth so much
My jump off never ask why I go out so much
My jump off never has me going out of my way
And she don't want nothing on Valentine's Day

My jump off don't argue or get rebellious
And she don't mind hanging out wit da fellas
My jump off's not insecure or jealous

Oh my god.

§

After work, I didn't go to the limo. I took a cab instead, just in case prying eyes were watching. I texted James before I left.

Please tell Bernard I'm catching a cab home so that he's not waiting. I don't have his number.

He texted back five minutes later.

Why?

Not wanting to go into it, I made up a vague excuse.

I've got some things to do before I go home.

He never answered back, anyway.

§

Once I got home, I ordered a steak and drank some wine. I refused to let it get me down too much, since that didn't describe us at all. I wasn't just some skank James was having sex with. We had a committed, emotionally invested relationship that had some "complications" he needed to take care of. Also, I was indignant because with everything that had been going on lately, we hadn't even been having much sex! I could understand if James was married to her - or in love with her, then I would probably fit the term, but it went deeper than that, I justified. I felt so humiliated. I needed to talk to Teresa or somebody. Remembering how I pushed her away, I started crying miserably.

§

That evening, James came home with his usual look as of late. Face haggard and worn, unshaven and suit hanging off of him. He looked like he was losing weight. Too consumed to dwell on it due to my own despair, I tried to give him a welcoming smile. I knew that I also painted an attractive picture since I hadn't bothered fixing myself up after rolling around and crying all evening. I was sure my hair was a bird's nest along with my puffy, red-rimmed eyes. Yep, because James took one look at me and came quickly to my side on the couch.

"Merci, what's wrong?" He grabbed my shoulders to look straight into my eyes.

Breaking down again, I dropped my head onto his chest. "Oh, James..."

"What's wrong - tell me," he demanded, holding me away to look into my eyes.

"One of my intern friends, Lance," he grimaced at the name, "told me there's a rumor going around on their floor that you and I are messing around. They said...I'm your new...jump off."

I sobbed loudly as he looked at me, disconcertment etched into his features, his lips forming a grim line. He hugged and rubbed my back until I began to quiet down.

"Merci, what else did he say? How did they find out?" I

ignored that he'd just basically affirmed it.

"That somebody's been watching me get into your limo every day."

He sighed. "Don't worry about it, babe." He pulled me into his arms, patting my head.

"How can I not worry about it? That's not all," I muffled into his chest, "he said if word got back to *her*, to be careful because she's crazy."

He chuckled, and not too reassuringly. "Don't worry about her either." He kissed the top of my head. "That's why you took a cab," he guessed.

"Yes, I don't want to ride in the limo anymore. Matter-a-fact, I don't even want to go to work anymore. I'm so embarrassed!"

Looking at me, he was quiet as if considering what I said. He smiled, trying to lighten things up.

"Tell you what. Take tomorrow off. If you still don't want to go in the next day, don't."

"Alright."

"Remember, I'm the boss so you can't be reprimanded." He kissed my forehead. I gave a watery smile and put my arms around him, hugging him to me.

"James, have you ever heard of the term, 'jump off'?"

In my arms, he went still. "What a stupid term, but yes I have."

"They said I was a *new* jump off, implying that's what they've always called your other… women."

Impatiently, he said, "Think about it, Merci. I haven't been there long enough to garner the so-called reputation that has been bestowed upon me. It's only been seven or eight months! People will start rumors about anyone, especially someone with power. It's mostly jealousy."

"But it's not a rumor. I am your jump off," I said sadly.

He chuckled bitterly and tilted my chin up and gave me a firm kiss on the lips.

Eyeing me sternly, he said, "Don't ever let me hear you call yourself that again. And seriously, let's not worry about it too much."

I agreed, feeling much better. James, on the other hand made a bee line to the bathroom. Apparently, he couldn't hold it and I was delaying his bladder with the latest sob story of *us*. When he came out, I noticed the area underneath his nose was red and irritated. He had a familiar glaze in his eyes. I caught on instantly.

"James, I know what you were doing in there." I crossed my arms. "Oh, you tell me not to worry about it, yet you're administering your own coping mechanism."

I looked at him pointedly, waiting for his latest excuse. He didn't have one.

"Yeah, babe, I really need this today. Not because of what you told me, but because of all of the extra stress at work." I'm pretty sure he was lying. "Merci, please leave me alone about this today."

Not waiting for my reply, he stalked out of the sitting room and slammed the door behind him in the bedroom.

Stunned, I could only stare at the closed door and surmise that things were not going too well for us at all.

§

That evening, I went in to check on him to make sure he hadn't OD'd. Satisfied that he was sleeping, I brought my pillow and a throw out to the sitting room to sleep. No sense being in the bedroom with him when he was out cold. The next morning, I felt a kiss on my head as he left for work. Disgusted with myself, I bathed, replaced the bathrobe with a clean one, and paced around the penthouse all day, bored out of my mind. After watching mindless infomercials and game shows, I checked the time, determining that it should be Teresa's lunch time. Nervously and after much debate, I called.

"Hi, Merci," she answered suspiciously.

"Hi, Teresa. Do you have time to talk for a second?"

"Well, I haven't taken a bite of my food yet, so could you make it quick?"

"Sure, sure." I cleared my throat. "Have you been hearing…things around the office?"

"You mean about you and James?" she asked bluntly.

"Yes."

I almost fell out. "Oh, God," I said.

She chuckled a little. I could hear her mutter under her breath, *Yeah, He's the one you need.* I ignored it while she continued in a louder tone.

"You know I didn't have anything to do with it getting out, right?"

"Teresa, I know you would never do that. That never crossed my mind," I reassured.

She paused. "Good. I have to go - food's getting cold."

Her abruptness was unexpected. "Oh, alright."

"Yeah, and Merci, I'm not going to preach, but you need to be careful."

"Alright I-"

She disconnected before I could finish. Apparently, she was officially done with me.

CHAPTER NINETEEN

The next day, I decided to stay off work since it was Friday. I reasoned that I should have my mind together (and some balls) to go back on Monday. Thinking we were going to spend a relaxing weekend together, James came in Friday evening and headed straight to the shower. Waiting in a chair by the bed, I had retired the bathrobe in exchange for some real clothes and tried to fix myself up in anticipation of some uninterrupted us time.

He exited the bathroom and hurriedly started dressing, intentionally avoiding my eye.

"Gotta go, babe," he said as he sat down on the edge of the bed and pulled a pants leg on.

"Where to?" I asked, disappointed.

"There's a family gathering at my parent's place in Winnetka, and I have to be there."

"Oh." I was hurt that I couldn't even suggest the idea of wanting to go with him. He continued getting dressed while I pondered what to say. Then it hit me with such force that I almost doubled over. I realized that in my position, I could never really say anything. Was this how it would always be?

"Well, okay, have a nice evening." Seeming to appreciate my non-confrontational manner, he came over to give me a kiss on the cheek, looking into my eyes for the first time since he got home.

"Thanks, baby, I needed to hear that." Then taking off out

of the room, he added, "I'll be home late, so don't wait up."

"Okay," I called after him.

Jump off, I was.

§

I ate, drank wine and even had the guts to light up one of the joints he had stashed. Still not brave enough to be unconcerned about the establishment finding out, I opened the secure window as far as I could, sitting by it and blowing out of the small opening. I could see over towards Millennium Park and even as far as Grant Park where people were just hanging out, ready to go to another fest and enjoying summer. Here I was, a side-piece, kept hidden away from the public due to my shameful status. I could've gone out on my own, but what would be the fun in that? I hadn't really made any close friends except for Teresa and she didn't want to have anything to do with me.

She was probably home with her family right now. I thought about how she would always invite me home every weekend but I refused because I didn't want to go to church. If my life was going to be like this, I may need to start reconsidering her offer, I thought. I chased that idea out of my head, though. The word "church" and the fact that I was smoking weed, didn't quite mix.

That evening, as I sat staring off into space and coming down from my high, I flipped on the TV to see an older movie playing called *Mistress*. I didn't miss the irony. Thinking I could learn a thing or two, instead of changing the channel, I watched the entire film, led by Victoria Principal. It was about a woman who'd been having an affair with a married man who'd been taking care of her. When he died, she found herself with nothing. So she tried to rebuild her life, but the stigma of being a kept woman followed her.

Utterly depressed about the film and my situation, I tried to find a bright light. At least the term "kept woman" sounded better than "jump off." If I was going to be in this situation, that's the term I preferred.

§

I woke up feeling the bed press down next to me. Stroking my hair, James was explaining something. I tried to open my cracked eyes but they were virtually glued shut. My head was pounding. The sun glared brightly behind my eyelids.

"I'm sorry I'm just getting home, we got kind of carried away with drinking and everything."

Groggily, I tried to sit up and open my eyes to respond. My throat was parched. As my senses returned, I realized what he was saying.

"You stayed out all night?" I croaked. I looked around to the bright sun behind the sheers. Daggers penetrated my skull.

"Yes, babe," he chuckled. "I guess I shouldn't have even told you - you would've never noticed." He looked around. "Damn. What did you do? Have a party of your own?"

I nodded. "Yeah, but it wasn't any fun without you."

He kissed my cheek and I frowned.

"Was *she* there?"

"Yeah, but don't worry. It wasn't fun without you, either."

I sighed. I was too tired to be jealous. Begrudging acceptance was becoming familiar to me.

Giving him a side-eye, I huffed, "Yeah, I bet."

He scrunched his nose, checking out my features closely.

"Babe, I hate to say it, but you look kind of terrible. Get dressed and we can go to Aria for breakfast."

Too excited to be offended by his rude observation, I smiled and got up to go shower. Yay, we were going out. Leaving the hotel room to go to a restaurant together - even if it was just downstairs - was a big deal.

§

The next week didn't start too bad at all. I had a routine and it seemed to be working out fine. I took a cab to work every morning, either before or after James left with Bernard. Instead of going out at lunchtime, I ordered in or brought the leftovers from room service the night before. After work, I caught a cab back to the hotel. Next day, repeat. James and I were never seen together, especially since he was rarely in the office anyhow. Everything seemed to be going well.

When he would come home from work now, he seemed to be more stressed out than ever. He looked like he had lost at least ten pounds since I met him. I was so worried about him being unhappy that I no longer reprimanded him for going into the bathroom to snort a line. Feeling comfortable since I didn't protest as much, he started breaking out his kit in front of me. As long as he didn't do too much, I reasoned.

Plus, I was in the habit of coming right home and fixing us both a drink. After room service, which consisted mostly of me eating it, we rolled out the blunts James introduced me to. A blunt, he informed me, was a joint but rolled in cigar papers. They were much bigger and I didn't need but a fourth of one each evening. He even surprised me by showing me how to roll them in blueberry and Jamaican rum flavored blunt papers. Yummy. I wasn't sure who his suppliers were and I didn't ask, but substances and paraphernalia seemed to magically appear about the place.

One day, he insisted I try a little orange pill that he said would enhance our sex life. I wasn't dumb because I knew it was the Ecstasy pill. I wanted us to have harmony in every aspect of our relationship, so I tried it. It really seemed to help and I noticed that it made the world appear brighter in general, but only for a while. To stop myself from fixating on my sordid status, I ended up taking a few of the multicolored pills to work with me and popping them after lunch. But just a few - I didn't want to get hooked.

Increasingly, James went to his place in Bucktown or his parent's place, and wasn't returning home. I chalked it up to more business dinners and the like as he prepared to take the helm at JWC. And now, I had acquired some skills of my own to cope with. It helped to keep my mind in a fog to shield it from any painful truths. More and more, I "partied" on my own.

No longer interested in finding out his whereabouts when he came home, I welcomed him and accommodated him in any way I could. He certainly didn't need me to chastise him along with everyone else. I wanted to be his comfort and solace. So I didn't ask questions anymore.

§

That's the way it went for the next few weeks. James came and went as he pleased and I comforted and soothed him from his stressful day in any way possible. When he was coherent, he seemed so grateful to have me as refuge. How could I also become a source of misery and refuse to support him?

Although the sex wasn't as passionate as it was before, it didn't matter because I loved him - truly and unconditionally. He was becoming an emotionless automaton operating on fumes. I knew the job was acutely taking its toll. Even our pills and substances weren't adding to sex anymore. In a rare moment of clarity, I flushed the ecstasy pills down the toilet. I was actually relieved that I hadn't gotten dependent on them. James didn't seem to notice their absence which was also good. What was the use if it wasn't helping the main reason we started taking them?

Most of the time, now, James would come home from work, do his "business" and immediately jump off to shower - leaving me at the hotel alone for the rest of the night. There was no way I could miss the irony. Although I was disappointed, I couldn't complain. I still had him, right?

§

One day he came home from work and I hadn't had a chance to get our drinks ready. Now, completely sober, I took a good look at James. Where was the fine, virile, athletic man I first met? He was nearly skin and bones. Although I knew he could probably hide it at work, I couldn't miss it when he undressed. Deciding I at least needed to be a responsible girlfriend, I made him sit down.

"James, we need to talk."

Kicking his feet up on the table, he looked at me impatiently.

"What is it, Merc? I can't talk for long. I've got to go home." Stung by his new definition of *home*, tears started to spring. I trudged on, regardless. This had to be broached.

"James, I'm worried about you. You're losing too much weight." Grabbing the worn room service menu, I picked up the phone. "What do you want to eat? You need to eat."

He got up angrily. "This is what you wanted to talk to me

about? I have things to do, Merci, and I'm not hungry right now. I'll eat at home."

Before I could say anything, he stormed into the bedroom and left me on the phone with the operator who was asking if I needed anything. I apologized and hung up. This was getting bad.

He left the hotel without so much as a goodbye. The reality of my situation really hit me, as I'd had no substance in me to block it out. I was in trouble. I took out my phone to call Teresa. She answered on the third ring.

"Teresa, I need your help."

"What's wrong, Merci?" I could hear the concern and it soothed me like a warm balm. It was so good to hear her voice.

"You were right - this is too much for me. Now I know that I made a mistake messing around with James."

I thought I heard her take the phone away from her mouth and shout *Praise the Lord,* but I couldn't be sure.

She cleared her throat. "Yes, Merci, I'm so glad you figured that out."

"What should I do? He's using drugs and drinking more and...so am I - but not pills anymore, just marijuana," I quickly clarified. I started crying in humiliation for how stupid I just sounded.

"Oh my God, Merci. The first thing you need to do is come home. I have the keys to your car here. Do you want me to come get you? I will, Merci - just say the word."

I thought about it. Was I ready to just abandon James? I loved him too much and he needed help just like I did. Teresa could sense that she was losing me as I continued to remain quiet.

"Merci? Can I come pick you up?"

"Teresa, I can't leave him now. He's in bad shape and he

needs my help. I can't just…abandon him. Everybody is on him at work and you don't understand the overwhelming pressure that's he's under. If he comes home and I'm not here, I'm afraid of how he'll react. He might…seriously harm himself or something." I heard Teresa sigh and deflate through the phone.

"Merci," she said tiredly, "how are you going to help him when you can't help yourself? You need to get away from him."

"He needs me and I'm not leaving him. Can you give me any more advice that doesn't include that? I can't - not right now."

"No, not really. Leaving him and praying for him would be the best thing for both of you."

Ignoring the "leaving him" part, I focused on what else she said. "I can pray for him. Can you give me some verses to help?"

"I will, but it's not going to be too effective if you're not willing to get into God's will by getting out of that situation of living with an engaged man while both of you are doing drugs."

"Please, T," I begged, not wanting to hear that - at all.

"Okay." She gave me several Bible verses that I wrote down in my iPad notes.

"Thanks T."

"Alright, Merc, I'm here if you need me. Please, remember that."

My eyes began to brim over with tears. It was so nice to have Teresa back, even if I wasn't ready to do what she was insisting.

"I will, thank you so much, Teresa."

I hung up and downloaded the Bible app that had been haunting my iPad. I read the corresponding verses. One of the verses was Galatians 5:1 about standing firm in the liberty of Christ and not getting entangled again into bondage. I thought that was a good one for James's spiraling drug addiction. I began to pray for James to get help and that I could be the best girlfriend I could be for him.

The next week, things really seemed to get better. My prayers seemed to be answered when James came back from his other home and we had sex without any substances. It was almost as good as it was in the beginning! He also started eating more and put on five pounds by the end of that week. I was so glad I had gotten those verses from Teresa. James, less grouchy, seemed to be his old self again as we joked and played around. The best news so far was that we weren't abusing substances as much. No longer did I come right in fixing us drinks, instead I encouraged him to eat. I didn't see any signs of coke, so we were strictly on marijuana. Slowly but surely, things seemed to be looking up.

CHAPTER TWENTY

Later that week at work, I got a strange text from an unknown number.

Hi Merci, I was wondering if after work, I could talk to you about ordering some materials for a remodel I'm doing. Can I meet you somewhere?

Who is this?

Oh, I'm sorry for assuming. It's Lorelei Sampson, James's fiancée.

My gut twisted as I read the rest of her text.

He told me it would be okay to enlist your contact skills and resources to get some samples ordered for a makeover. Can we meet after work, today?

Today? I considered her request. So, James told her it was okay to use my help. I figured I could trust this whole deal if he thought it wasn't a problem. Not wanting to sound suspicious by delaying any longer, I hurriedly texted her back.

Sure, where do you want to meet?

Café Spiaggia's at 5:45.

Alright, I'll be there.

I'd heard of the expensive, Italian restaurant and always wanted to go, but not like this. Nervously, I fidgeted as I gathered my pad, pen and a design book to take.

Not totally insane, I texted James to verify.

Baby, did you tell Lorelei I would help with her remodeling project?

Not surprisingly, I didn't hear back. I hadn't heard from him since he left for work this morning so I figured he was swamped today. He obviously had pulled another all-nighter since he didn't come in until seven in the morning.

I knew that James kept a flask of cognac in his desk, and since J.J. had left early for the day, I went in and slipped it in my purse after taking a couple of swigs for liquid courage.

Deciding to take off on good faith, I fixed myself up in the bathroom mirror, inspecting my makeup closely. I was glad I had on my new Prada pink dress with my matching Balenciaga handbag and pink Jimmy Choo bunting sandals. My eyes were done up in James's favorite smoky eye look, and my pink, *Lickable* Mac lipstick matched my dress. Satisfied as I preened in the mirror, I decided I looked great. I knew that if she looked like she normally looked with her outdated eighties makeup and hair, I would be killin' her today.

I jumped in a cab and headed up Michigan Avenue to Spiaggia's. I was a bit relieved that we were dining at the new café as opposed to the extravagant, adjoining restaurant. Something just didn't feel right about having a beautiful sit down dinner with your boyfriend's fiancée. This way was less formal.

I entered the café and asked for *Sampson*. Before the hostess could look on her list, from the corner of my eye I saw Lorelei sitting down at a small table facing in my direction. I didn't think I was supposed to catch the menacing scowl that quickly morphed into cheery grimace. She waved me over. I tried not to overdo my sashay as Lorelei eyed me up and down, her expression showing nothing but mild interest. If I thought she was going to comment on my designer clothes, I was wrong. She had on a teal shantung suit adorned with pearls which I could appreciate. Her hair was twisted in her patented throwback upsweep, her cheeks were heavily rouged and she had eyelids of blue. She looked like a colorful dragon. A small giggle tried to escape my throat but I suppressed it. Its blue eyes turned frigid as it spoke.

"Hello, Merci, how are you?"

"I'm fine, Lorelei, how are you?"

"Great."

A server showed up. Lorelei eyed her with poorly concealed disdain. She muttered to me, "You've never been here before, right?" Before I had a chance to reply, she said, "We'll have two Fritto Mistos and," she turned to me, "what would you like to drink?"

Oh, I get a choice? I decided to let go of the fact that she ordered for me because I wasn't sure what would come out of my mouth. I needed to be cool. Already resenting the woman who stood like a *Titanic* iceberg between me and my man, I didn't trust myself with any more alcohol. The swigs of cognac had more than done the job.

"I'll just have lemonade." She looked at me with barely

hidden disapproval. I didn't care as I lifted my eyebrow in challenge. She looked away first and to the server.

"I'll have a Cosmo." The server scuttled away, no doubt intimidated by her nails-on-a-chalkboard voice.

Lorelei set her severely drawn eyebrows on me. "Now, Merci, tell me about yourself."

"Well, I'd rather we talk business."

She looked incredulous at my brazen response.

Thank you, Hennessy.

The server returned with bread and water and disappeared. Lorelei seemed to be taking time to gather herself. She appeared to be taking deep breaths.

Whatever.

"Alright, I noticed you brought a design book. Let's have a look," she gritted out.

Smiling brightly, I took the design book out and opened it. I took out my pen and pad while she skimmed through it, pointing to colors and samples she wanted me to order. I dutifully wrote down her instructions, proud of myself as I performed the tasks in a professional manner, despite being tipsy. Apparently, since becoming a drinker with James, I was becoming quite the natural.

Our orders arrived and we pushed our materials away to eat. I looked down at my plate and gaped. Calamari, brussels sprouts, fennel, jalapeño and some type of sauce. Out of my peripheral, I could see her severe smile as she started eating her food.

"What's the problem, Merci, don't like what you see? It's quite good."

"Well, it looks fine - I just don't like brussels sprouts." Upset once again that she took it upon herself to order my food, I couldn't help but lash out a bit. "Spaghetti would've been just fine."

It gave a sharp laugh that went into another frequency. She was irritating as hell. No wonder James couldn't stand her, but I remembered that her imitations also made him laugh. I was becoming more depressed by the minute.

"Well, don't eat them, but please don't pass up the other items. They're delish."

I nodded and tried to eat. Sure enough, the food was tasty. I even ventured to taste the dreaded brussels sprouts. They were surprisingly good. Lorelei picked up on this.

"See, I told ya. Good, right?"

I nodded contritely and continued to eat. The food here was wonderful.

After we were done eating, we continued getting the samples chosen. Once we were finished, I closed the book to return it to my bag. I was ready to get out of here. She waved the server over with her credit card. I didn't want her paying for me, so unthinkingly, I took out mine, placing it on the table while I stuffed the book in my bag. I saw her eyeing the card but I realized my mistake too late. She feigned ignorance. Maybe she really didn't see it?

"Merci, why don't we have dessert?" she asked.

I smiled. "No, not today, I really need to get home."

"Oh, alright." She paused as her mind seemed to be calculating something. "I'm sorry dear, but it looks like you have something in your teeth. I'll get us refills while you go to the restroom and check that out. Looks nasty. Then we can look at the dessert menu when you return."

Embarrassed about possibly having brussels sprouts in my teeth, I nodded and raced to the restroom.

Looking in the mirror to examine my teeth, I didn't see anything. Maybe I got rid of it while continuously running my tongue over them before I got here.

Inspecting my makeup, I began to worry. Had she seen

James's credit card? I was almost sure I had placed it back in my bag before she could read the name. I reapplied my lipstick and returned to the table. There were two fresh drinks.

"I got you another flavor of lemonade to try. Please look at the menu, *dahling*."

What was this - *Green Acres*?

"Alright, but I really don't want dessert." I took a huge swig of my lemonade. It was some type of Blueberry and it was delicious.

"Are you sure?"

"Yes, I just want to go home."

"Alright, let's just finish up. By the way, how are you getting home?" I didn't miss the derisive note on the last word.

"I'll take a cab."

A drawn eyebrow lifted curiously. "All the way to Hyde Park? That will be some fare." How did she know I went to school in Hyde Park? She waited in challenge, it seemed.

Caught, I came up with a response. I was starting to feel a little woozy. Why was the cognac working again?

"It's no problem, I have the money."

"No, I can't let you pay that much, I know you're a poor college student."

I would've protested more but I started to feel like I could pass out. Her face was swimming.

"Merci, are you alright?" I thought I saw an evil, bright smile on her face but I couldn't be sure.

"Yes." I answered dazedly.

"Oh dear, you don't seem to be in any condition to hail a cab or anything. My driver, Gino is outside - let's go. I'll have him take you home."

Now weak, I relented as I let her guide me to the door,

not sure what was happening. The whole room was spinning and I could see the curious faces of other patrons while I leaned on Lorelei's tiny, bony shoulder. Once outside, the lights from downtown seemed to turn into big, blurry pieces of snow. How could that be - it was still summer? I heard Lorelei telling someone something as I was shoved into a back seat.

Everything went black.

§

When I came to, I was on something hard and wet. I could see bright lights coming at me and zipping by. Muddy water was splashed all over me. I tried to open my eyes but I could only open one, the other one was virtually shut. All at once I felt throbbing and searing pain on my face and body. I sat up to look down at myself only to see that I was muddied and dirty, my legs scraped and that there was blood on the neck of my pink dress. Trying to survey my surroundings, I could see that I was on the pavement under a viaduct and cars were speeding by, coming so close it looked like they could hit me as they splashed me. It was dark, wet and smelled of urine.

Where was I?

"Help me, Lord," I mumbled as I looked around.

I looked down for my purse, thankful I still had it. I tried to recall the last thing I remembered. I was at dinner with that witch and then – nothing. I put my feet under me to try to get up but as I did, I twisted my foot and broke the heel on one of my shoes. I winced in pain but now that I could see a little bit, I had to get from under here. Stumbling, I made it out from under the viaduct into some street light.

Two guys that had on big clothes were coming my way as I tried to amble out from under the darkness.

"Hey, girl - how much," one of them asked with his arms wide open in question. The other one laughed as my heart hammered in dread.

"Nah man, you don't want none of that. She a mess - let's go. Plus, I got this hottie named Trish waitin' for us back at the crib."

Thank you, God. They laughed and kept going as I made my way towards more light. There was a parking lot outside of a White Castle so I went in that direction, squatting between some cars. Once I felt I was safely away from trouble, I assessed what had happened to me.

I hadn't had anything to drink but lemonade since I left the office, so obviously I was drugged. Did she slip me a roofie or one of those date rape drugs? When did this occur? I wracked my brain trying to figure out the timing and I could only deduce that it was when I was sent into the restroom. That's right - there was nothing in my teeth. It was a ruse I fell for. I gently touched my face and my eye felt tender and swollen. I had been beaten up. I looked around at my surroundings noting that it wasn't a great neighborhood. Immediately paranoid as I recalled the infamous Chicago statistics, I got up and hobbled into White Castle to use the bathroom, examine my injuries and make a phone call to James.

What I saw in the mirror almost made me collapse. It was confirmed that I had been battered. Now, I started to really feel my swollen lip, scratched face and blackened eye. I looked like I had been in a bad fight and lost. Getting some tissue, I tried to wash off my face, hoping that excluding my eye, most of it was just surface scratches, which thankfully, it was. Had Lorelei done this to me? Should I go to the police?

I reached into my bag to call James. My phone was gone. I scrambled around my small bag hoping to be mistaken but it was really gone. What else was missing? His credit card. This chick had dumped me off somewhere questionable with no phone and no money. Nobody used pay phones anymore. I still had my wallet but it was emptied.

What an evil wench.

Tearfully, I went to the counter and asked the cashier, who was looking at me like *she* was scared, could I use her phone.

"Sorry, I don't have one," she whispered, terrified.

I shook my head and left.

Outside, I wailed. "Please God, help me," I begged.

I went to the next door establishment, which was a small food store. There was an old man behind a bullet proof window, eyeing me cautiously.

"May I help you? We don't have a restroom."

"No, I just," I started sobbing which hurt my left eye even more. I was in such despair."Please... I don't want to use the bathroom." Still not moved, he kept looking at me closely.

"Then what can I help you with?"

I hiccupped as I tried to speak. "I just got kidnapped and left in this neighborhood."

"*This* neighborhood?"

I realized I had offended him. "No, sir, I didn't mean anything by it." Knowing I was blowing this, I sobbed loudly. "I'm from New Hampshire...and...and... I don't know anything about Chicago except where I go to school in...Hyde Park. Please hear me out. I was drugged, beaten...and...dumped under the viaduct a block down. My phone was ripped off and I have no way to call anyone." I hiccupped. "Please, help me."

He studied me for a moment, no doubt taking in the mud

and blood on my clothes, my scratched face and legs and my black eye. He sighed and came out of the door from behind the counter. He looked like he was about sixty-five years old. Grey headed and pudgy, he smiled sympathetically.

"Alright, sit down here." He pushed some stacked crates together and made me sit down, which I gladly did. "I can see you're telling the truth."

Crying, I could only shake my head. He handed me an outdated flip phone.

"Make your one call. You can wait here until they show up."

"Thank you so much."

Gratefully, I dialed James's number. I waited for eight rings and got nervous when it went to voicemail.

"James, I need you to come get me. I'm at-" I looked at the man for him to tell me where I was.

"Sixty second and Templeton - Sam's Food & Market."

I repeated the address back and added quickly, "Your fiancée drugged and dumped me. Please come pick me up right away."

I disconnected and noticed that the man was looking at me shaking his head.

"Are you Sam?"

He chuckled like he got that all of the time. "No, I'm Ray. Sam was my brother."

"Oh. Thank you, Ray."

He looked at me with wise, narrowed eyes. "So you done got yourself mixed up with a taken man," he stated more than questioned.

I couldn't answer as I was stunned that he had picked up on it so fast from my brief message.

"Young lady, you're young and perhaps don't know any better, but don't ever mess around with what belongs to someone else. What she did to you was wrong, but expect something like that when you're also doing wrong. Get yourself away from that situation as fast as you can. No good can ever come from it."

Sadly, I nodded. He sounded like Teresa, but I was listening. Apparently, he and Teresa were right and I was the dumb one. After what had just happened to me, I was definitely going to take heed of his words.

After forty five minutes, there was still no sign of James. I figured he would've immediately called back on Ray's phone after he got the message. A few customers came in for purchases and looked at me strangely. After they left, Ray stuck his head out of the door again.

"Where is he?"

"I don't know. Can I please use your phone again?"

"To call *him*? He obviously ain't comin' to pick you up."

I thought about that. Why hadn't James called? Come to think of it, why hadn't I heard from him all day?

"No, I'm calling my best friend."

I reached Teresa and she took the keys to my car and was at Sam's in less than twenty minutes. She gaped at me in horror as I thanked Ray profusely.

As I held on to her as she helped me out of the door, he called out, "Remember what I said, young lady - no good can ever come out of it. End it."

I smiled gratefully. "I'll remember, thanks again, Ray."

"Alright." He gave me a warm smile and I was gone.

In the car, I slumped in the seat.

"Merci, we need to go to the police."

I thought about it but I didn't want to go in this condition.

"Later. I don't want to be out like this anymore."

Not saying another word, Teresa drove us back to the Hyde Park campus. I wasn't even surprised or displeased that we were going back to the dorm. She was quiet until we were about eight minutes away.

"Merc, I'm so sorry this happened to you."

"Go ahead - tell me 'I told you so.'"

"No, I don't have to. Clearly, between me and that man, Ray, you already know that."

I chuckled bitterly.

"Your bruises don't look too bad. Tell me everything that happened."

"Can we get home first? Then I'll tell you the whole deal after I've had a shower."

CHAPTER TWENTY ONE

Once I was at the dorm, which felt extremely comforting, I dressed in my familiar dowdy pajamas and settled in my bed. It was cold since I hadn't been here for almost two months. This seemed more like home. I recounted the whole, sordid tale to Teresa who had her mouth open in astonishment the entire time. Once I was done, I leaned back onto my bed, exhausted. She was ready to take me to the police station but I was too tired and in pain and thought we could go tomorrow. She applied a salve to help with my eye and brought an icepack to apply.

"That is so bogus. She's obviously a thug from Brooklyn. I think she's the one who beat you."

"Why?"

"Because if it was some dude, you would've been more bruised. She probably started pummeling and scratching your face while you were passed out," she said in disgust.

"What about my legs?"

"Your legs probably got scratched up when you were dumped under the viaduct. You probably rolled when they threw you out of the car. "

That almost sounded funny. "Hmm, makes sense."

"She obviously took your phone and his credit card so you would be stuck. We need to at least call the police and report this."

Suddenly, I thought about what else was missing from

my purse. I sighed.

"We can't. I had James's alcohol flask in my purse and she took that too. I could get him into serious trouble if she decided to retaliate by blackmailing him about giving alcohol to a minor. It even has his initials on it. I'm sure that's why she kept it."

She frowned. "You had his flask? Oh well."

"What do you think happened to James? Could she have done something to him, because I haven't heard from him all day?"

She pondered this and shrugged. "I have no idea. You're going to have to figure that one out since you know him, and I don't.

"I just don't understand why this happened. I did what you said and started praying and then - this. One of the verses, Galatians 5:1, really seemed to be helping pertaining to his drug issues."

Teresa's eyes narrowed in remembrance. "That's the verse on getting free from bondage. Merci, that verse was probably not just for him - it was for you, too."

"Oh, that didn't even occur to me."

"While this was a bad thing, it could turn into something good. Don't get me wrong, God didn't do this or was trying to punish you for what you were doing wrong. He is a good and merciful God that looks at His children through the grace of Jesus Christ. So ultimately, if you listen and obey, God can use this as a wake-up call to keep you out of a bad situation that was on its way to worse. He's delivering you out. I told you, you couldn't really be in His will and in that lifestyle. You were open for the enemy to bring all sorts of bad things into your life, including this. As bad as it looks, I believe this could be answered prayer *if* you obey."

In my familiar bed, I still couldn't sleep. In addition to my painful eye bruise and lacerations, I was wondering where James could be. Since I had no phone, there was no way for him to contact me. What had really happened to him?

I thought about my experience all night. I had called on God to help me and He sent me to Ray for him to assist me. Then James, whom I thought I could count on, didn't come to pick me up - it was Teresa. It looked like God had really rescued me and was warning me to stay away from James's mess. I could've been killed tonight. I decided that losing my life wasn't worth it. Teresa was right. This was definitely a wake-up call. James and I were really done. He could marry that gangsta-thug chick if he wanted.

§

The next day, I stayed home, not wanting to be bothered with anything related to James, Lorelei or Jansen Worldwide Capital. Teresa agreed that I should rest and she went to work. I sat in bed, reading and watching TV. I even read a few verses from the unopened Bible Mom had packed for me last year. I was very thankful to God for taking care of me last night. Teresa explained it so well that from her point of view, although the enemy meant it for bad, God had turned it into good so I could be wiser in the future to avoid getting myself caught up again. He had rescued me from a something that could've gotten worse.

Later that afternoon, I heard banging on my door. I opened it to see James in a black suit and tie looking hysterical as he frantically inspected the length of me, his eyes wincing as it settled back on my face. He grabbed me but I shoved him away with all of my strength.

"Merci…" He looked at me in revulsion as he tried to cup my face.

"Don't freakin' touch me!"

"Oh, baby, what did that bitch do to my baby's beautiful face?"

"Leave me alone," I hissed.

He stepped back at the vehemence in my voice. He raised his hands in surrender.

"Please, Merci, talk to me."

"No, I can't do this anymore. You didn't call all day yesterday and you didn't come when I needed you." I pointed to my face. "Your fiancée did this."

"I know." He dropped my retrieved cell phone on the bed. "I was going to report her but she threatened to ruin my career by exposing me to the media for providing alcohol to a minor. She had my flask that she said you had-"

"Yeah I know. I figured as much. James, we're done."

He looked at me incredulously. "You won't even give me a chance to explain?"

I sat down on my bed, crossing my arms. My room seemed miniscule with a towering James in it. It dawned on me that he'd never been here before.

"Okay, you've got ten minutes."

He sat down in the desk chair. "When I left the night before - and you're going to get mad - I was with her."

"What?"

"Please, Merci, let me finish. I apologize, but we got a little drunk, and there she was, declaring her love for me again. When she tried to get touchy-feely, I drew the line. She got downright angry and cursed me out, saying she knew all about us and I would never get away with it. I left right away, but since I was still drunk, I didn't notice she had stolen my personal phone. I still had my business phone and didn't notice until I was already in an all-day meeting. That's why I didn't call you because stupidly, I forgot to program your number into my business phone-"

I stood up in bewilderment.

"Wait a minute. All this time, you never programmed my number into your business phone? I gave it to you before NeoCon because you said you might need to reach me regarding samples - that was business. Why wasn't it programmed then?"

He tried to smile affectionately, "Baby, you were always 'personal' to me."

"That's a load of bull."

"It's true. But, baby, please let me finish."

I sat back down on the bed while he continued.

"So, obviously, she saw your messages to me and it pissed her off. She is downright devious. I didn't find out until I went to the hotel and you weren't there. I wracked out my brain trying to figure out where you were..."

While he bloviated, I checked my phone and saw twenty-three missed calls from James - this morning?

"Then I tracked her down this morning and got our phones and my card back. She spilled all but is unremorseful and dared me to go to the police. She said she would ruin me. I came as quickly as I could, baby. Me and her are really done - done for good."

Unimpressed with his side of things, I glared at him.

"As quickly as you could. Why wasn't it last night?"

He looked ashamed. "Because I spent another night in Bucktown, drunk after another outing. I'd been schmoozing the board members and I didn't get back to the hotel until this morning."

"This...morning? So you didn't notice I was gone until this *morning*?" I looked at the clock on my phone. "And it's already eleven thirty," I said, flabbergasted.

"Well, I had that important board of directors' meeting to

attend this morning, and I had to go there first."

Fed up, I shook my head.

"I've been such a fool. I'm tired of being last on your list. God says in His Word that I deserve better. I've done everything for you and changed my whole life and values for you. Indulging in things 'Merci Townsend' would never have done. And you know why? Because I loved you. You've never once told me you loved me, but I'm done being stupid. I could've died last night and you know what, James? I realize now that I love me, more."

He looked shocked. "You love me?"

I threw a pillow hard at his head. He caught it before it connected.

"Of course I do, don't act like you didn't know."

"I wasn't sure because you never told me either." He looked overjoyed. "Merci, I love you too."

My heart hammered and I felt myself beginning to fold, but I held strong. I wasn't going to fall for it.

"No, James, It's too late. I don't believe that - because your actions certainly don't add up to a person in love."

"But I do, Merci. I've loved you since we went to NeoCon together. It was then that I knew you were going to be my best friend and partner for life. At the time, I wasn't sure of what to make of those new, foreign emotions, but later, I realized what they were."

Shaking my head to deflect his confession, I put my hands up in protest.

"Oh, no you don't, James. Truthfully, I don't want to hear it. It's too late. Lip service is one thing, actions are another. I don't care why you decided to keep being engaged to her - if you loved me, you would've ended it. I don't care if you and your family have millions invested - if you loved me, it wouldn't have mattered. Love is more precious than money and everything else. I changed my whole lifestyle for you, started indulging in drugs, alcohol and snuck around the back like a sleazy whore, just for you - just to make you happy. Only because I loved you. That's how far a fool could go for love. But you weren't a fool for me. I was a fool for you and it almost killed me. If I ever fall in love again, I'll never lose myself or nearly destroy myself for love."

He looked down at his lap, contemplative of my words. He didn't speak for several moments.

"You're right, Merci, and I'm truly sorry for everything that has happened. I was wrong." He was silent for another moment. "It's true. If I loved you properly, you wouldn't have had to go through any of this."

"I'm glad you see that. Now, get out." I tearfully looked away while he was quiet for a minute.

"I'll leave, Merci, but remember this - I love you and I'm going to show you how much I really love you."

"Yeah, yeah. Bye," I said nastily.

Then, he was gone.

§

After he left, I stayed in bed that day, trying not to cry too much since my left eye was still sore. My heart ached so badly with everything that had happened. This was it. James and I were really over. Now that I had time to think about it, I didn't have anything left to turn to. I knew that I had God, but right now, I didn't want to do anything but wallow in my misery.

That evening, I received a text from James.

I love you.

My heart sputtered and I felt myself growing weak. I wanted to respond in kind so bad.

Then, another text.

I love you. Even if you don't believe me, it's true. I meant what I said. I'll show you.

A fresh wave of tears spilled over, and clutching my phone to my chest, I went to sleep.

§

After that weekend and with only one week left of my internship, I decided to stay home since I still looked a mess and didn't want to be in the vicinity of JWC. James was the only person I needed to check in with, anyway. Then I began to worry about whether my internship would be invalidated since I didn't plan on finishing off that week. Did I need to call him? Before I could think more about it, he called first.

"Hello, Merci. Why aren't you here at work? Is the swelling still bad?"

Ignoring his question, I tried my best to sound professional.

"Hello, James. I'm not feeling well and with only one week before the end of my internship, I don't think I'll be in any condition to return. Will this be a problem and will I still receive credit, sir?"

I could hear him sighing over the phone. His voice dropped a few levels.

"Merci. Again, I'm so sorry. Of course I'll talk to HR to make sure you get your credit."

"Thank you." I could hear him call out my name but I quickly hung up. I wasn't trying to stay on the phone any longer than necessary. It hurt to hear his voice.

I received a text.

I love you and I'm going to show you.

I didn't respond.

§

The next few weeks passed slowly as I continued to ignore James's apologies and love declarations. It wasn't easy but I managed. Teresa encouraged me by saluting my resistance, and that following weekend, I drove us to her home so I could visit her church. The Rothschild family was so warm and "regular." They kindly took me into their beautiful home, making sure I knew I was welcomed. I didn't know what I expected since I knew they were wealthy, but their house was only a bit more extravagant than my parent's. While it was huge, it wasn't pretentious. I recalled her father's words about the money not belonging to him, but to his grandfather. It was easy to see where Teresa got her values from. They reminded me of my family.

In church, the pastor preached about how God can deliver you from a situation, but if you don't stand firm in His Word, you can easily fall back in. Watch for the enemy's devices so you can be familiar and be on guard. His message was very interesting.

On our way back, we drove mostly in silence. I was contemplating the turn of events in my life.

"What did you think of today's sermon?" Teresa asked.

"I thought it was good. I enjoyed it very much, thank you."

"You're welcome. I thought it was important when he talked about how easy it could be to fall back into the same destructive pattern if you aren't watchful - aren't careful."

I knew what she was alluding to so I sighed. "Yes, Teresa, I was listening to him and I know you're thinking about me and James."

She smiled sheepishly.

"Don't worry, we're done," I said.

She smiled sincerely and kindly changed the subject.

We were due to start classes next week and we had to clear out of our rooms. Teresa and I decided to separate due to how cramped our room had become as we accumulated more things, so now we were right down the hall from each other. I took my time getting my place together, placing things where I wanted since I no longer had to consider anyone's preferences. I had to admit that I was happy to have my own space, although I would miss her.

CHAPTER TWENTY TWO

School started uneventfully and before long, I got into the swing of going to class again. The problem was that since I only had four classes, I had a lot of down time to think about James. I tried to get into praying and reading the Bible as well, but I admit I wasn't as interested as I should've been. Teresa suggested attending a campus Bible study on Wednesdays that she had been going to. I told her I would let her know.

I was receiving fewer of his texts every day. Although I didn't reply, it was nice to read them and I had forgiven him. Now I was wondering if his feelings were waning for me. I thought of our whirlwind romance downtown and wondered if it really happened. I thought of the fancy clothes he bought me that were recently sent to the dorm in a box that I couldn't bring myself to open. Every time I saw something related to fashion, I turned it off. It all reminded me of my time with James. Now, I was strictly jeans and t-shirts, my glasses and a haphazard ponytail every day. I didn't really care how I looked anymore. Teresa said I was still heartbroken and soon I would get over it and back to my fashion forward self.

§

One evening, while relaxing and reading a book, I heard an

incessant banging on my door. Thinking it was Teresa wanting to bum a few snacks, I opened it with a big smile. It was James. His curly hair was overgrown and disheveled and he looked like he'd lost weight again. He had on loose jeans and a blue sweater. His face was a bit gaunt, his high cheekbones now sharp, prominent angles. His bloodshot eyes were wild and he was unshaven. I had never seen him looking so unkempt.

"Merci, it's really over." Astonished, I just gawked. "Please let me in. It's done for real this time." Not waiting for an answer, he moved around me into the small room. In a fog, I closed the door behind him.

"James, what are you doing here?"

He sat down in a desk chair. "It's over with. I'm no longer working at JWC."

I sat down on my bed. "What are you talking about?"

"I quit Jansen. I told you I broke it off with Lorelei for good after what she did to you. That morning, the board appeared ready to confirm me as CEO, but within days they got wind of our breakup. The final vote was at the board of directors' meeting this morning. I got voted down. I'm free."

I gaped at him in disbelief. "So, you wanted to be outvoted? I don't get it."

"Yes. I knew that it would turn out like this because I'm looked at as unstable. With the impending merger of JWC and Sampson Electronics, the shareholders got over confident. When they heard of our breakup, they no longer had assurance or felt they could trust me on my own to run the company," he said bitterly. "That's fine with me."

"I can't believe what I'm hearing. What are you going to do now?"

He looked at me in bewilderment. "What do you mean? Do you hear what I'm saying? I'm free."

I still looked at him in confusion. "So, you're out of a job?"

"Yes, and happy about it. I told you I was going to prove to you that I loved you. I knew it would turn out this way and I'm totally yours now. Free and clear without any job pressures or 'commitments' to come between us."

I still wasn't sure if I understood him correctly.

"Alright. If you didn't get the CEO position, why did you quit? Weren't there other positions you could've taken?"

"I could've, but this was my opportunity. I told my dad I was out."

"How did he react?"

"He's livid and scrambling to get my brother, Andrew, brought in for consideration."

"Isn't Andrew still finishing up school?"

"Yep, but he's desperate and Drew is all too ready to jump in."

I eyed him skeptically. "I know that there were other consequences you're not telling me about. What's really happened, James?"

He sighed loudly. "My father said he could tell that I'm on something and that I needed to get help. He also said the board members noticed a change in my appearance, as well." He put his head in his hands and my heart went out to him.

Softly, I asked, "What else, James?"

"He said that if I didn't get help right away so that I could come back to the company, that he and I were done. I told him that was fine with me because I didn't want anything he had to offer. So, basically, he cut me off."

"What does that mean, exactly?" I asked cautiously.

"He had The Fairmont kick me out, since that was really his connection with the franchise and they value his money and influence, not mine. It was never in my name," he said, shamefaced. "He took my place in Bucktown since that belonged to him too," my eyes bugged out, "and told me that after today, Bernard would no longer be my driver since that was a company privilege. Of course he cut off my JWC salary and told me I could forget about receiving an inheritance."

My heart dropped. "James, was this all worth it? What are you going to do?"

"Absolutely, it's worth it. I'm going to start my own architectural and design firm," then he attempted to look at me pointedly, his red eyes unfocused, "and be with you."

I stared back at him in a daze. I wasn't sure what to say. On one hand, I was delighted because it really seemed as if he was free. On the other hand, he looked a mess, and now his life was a mess. Should I still support him? Isn't that what I was supposed to do if I still loved him? Which I did.

"Okay, I'm pleased you're happy, but obviously, you're still indulging. What's been going on with you?"

"Yeah, just a bit but I'm handling it. It was just until I got out of that place - so much pressure. Now, it shouldn't be that much of a problem." I looked at him doubtfully but changed the subject for now.

"Where are you going to stay?"

"I want things to be back the way they were before. I want to be with you." For the first time, I noticed a green duffel bag on the floor between his feet. I eyed it in disbelief as alarms tripped off. I got up and started pacing.

"James, I'm trying to get myself together and while I still have feelings for you and have forgiven you for the mess you got me in, I don't want to be involved in that stuff anymore. I value my sobriety and being clear-minded again. I don't know how this is going to work."

His arms reached out and caught me around my waist, placing me squarely on his lap. He moved my ponytail aside and started kissing my neck. Familiar goose bumps popped up all over my skin and my heart rate accelerated. Even looking jacked up like he was - he still had the same effect on me. I tried to squirm away but he held on tight.

"Baby, please help me. I can see that you've made some positive changes and I need that in my life, too. I need you. With you, I feel I can accomplish anything." He kissed over to my cheek. "Feel that? We were made for each other."

I pitifully gave one last protest. "No, James," I murmured, trying to clear my muddled head, "what are you saying? You want to stay here with me? I'm in school for goodness sake. I can't get distracted."

"Just for a little while. I'll get my place soon. I still have some money saved up but until then, I just want us to be together. Anywhere, I don't care - as long as I'm with you."

I had a thought that should've occurred to me earlier. I turned my head around to face him.

"How did you know I moved out of the other room?"

He gave me a kiss on the lips. "You know I can find out anything about my baby," he looked around, "this is very convenient, too."

Why did I even ask how he found out?

§

James was totally exhausted because once he sat down on my bed, he keeled over and was out. This gave me time to consider this massive, new development. What was I getting myself into – again? I considered every angle. I still loved James and he loved me. He wasn't engaged anymore. He had a slight drug problem and he needed my help.

While I knew it wasn't right for him to be living with me, I felt it was my duty as someone that loved him to help him. *But he could get his own place and you could go over there to help him*, a voice reasoned. No, I had classes to go to and I couldn't watch him if he wasn't here. He needed to stay with me so I could keep an eye on him, I justified. So there it was - my decision. James would be living with me until he curbed his addiction, found a place and started his company.

Overjoyed with my decision, I laid down in the bed next to him and snuggled up to him under his arm. He felt so frail compared to before. This only furthered my resolve about my decision. I kissed his hollow cheeks and hugged him. Now, I had to take care of him.

When James woke up a few hours later, I encouraged him to eat some ramen noodles I'd heated up.

"Are you crazy, I don't eat that junk. I'm James Jansen III."

I put my hands on my hips. "Where are you, James Jansen III? You are in a poor college student's dormitory. So either you go out to get something to eat or you acclimate."

He looked at me with resigned amusement and took a bowl, tasting it.

"Hmm, not bad. I remember this stuff."

I smiled knowingly and ate along with him.

"But seriously, babe," he said through slurps, "we can do better than this. I'm not totally destitute."

"I know, but you were so tired and I knew you wouldn't feel like going out."

He looked around. "We need some better food up in this joint. I tell you what, let's go grocery shopping tomorrow."

I pointed over towards my miniature fridge. "Do you see that thing? We can't buy that much to fit into it anyway."

"Then I'll have to buy us a bigger fridge-"

"No, James. You need to save what little you have."

"But-"

"If you're going to be staying here, we need some rules. First, I have to go to my classes every day they're scheduled. I refuse to let you be a distraction. Also, no drug usage of any kind in my place - you'll get me kicked out. Next, you need to save your money. So while you're staying here, there will be no extravagance of any kind. You need to continue to look inconspicuous like a student-"

"Please - do you know how much money we give to the University of Chicago?"

I placed my hands up. "That's in the past."

He nodded in reluctant agreement. "Yeah, you're right."

"And last, you need to be actively working on developing your business plan while I'm going to class and studying."

The next few days, it seemed to be working. James had only brought jeans, shirts and sweats, so that worked out. Nobody seemed to be checking on whether he was a college student here anyway. Most people at UChicago seemed to mind their own business. I was happy about that discretion. We had sex a few times but something was off. The fact that he wasn't quite well had a lot to do with it, but there was something else that just felt...wrong.

§

We decided to go grocery shopping. His red Ferrari Modena was back at Bucktown and needed to go into the shop for repairs. We both agreed it would look too ostentatious here anyway. As we approached my small car, I could see his disapproval but chose to ignore it. I knew he wasn't pleased, but I had to admit it was comical to see James scrunching up his nose while trying to fold his tall body into my compact.

As I started driving, out of the corner of my eye I could see him looking around, scrutinizing the interior of my little Focus like he was revolted.

I looked at him pointedly. "What's the problem, James?"

His lip was curled up in distaste. "Your car...is so... small."

I pulled over and screeched to a halt, abruptly putting the car in park.

"Look, buster - you got any other options?"

Slightly startled, he said, "No, I don't. Calm down - I was just making an observation."

I continued to glare at him while he turned his head to casually look out of the passenger window. Satisfied that he didn't have any more comments, I drove off towards the store.

I'm sure he was wondering how it all had come down to this.

My, how the mighty have fallen.

§

We bought a few dishes that we could quickly throw together after I insisted we didn't need Filet Mignon and oysters. I lost the fight regarding wine and let him buy at least one bottle to stuff in my little refrigerator. When I returned from class, sometimes he would have a meal prepared for us to eat. Touched, I was thankful and hopeful that he would eat more to gain his weight back. Most of the time, he would be on his laptop while I ate, typing away. He also tried to remain quiet while I was studying. Although there were plenty of issues that needed work, I felt pretty good about our arrangement.

CHAPTER TWENTY THREE

One day when I returned from class, he wasn't in the room but I could see that his one pair of sneakers were still on the floor. Maybe he was in the bathroom. I knocked and heard some quick shuffling.

"James, are you okay?"

I heard him sniffle and flush the toilet. "Yeah, I'm okay. Be out in a moment," he called out too loudly.

I went into the room to heat up the hot plate and looked on my shelf for what we might eat tonight.

James came out wiping at his nose and I saw the telltale signs of redness in his eyes and under his nose.

I casually looked at him. "You just snorted coke," I stated.

"Yes, I did. It's been a rough day."

My ire rose. "James! I told you, you cannot do that stuff in here. You want to get me kicked out?"

"That won't happen, I'm an established alumnus here-"

"I don't want to hear that crap. Not anymore you aren't."

He looked stunned. "What does that mean?"

Instantly contrite, I tried to backpedal. "I didn't mean it like that. I meant that as for now, both of us are college students as far as anyone is concerned."

He seemed to accept my words but I wasn't letting him off the hook that easily.

"James, you can't do that here. I thought you were done. Why was today so rough?"

"I got a call from my father and we got into a big argument about what I was doing with my life. He didn't like my ideals and tried to convince me to get help so that he could get me back in JWC. He started telling me about the other positions I could fill, but I adamantly told him I wasn't interested. I told him that he should support my wishes like he does Andrew's, and we had a big blowout. Merci," he pleaded for understanding, "I couldn't deal with it and I just needed a tiny bit to calm down."

My heart went out to him as I woke up and realized that the strong, virile man that I fell in love with had a serious drug problem.

"James, you can't just lose it and turn to coke every time something doesn't go your way." He looked at me thoughtfully. "I've been finding out from reading the Bible that everything is not going to go your way all of the time, but God is trying to develop us to have patience and peace, so that we are never anxious about anything."

As soon as I mentioned *God*, he rolled his eyes. "Here we go. I don't want to hear about that now, please."

We sounded like me and Teresa. The irony.

"You said you wanted my help, right? Well, this is the new me. That night your fiancée beat me up and stole my phone," I spat, "I had no one to turn to and I had to call on God, and guess what? He showed up and rescued me - and you weren't anywhere to be found."

"So now you're all religious?"

"No, spiritual." Thanks, Mom and Dad, I chuckled to myself. "Or at least, I'm trying to get there. I can't deny that I need God's help. I always thought I could make it on my own. I can see you're the same way. And as long as you're here with me and want to be with me, then you need to accept that I have a growing relationship with Him."

He looked at me as if I was pathetic. "That's nice, baby, really it is, but please - I don't need this right now. I know I let myself go today, but I'll be fine."

I shook my head and gave him a patented Teresa response.

"I'll be praying for you."

§

It was becoming clear that James was in denial about his drug usage and wasn't going to hear what I had to say. As a couple, we were headed in the wrong direction and we needed help. I went out into the hall and texted Teresa.

Hey T, how's it going?

Fine girl, how are you? I feel like I haven't seen you in weeks and you're just down the hall. Classes going ok?

Yeah, they're going fine. Listen, when is Bible study?

Really? :) It's in about fifteen minutes actually. I was just getting ready to set off. You coming?

Yeah, I'll meet you on the steps.

Cool.

I went in to grab my Bible and saw that James was staring dazedly at the TV, the effects of coke obviously holding steady or either he had snorted a few more lines.

"I'm going out. Be back in a few hours."

"Okay." He never took his eyes off the TV, rocking slowly

from side to side.

He had snorted more lines.

§

Bible study was over in Brent House and consisted of about twenty people with name tags that were handed to us to fill out on arrival. The study leader, Greg, instructed us that the first verse of today's lesson would come from Romans 10:17. *So then faith cometh by hearing, and hearing by the word of God.*

He was explaining that you had to hear and read God's word to build up your faith and then it would grow inside of you like a seed. All of us were dealt the same measure of faith but we had to develop it by staying in His Word. And if you stayed away from His word, it could diminish your faith. It was like a battery that needed to be recharged.

Liza, a brunette that was sitting across from Teresa and I, raised her hand.

"What if you don't want to hear it? I'm having a problem of staying in the Word. I know I need to but I honestly don't want to. What do I do?" My ears perked up at this.

Another guy named Jack raised his hand to answer and Greg nodded for him to proceed.

"That happens to all of us because we are in our flesh which is still sinful, even though our spirits have been made new. In 2 Corinthians 5:17, it says *Therefore if any man be in Christ, he is a new creature: old things are passed away; behold, all things have become new.* So, we're all new on the inside, but still susceptible to outside influences because of our flesh. That's why we are to walk in the spirit and we will not fulfill the lusts of the flesh as it says in Galatians 5:16."

I think I liked this Galatians book.

"How do we overcome that?" she asked.

Greg turned to her. "The only way that I'm overcoming it is by, just what Jack said, walking in the spirit. In the beginning, I wanted to do the right thing but I really didn't want to be bothered with getting deep into God's Word. I thought I could control what I needed to control within my own power. I still found myself indulging in a lot I used to do. In other words, I was still sowing to my flesh even after I was saved. I could feel that my spirit was unfulfilled and that nothing was working out for me like I wanted.

"So, I surrendered to God and crawled my way like a man dying of thirst to my Bible. My flesh rejected it and tried to rise up, but I pressed my way. I forced myself to turn on spiritual teachings on the TV and radio, even when I really didn't want to, and saturated myself in the Word. And you know what? My spirit took over. I found out that there's an unspeakable joy when I'm walking in the spirit, not the other way around. I started to thirst for the Word and my spirit overruled my flesh. That's the only way it's working for me. I'm a constant work in progress."

"Wow, thanks. I forced myself to come here tonight, even though I didn't want to." She turned to me and we laughed. Liza said just how I felt and I admired her honesty. It was good to know I wasn't the only one.

"That's because God was drawing you. He has a set plan for all of our lives. We can either do it our own way, which could lead to some contentment, or do it His way, which is life - and life more abundantly which I feel means life beyond our wildest dreams. That's in John 10:10." I scribbled all of the scriptures on my pad.

The next verse was Romans 10:9. *That if you confess with your mouth the Lord Jesus and believe in your heart that God has raised Him from the dead, you will be saved.*

This is where I was confused. I raised my hand.

"I accepted Christ this way when I was younger. But I'm - I've been involved in," I gulped, looking over at Teresa, "some issues recently and I'm not sure if I'm still saved."

"You sound like you backslid, which could happen to most of us. I heard someone say that a Christian who backslides is like a child who disobeys his parents. It does not affect his sonship but it affects his fellowship, his joy, and the approval of the Father. Have you repented of your sins?"

"Not exactly," I hedged.

"Let's meet after the lesson and I'll pray with you."

After the lesson, while everyone was gathering around doing small talk, I hurriedly left out of the door.

Teresa was on my tail. "What happened, I thought you were going to pray with Greg?"

"I will, just another time."

She stopped in her tracks. "Why, Merci, what's going on? I thought you were enjoying it?"

I went over to a nearby bench to sit and she followed. I drew a deep breath in fear of her reaction.

"T. Please don't get mad. James is back."

Her eyes got huge. "What? When? Where?"

"I told you he left Lorelei for good, but now he quit the company and is trying to start his own architectural and design firm."

"Alright, where is he?" She raised an eyebrow suspiciously as I tried to stall.

"His dad completely disowned him and he's looking for a place right now."

"And?"

"And he's staying with me." I turned my head and flinched for her retaliation.

"What??" she bellowed.

I turned back around to bite. "I know, but it's just until he gets his place."

Teresa was shaking her head. "No wonder you didn't want Greg to pray, you're still living disobediently."

"I know, I know. I was too embarrassed, but honestly, I don't feel right about it. I feel - convicted. Even the sex is not the same. I don't even want to have it."

"Why are you letting him stay there?"

"Because as much as it pains me, I still love him and I feel sorry for him. He needs me, T. He's a mess and still has a…bit of a problem."

"What, drugs? Oh no, Merc, you have got to get out of that situation. I know you care for him, but having a man addicted to drugs living in your dormitory? Do you think God is pleased?"

"I know He's not, because I'm not."

"What are you going to do?"

"I'm going to give him a chance to get it together and then he's out."

"Alright, Merc, I hope you know what you're doing. You need to repent and ask God to help you in this. He will."

"Okay, I'm going to do that tonight."

§

When I returned to the dorm, James was out cold. His tall frame looked so frail and pitiful curled up in a fetal position on my small bed. He was so still. My heart sped up as I wondered if he was okay. I waited nervously until I saw that he was still breathing. Filled with intense sadness that it had come to this, I laid my hands in his curly hair and kissed his temple.

"Dear Lord, please forgive me for my sins. I know I

haven't been living right but please accept me back into your good standing. I truly believe that you died for my sins and were raised from the dead on the third day. I thank you for taking care of me all of these years, even though I thought it was me taking care of me. Forgive me for that vanity. I now know that you've always had your hand on me."

I looked down at James.

"Lord, please help James. He is struggling right now and even though he has rejected you, in his heart he's a good man that needs you. As a recommitted Christian, I stand in the gap for him. Please give your angels charge to watch over James wherever he goes and let him know that he needs you. I know you're not happy with the situation I'm in right now, but please work it out. Please don't let any harm befall me or James. In Jesus' Name, Amen."

I felt lighter than I ever had and went to my computer to finish up some school work I needed to turn in tomorrow. I must've drifted off because when I woke up, it was morning. I didn't know I was so tired.

I turned around to look for James on the bed but he wasn't there. I got up to go to the bathroom, since I figured that's where he was, but the door was open and it was empty. When I came back out, I saw a note in jagged handwriting on my bed that I had apparently missed.

Dear Merci,

Last night I dreamt that I died, so I called Bernard, against my father's wishes, to come get me. I'm entering rehab. I now know that I'm in no condition to be a good boyfriend to you. I want to keep using and I know that I'll never get anything accomplished, personally or professionally, with this new bad habit that I've acquired. Please forgive me for leaving without notice. I felt I didn't have a second to delay getting the help I need. Hopefully, when I get myself together, you'll be there, waiting. But if not, I understand. I truly did love you, Merci. Love, James.

I sunk down to my knees and sobbed disconsolately. He was gone. Why had this happened? I had just prayed for him.

After crying for about thirty minutes, I heard a still voice say,

I'm answering your prayer.

To He, Who Has Ears To Hear, Let Him

Hear! Part III

CHAPTER TWENTY FOUR

I went back and forth from accepting that God was really answering my prayers to being angry at James for leaving. I got lonely and depressed from time to time, but turned to the Word for comfort. The more I was into the Bible, the more I believed that this was all a part of God's plan and for me to leave it alone. I prayed for God to help me get over James if he wasn't coming back. I refused to contact him first since he was the one who bailed. It had already been two months and I hadn't heard a word from him. Isn't rehab usually thirty days or so?

Another month passed as I tried to stop checking my messages for any response from James. One weekend, I went with Teresa to a pumpkin patch for a hayride near her home. As we were jumping off the wagon and laughing, we heard a loud voice.

"Hey, chickadees, what's crackin'?" It was Darren from JWC. Teresa smiled wide and they gave each other hugs. I stood back timidly, too embarrassed to move as I was reminded of my sordid reputation at Jansen.

"Hey, Darren, what's up?" Teresa asked.

He looked at me and held open his arms. "Oh, what? I don't get a hug, Merci?"

I smiled sheepishly and gave him a quick hug.

"So, Darren, you live around here?" Teresa asked.

"Nah, I came up here with my buddy, Matt. He lives nearby. What about you?"

"My parents live over in the next town. Are you back in school or what?"

"Oh, you didn't know? I actually graduated last spring. JWC hired me on and I'm still there - but in the mailroom, mind you," he added with a smirk.

"Oh, that's cool."

"Yeah, right."

Teresa, always the optimist, nudged him playfully. "Hey, it's a start. What's been going on there?"

He looked at me and hesitated.

"Well, there's a rumor that James Jansen is coming back and that he's engaged again."

I thought I was going to vomit. "Excuse me, guys." Teresa looked at me pitifully while I took off across the patch, almost tripping over a pumpkin or two.

Engaged? That quick? He and Lorelei got back together? Well, serves him right if he wants that witch. The witch that almost killed me. I'm truly done now. Teresa caught up with me.

"You okay, Merci? We don't even know if that's true or not. He said it's a rumor."

"You know what, it doesn't matter. I'm so done right now. It's probably just what I needed to hear to totally let go."

She looked at me doubtfully. "You sure?"

"Yes, I'm sure. Let's go."

§

After that, I threw myself into my schoolwork and went to Bible study with Teresa every week. I found a church home not far away from campus and decided to join instead of having to travel home with Teresa every weekend. The small church named Living Life Christian Center was perfect for me. The pastor taught, more so than preached, and that's just what I needed as I was learning the Word and applying it to my life. I found that the young minister, Pastor Lawson, taught useful principles on how to live from Monday through Saturday, not just on Sunday. I made the decision to give my life totally to God by putting him first. I meditated on Matthew 6:33 and just what that meant. *But seek first the kingdom of God and His righteousness, and all these things shall be added to you.*

I remembered the first Bible study I went to with Teresa and how Greg taught that by living life your own way, you might get some happiness but if you live it God's way, you would get life - and life more abundantly. This was coming true for me. As I began serving and seeing things God's way instead of my own, my desires changed. I was becoming content with serving God in any way I could.

My heart began to be heavy when I thought about children starving, or not having water, or the homeless. I realized how important it was for His Word to go forth to all of the lost people, like I had been. When I served at the local soup kitchens or helped a child put on a brand new pair of shoes, there was no greater happiness that I had ever felt. Even the times I thought I was happy with James, couldn't compare. Now I realized I wasn't happy, but consumed with an obsession fortified by lust. First Corinthians 13:47 explained what true love was, and although I knew my feelings for him were real, the situation was based on deceit, lies, indulgence and we were headed to destruction.

§

So here I was today, thinking over the last six months of my life. I thank God for delivering me out of dire circumstances that could've gotten worse. I was thankful that my parents raised me in the church, even if I chose to ignore God's hand over my life for the first nineteen years. He was always there with me. The seed was planted and I knew that when I was in trouble like I was under that wet, dark viaduct, to call on the name of the Lord to help me. I thanked Him for giving me a spiritual roommate like Teresa, who always lovingly coerced me back to the truth. Even though she admitted she wasn't perfect with it, she didn't beat me over the head with her faith and I appreciated that. Her job was to tell me the Truth and let God do the rest. I had hoped that I did it the right way for James, but in light of what may have happened, I wasn't so sure.

I went home for Christmas and enjoyed spending time with my parents. They were impressed with my growing Bible knowledge and rejoiced at my growing relationship in Christ. I went to church more than they did for the three weeks I was home.

§

In January, thankful for my parents and to God for a joyous holiday, I got up in my church in Chicago to testify. Now that I was in His Word, I had peace and a boldness that I didn't have before. After all, when He instructed us to do something, we couldn't be fearful anymore. *God does not give us the spirit of fear*, after all. It took a while for me to get that, but after meditating and speaking II Timothy, 1:7, it took effect and changed me.

As I stood at the front of the church, a peace pervaded my senses. I wanted to help someone. I had nothing to be ashamed of since we all went through hard things - embarrassing things.

"I was raised in the church and always attended with my parents every week. But how many of you know that just because you're raised in the church doesn't mean church is in you?"

I received some Amens.

"That's how it was for me. I always got good grades and was a model student, always exceeded my parent's expectations and my own, knew what my goals were, always accomplished them and was pretty self-sufficient. Did you hear that word? 'Self.' That was the problem. It was all about me and no one else. I thought since I had it all together that I didn't need anyone else, including God - especially God."

I paused, willing myself not to cry.

"Earlier last year, I entered into a relationship with an engaged man." I could hear a pin drop but I didn't care. "At the time, I was full of excuses on why this was okay, including the excuse that he was going to break up with her soon. I was stupid. I won't insert 'young' because even though I was, this could've happened to anyone, at any age. Well of course, nothing turned out right. First of all, I wasn't in God's will so the door was open for all sorts of things to come into my life. He started doing drugs and I did too, just to keep up with him and make him happy. The final straw happened when his fiancée drugged me, beat me and left me out under a viaduct at night to die." The congregation gasped. "Not being from Chicago originally, I didn't know where I was. I had no phone to call anyone and I was beaten and bruised. So who did I call on? The Lord."

At this point whoops and hollers were rising. People started to get up, clapping.

"He was the only one I could call on, and he had a kind man in a nearby store help me out and let me use his phone. And then my roommate came to pick me up. I could've been dead, but God took care of me when I called on Him. I'll never forget that. Hallelujah!"

I broke down and a woman came forward to catch me as I sobbed in her arms. The church was in an uproar. I looked up through my tears and saw a few young girls, younger than me, crying. Oh Lord, I hope I helped. I could feel His smile on me. *You did good, servant.*

As I was leaving church, I was bombarded with hugs and thanks for my brave testimony. A few of the young girls I saw, told me of a similar situation or one they were contemplating getting into. I was so thankful that God led me to get up there at a time such as this. On my way out, I saw an older man with a black suit on in front of me blocking my way. He cleared his throat and took off his nice fedora.

"Young lady, I knew you'd do alright." I looked for a moment and then I gasped in surprise as I realized who it was.

"Ray!"

I launched myself into his arms. He patted my back and laughed warmly.

"Young lady, I didn't even recognize you until you started telling that story. My, my, my, how good is God? I prayed for you that night."

I could hardly let go of him I was so happy. "I didn't

know you went here. Oh, Ray, thank you so much - for everything. That night changed my life and you were a part of that."

Fresh tears started rolling and I saw him brush away a stray tear.

"You're going to make me cry all over again and I already did when you were speaking."

I chuckled and continued to hug him, speechless with joy.

"I was just visiting. I go to another church but look at God, bringing me here to show me that my prayers were not in vain. This is nothing but confirmation. Praise The Lord."

I beamed in amazement, shaking my head.

"Praise The Lord!"

§

Over the next few months, I learned that God created us in His image and that the power that he had with His Words, was the same power that He gave us. So I began to pray and speak over myself pertaining to receiving a good man of God. I meditated on Romans 4:17 and *called those things which be not as though they were.'*

Later that month, a guy named Lawrence joined church. He looked like he was about twenty-four, six feet tall, nice smile, hazel-green eyes, sandy hair and handsome. A few of the other ladies were excited about him joining and he shyly basked in their attentions. I taught Sunday school and he signed on to be an assistant. I instructed him on what his duties would be while I taught. After the lesson, he came to sit down across from me as I gathered my materials to leave.

"Thanks for showing me the ropes. Some of the kids got a little disorderly, but it was fun."

I laughed. "I really needed help so I'm thankful that you

enjoyed it."

He hesitated. "If you're not doing anything, would you like to go to lunch after service?"

I thought about it and didn't see the harm in having lunch. "Sure, why not?"

We went to a diner not far and sat down to order. I would look up periodically to catch him staring at me. He tried to play it off but I was too fast.

I smiled. "So Lawrence, what do you do?"

"I'm in training to be a police officer. I'm a cadet."

"Really? That's cool." I went back to reading my menu. "So are you in a police academy?"

"Yes, down on Thirty fifth and Michigan. It's a lot of hard work but I like it."

I looked up at him. "It's so important to do what you love."

My mind involuntarily went to James and a similar discussion. I immediately balked at myself for comparing anything like this to my relationship with James. I wasn't looking to get into another relationship unless that person was the one for me and I didn't feel any inclinations about this guy, Lawrence.

"What do you do, Merci?" he asked with a warm smile. I couldn't deny he was handsome, though...

§

Over the next month or so, Lawrence and I went to lunch after service. Just so he wouldn't get the wrong idea, I made sure we each took turns paying the bill. We were just being friends and I was fellowshipping with my new brother in Christ. Lawrence was easy to talk to and he seemed to have a similar, modest lifestyle like my own. He grew up in "The

City" as Chicagoans liked to call it and didn't live too far from the church. On one of these outings, Lawrence decided to move it along a notch.

"Merci, you do realize that I'm interested in you? Would you officially like to go out with me?"

I was thrown off guard but not that much. I could tell by the way he looked at me appreciatively that he was interested. Not to toot my own horn, but a lot of guys were. I was a little surprised that he acted on it, though. I had already mentioned to him that I had been through a hard break up without going into details. I knew he hadn't joined the church yet when I gave my big testimony, but I still wondered how much he had found out. Some church folks liked to gossip, too.

"Lawrence, I'm just not ready for that yet. I'm focusing on my relationship with God first."

He looked disappointed. "I understand that. Okay, friends it is."

I smiled gratefully. "Friends."

Our lunches turned into the movies and then we actually went to dinner one Sunday night. Had I been hoodwinked? I noticed Lawrence smiling a lot more in satisfaction as if he knew something I didn't.

I was bored a lot on the weekend and I didn't see any harm in going to the show or out to eat with a friend.

CHAPTER TWENTY FIVE

It was Friday, March sixth, and it was my twentieth birthday. I was so happy not being a teenager anymore. Now, the teen years that culminated with an ugly status were most definitely, a thing of the past, thank God. In my life, I was entering into a new era in so many ways.

Lawrence slyly suggested we go eat at Buffalo Wild Wings, or as they called it, B-Dubs, to celebrate. I went to get my mail before I got dressed for tonight and saw a huge box from my parents with all sorts of items, including my favorite chocolate almond candy, my favorite pumpkin spice body wash, more toiletries and some long thermal underwear. My parents were so funny - still obsessing that because I was here in Chicago, I was probably freezing. They were right, though. It was still cold here. There was also an envelope with no return address. I opened it and pulled out a beautiful, simple card with a ballerina dancing on the front. The inside of the card was blank except the handwritten scrawl that read:

Thinking of you. Happy Birthday, Merci
- James.

My heart raced as I stared at the card and plopped down onto the bed. I couldn't believe after all of this time, he sent me a card out of nowhere. I looked at the envelope and there was no return address - which probably meant he used inside help. Where was he? What was he doing? Was he still engaged to Lorelei? How did he remember my birthday? I remember mentioning it to him but I didn't think he retained it. I knew his birthday was May 3rd, but girls remembered those kinds of things. Before I could get that thought out, I had my answer. James Jansen knew everything. Not wanting to get caught up or explore it any further, I threw the card on my dresser and got ready for my evening with Lawrence. It was a nice gesture but that's where I was going to leave it.

§

By April, Lawrence had worn me down and we started to date. I had to admit I could do worse. He was, after all, handsome and a church going man to boot. He also seemed very cool and was pleasant to be with. I knew I had prayed and asked God for a man and now Lawrence was here. I didn't know if God was telling me he was the one. Actually, when I prayed about it, I wasn't getting anything right now. But I didn't see anything wrong with hanging out.

I considered how young I still was and how I shouldn't have rushed into things with James. Actually, James was my first real relationship experience and it was *too real*. I hadn't truly had the chance to enjoy being a young person that went on normal dates. James hadn't really taken me anywhere because of all the secrecy involved. Lawrence and I went to quite a few of the food places I had wanted to check out in Chicago. It was nice to be out, to be young and free.

I allowed Lawrence to kiss me a few times but I pulled back when he started to get carried away. His kisses were pleasant enough but I let him know that nothing was going further than that. If he didn't like it - too bad. I had peace knowing that I didn't have to give in to anyone or anything that wasn't pleasing to God because He could always replace them, if need be. If they weren't happy with my abstinence, they could step.

One particular evening as we were coming home from the show, Lawrence drove us to the lakefront. It was still chilly outside but I could see the leaves budding for spring. It was a clear night and Lake Michigan was calm and serene. He put his arm over the back of my seat, pulling me close.

"Merci, I really like you a lot. As a matter a fact, I think I'm falling in love with you."

I was glad it was dark so he couldn't see my eyes widen in panic.

"Lawrence, I like you too." I couldn't think of what else to say but he wasn't fooled.

"But not like I like you? Look, Merci, I'm trying to do the right thing here as a man and as a Christian, but I want to take it further than this."

"I'm not ready for anything like that-"

"I know, because you had a bad relationship." I stiffened as my guard went up. "I heard all about how you were somebody's side-piece but-" I slung his arm from around my shoulder.

Oh, he went there?

"Lawrence, take me home now! I don't have to listen to this."

He backpedaled a bit. "What's the problem? That's what happened, but it's in the past."

I wheeled on him and fired. "I know, but did you have to put it like that?" I shouted. "I know that's my past but you don't know exactly what went on and there was a more delicate way you could said it. Take me home, now."

His hazel-green eyes turned feral and he grabbed my shoulders and started shaking me.

"What was so good about him, huh? What was so good that you could give it up to him and not me? Why do you have to act all goody-goody now?"

I was so stunned that my eyes teared up. "Let go of me, you jerk!" I scrambled to get out of his grip, but he held on firmly, ranting and shaking me so hard, I began to feel dizzy.

"I'm tired of suffering, waiting for you to get over him and whatever you went through. You are mine, Merci, not his anymore. Give me what's mine!"

I hauled off and punched him dead in the nose. While he stared in disbelief, holding his nose as blood started to drip - I grabbed my bag and got out of the car. I ran as fast as I could over the bridge and down to the main street. I turned around to peek but he didn't seem to be following. We were in Hyde Park so it wasn't that far to my dorm. I kept running through the cold until I opened my door and locked it swiftly behind me. I crawled onto my bed and cried miserably. Why had this happened?

"God, why?" I asked. "He was so nice, why did he turn on me like that?"

I cried and waited for an answer.

Calm down, I never said he was for you.

"Then why did I go out with him? I thought he could be the one."

But I never said that.

I realized that God, in fact, had never told me the Lawrence was the "one." My mind started considering it when he seemed perfect for me and he was from the church, but I never got confirmation and I never felt peace about him being for me. Now I knew why. He snapped on me out of nowhere, spoke to me foully and seemed to have a violent streak. That Sunday, I was a little apprehensive about returning to church but God let me know he would protect me, no matter what. I was ready to face Lawrence if need be, but he wasn't there. He wasn't there the following week either. It looked like God was looking out for me again.

A few months later I read a police blotter report online.

DOMESTIC BATTERY: Lawrence Redfield, 24, of the 1900 block of 51st Street, Chicago, was charged with domestic battery after a May 31st disturbance at his home, police said. He was charged with assaulting his girlfriend, Jennifer Newsome, 20.

I reread it several times to make sure the identity and address added up to the Lawrence I knew.

I sat back and exclaimed,

"Thank you, Lord! Thank you for delivering me, yet again."

That police career wasn't looking too good…

§

After that, my prayers became even more fervent to be in His will completely. I didn't want to be deceived into thinking that I had found the right person if he wasn't for me. I didn't want a man at all if I was susceptible to being deceived like that. I began to listen even more closely to what the Holy Spirit was telling me. I prayed in the Spirit every day.

§

That summer, I went home and enjoyed New Hampshire with my family. I relaxed a lot and brushed up on my book reading. It felt nice to come home and enjoy the familiar, peaceful surroundings after my chaotic year. Layla was also home and I wasn't sure if she would appreciate the new me. I wouldn't beat it over her head but I would let her know where I stood. If she wanted to hang, she had to put up with a more spiritual, Merci. If she didn't want to hang out, that was okay too. Layla was surprisingly receptive.

"Have you been praying for me?" she asked.

"I have. How did you know?" I replied, surprised.

"Because, a lot of the things I used to do, I don't want to do anymore. It's like - it's tired. There's a guy that I like that goes to this really cool, laid back church where you can come as you are and the other kids there are totally cool. They don't judge at all. Every one of them had issues like me at one time."

"That's fantastic, Layla! That sounds like my church back in Chicago. Real laid back and down to earth. That's the awesome thing about God. He knows that we were imperfect sinners because no one is perfect but Jesus Christ himself. So why do you need to be judged twice for the wrong you've done? God is the only judge. He wants us to come to Him as we are. God is the Best thing that ever happened to me, Layla."

"Me too - I accepted Christ last week."

"What!" We hugged each other and cried. After a few minutes, we wiped our faces and I laughed.

"Well, sister, have I got a story for you," I said.

I told my entire tale to Layla whose mouth was wide open the whole time. She couldn't believe that "good girl - Merci Townsend" was involved with an almost married, twenty-nine year old man, and had indulged in drugs, alcohol, got mugged, beaten and left for dead by his fiancée.' Layla looked at it as a cautionary tale, just like it should be. I went through that so someone else wouldn't have to.

CHAPTER TWENTY SIX

Two Years Later

After graduating from the University of Chicago, I decided I wanted to plant roots in Chicago permanently. At twenty-two, I loved my church home, liked the rhythm of Hyde Park and wasn't too thrilled about returning to the slow pace of Stevensville. I found a decent co-op for rent near campus and Teresa wasn't far in her own place down the street. I changed my major to interior design, not because of *him*, but because I truly got excited over materials and fabrics. My parents didn't have a problem with it because they knew I would work hard and I had retained my scholarship. I received my degree in Interior Design that spring and I was ecstatic.

Since it was tough to find a job, period, I took on a paid internship as soon as one became available for me, which was amazingly quick. Thank you, Lord. To my surprise, it was a design firm located around Fourteenth and Michigan, Lee Warwick and Sons. I knew exactly where it was. The first time I was in the area was right before I changed my major. We had a field trip to IIT of Architecture, the same school James went to, and continued down to Fourteenth Street to see some of the new developments in the area. At IIT, it was finally nice to see the school first hand and it was the first time I realized I got excited about design on my own. That's when I felt that God was leading me into a different path than what I thought I wanted. The Bible said, He would give you the desires of your heart. I never thought I'd be interested in the art of Feng Shui or design aesthetics, period.

§

Driving down to the South Loop was a relatively quick drive. As I entered the trendy loft style building, immediately I felt this was the type of place I was meant to be. On the walls were cool drawings of etched buildings and interiors. There were a few showrooms that displayed beautiful, modern design concepts. I did my research and found out that Warwick and Sons was one of the only architectural firms focused on interiors. It seemed like the best of both worlds. The firm offered services that covered every aspect of the work environment from initial strategy and design through to implementation. I was already eager to do my best so I could possibly get hired permanently.

I was met by the executive assistant, Sienna, who seemed really nice. She introduced me to Mark Warwick, whom I assumed was one of the "Sons." He was also very welcoming. I was placed in a desk up on the second level of the loft that included a few other desks, one of which was Sienna's. I had a nice view of Michigan Avenue in which the street was a mix of other cool, little brick establishments, coffee shops and newly built townhomes. I loved this area. My job was going to be assisting Sienna with categorizing the concept boards and creating sample boards. Happily familiar with samples, I eagerly listened and learned all she had to tell me. She seemed surprised when I began to question about specific materials for the sample boards.

"So, Merci, you seem familiar with samples. Did you gain more experience other than what was listed on your resume?"

I listed my internship at Jansen Worldwide Capital but didn't list specifics since I was apprehensive about questions on why I had that assignment as opposed to learning about business development - among other reasons. Now, I realized it was foolish to leave it off - I had nothing to be ashamed of. It is what it is.

"I interned at a company a few years ago where I assisted the CEO in a preliminary remodel of the company. I was in charge of ordering plenty of samples."

She looked impressed. "Wow, that's really cool that you gained that experience."

"Yes, it was very valuable. It actually started my love for interior design."

She laughed. "Yeah, it usually starts with seeing the possibilities when you encounter materials and concepts first hand. What company?"

"Jansen Worldwide Capital, a business development capital firm downtown." I didn't need to expound, did I?

Her eyebrows wrinkled in thought. "That sounds familiar. Oh well, I'll let you get started and you can take your lunch at one o'clock. I take mine at twelve. Mark always wants one of us to be here."

"No problem," I replied cheerfully.

Mark Warwick's office was a few yards in front of Sienna's desk and it had frosted glass doors and windows. The entry to his office was on the side where we couldn't see, but apparently someone was in there now. I could hear the cheerful banter of male voices. Sienna announced that she was heading off to lunch. I waved goodbye and went back to work. At twelve-fifteen, I received a text from an unknown number.

Hi, Merci.

Who is this?

It's James.

James Jansen? I was completely stunned. I had a new phone and number, and there was no way he could've gotten it. I hadn't talked to James in over two years. The last time I heard from him was when he sent another random birthday card for my twenty-first birthday - still with no return address. My heart thumped and I prayed for composure.

Hello, James. How did you get my number?

You know I have my ways, lol. I'll explain if you have lunch with me.

I looked around in suspicion. He could've been in this place for all I knew.

I take it you know where I am and that I'm due to go to lunch soon - since you know so much. ;)

I do.

This freaked me out but I stayed cool.

Alright, where should we meet?

Right outside of where you are now.

OMG, he really did know where I worked!

Okay, I'll be able to go as soon as the assistant comes back.

Alright, see you then.

My heart hammered in my chest. How in the heck did he know where I worked? I couldn't figure it out. Oh my goodness - I was having lunch with James Jansen. By the time Sienna returned, I wanted to bite all of my fingernails clean. I was praying for composure, that I would be cool, and to look at our reunion as two old friends catching up. I went to the bathroom to freshen up and reapply my makeup. Who was I kidding? I still wanted to look good in front of him. I wanted to make sure he knew that I wasn't wallowing in despair ever since he disappeared and got engaged - or married - or whatever. I wasn't going to let myself be affected. Or at least, I didn't want it to show.

Today, I had on a black and white, scarf print, shift dress reminiscent of the sixties made by Mango. I didn't dress as fancy as I did when I was with him, but I slowly got back into appreciating good clothing. I had on my black, four-inch, Mary Jane, Jimmy Choos. It was a simple, vintage look. My hair was tied back in a matching printed scarf, where the back of my hair was loose. I had on big silver hoops, my makeup was minimal and romantic - and this was me. Thank you, Lord for the peace that overcame me at that moment. No longer manic, I made my way down the steps to the first level and out of the door. There was James Jansen III, in the flesh.

He had his arms crossed as he leaned against a black car. He had put back on his weight, his curly hair was cut lower than before and he had a five o'clock shadow mustache and goatee that suited him perfectly. He had on a grey, mock turtle-neck, cashmere sweater that couldn't help but emphasize his athletic arms and chest. Black jeans fitted across his once again muscular thighs and casual, but stylish loafers adorned his crossed feet. His chestnut eyes were clear and perceptive. With the added maturity and wisdom that was evident in his eyes and strong jaw, he exuded a more confident, imposing presence than ever before. At thirty-two, James Jansen III was more handsome than ever. My heart sped up involuntarily. Why did he still have this effect on me?

He assessed me slowly and when he made his way back up to my eyes, he gave a warm, friendly grin. I smiled back sincerely.

"Wow, Merci, you look fantastic. It is good to see you." I didn't move and neither did he.

"James, it's good to see you, too. You're looking well."

Understatement.

Staring a little longer than he expected, he seemed to shake out of something and blinked. "There are many nice places to eat around here. Where would you like to go?"

I eyed the car he was leaning on and opted not to put myself in close proximity at this time. Now, more gorgeous than ever, I needed to be on guard.

"Some place close within walking distance. It's a nice day."

He caught on and smiled, lifting up off the car. He was still so tall... and so fine. I need to be really careful, I thought.

"Alright, I know just the place." He started walking and I took his lead, keeping up with his casual stroll.

"James, how did you know where I worked?"

"Remember the buddy I told you that I went to school with, Mark? You're working for him."

Stunned, I narrowed my eyes at him suspiciously.

"Did you have something to do with me getting the internship here? I thought it was awfully fast when I got picked out of thousands of design graduates vying for this same position." He feigned innocence but didn't deny it.

"Let's talk more once we're seated." We turned right into a place called Ameritalia, an Italian restaurant.

Once we were seated, I ordered a salad with the same name as the restaurant. I wasn't that hungry because I was still in shock that I was having lunch with James again. The house salad had tomatoes, cucumbers, banana peppers, red onions, and herb flatbread tossed in garlic parmesan dressing. It was delicious. James ordered something called a Parmburger. It consisted of a parmesan crusted beef patty with provolone cheese, a seared beefsteak tomato, red onion, fresh basil, and garlic aioli on a home-style bun. I laughed at his choice and he laughed along.

"Ever since you turned me onto burgers, I try them everywhere I go-" He noticed my face had flushed in embarrassment as uncomfortable memories surfaced.

His amused eyes turned grave. "Too soon?"

"Yes," I said as I looked elsewhere and forked a tomato.

"Alright, let's just eat." We ate in silence for the first ten minutes. It wasn't uncomfortable, though. I needed to get my bearings.

After we were halfway through, I felt a little better. I had been praying under my breath to be cool and now I felt like I should just ask whatever I wanted to know.

"So, James, what have you been up to for the past couple of years?"

He raised his eyebrows at my direct query. I don't think he expected that so soon. Well, we certainly couldn't pretend that everything was left hunky-dory. He put what was left of his burger down and wiped his mouth on a napkin.

"Well, I've been doing what I said I needed to do in the letter I left you."

I smirked. "What - you've been in rehab all of this time?"

"Of course not, that lasted only three months."

"What happened then?" I braced myself for the mention of his engagement or marriage or whatever.

"I left rehab and left Illinois."

That was unexpected. "Really, where did you go?"

"I went to the Bay Area in California to complete my masters in design."

"Really?"

"Yes, I stayed there for two years and got it."

"That's great. What about Lorelei?"

He frowned. "What about her?"

"I heard that you two got back together."

He looked appalled. "No, we didn't - not even close. My brother got engaged to her for a moment but that's another story."

I was astonished. He took a swig of water. Just then, I realized that he hadn't ordered a drink.

"So, it really was a rumor," I said in awe.

"Yeah, they were alluding to another Jansen, not me."

I was completely blown away at this news. Trying not to stall our conversation as I recovered, I tried to think of other questions.

"How was California? Where were you exactly?"

"I was between San Jose and San Francisco." He looked at me pointedly. "Merci, it changed my life."

My eyebrows went up in surprise. "What do you mean?"

"I accepted Christ and it changed my life."

Knock me over with a feather, James Jansen got saved? I was so ecstatic I wanted to hug him and I wanted to cry.

"James, I'm so happy for you! Praise the Lord. How did it happen?"

"Well that could take a long time to discuss." He looked at his watch and then back at me. "Merci, I know it's your first day and you can't be late back from lunch." His eye crinkled in amusement as if remembering something from long ago. I remembered too. "Is it possible that I could call you?" he asked delicately, as if he thought I was a cobra about to strike.

I smirked but he continued before I had a chance to answer.

"As friends, please. I would love to share with you what I've gone through. Can I call you tonight?"

I decided it was no harm in that, especially since he mentioned the "friend" word, first.

"Alright, since I still need clarification on how you found out I was here."

He smiled cheekily.

Afterwards, James walked me back to Warwick and Sons and I went back up to my desk and started working. Mark, who was slightly balding with kind eyes, came out and answered the question for me while handing Sienna some documents.

"Merci, my old buddy was here today and you come highly recommended. James Jansen is the one that referred you. He said you were meticulous when you helped him at JWC, so I know you'll do a good job."

I could only smile and try to keep shock from overwhelming my face. James was in here? Today? He must've come in through the side entrance of Mark's office that wasn't visible from our vantage point. James was still slick. He was probably looking directly at me when he texted me, obviously acquiring my number from Mark. Sienna looked at me as if something clicked in her head.

"Thanks, Mark, I'll work very hard." He smiled and went back into his office. Something else added up - he was the old boyfriend of Leslie from NeoCon.

CHAPTER TWENTY SEVEN

That evening, I prayed while I waited for James's call. I waited to feel any ominous or foreboding feelings about us chatting again, but I felt none. We were just going to talk as friends. The enemy taunted that he'd heard that one before, but I ignored it. I really felt that this was okay.

My phone rang at eight thirty. I had already programmed his new number into my phone as a contact. Not because I was frantic like when I was a teenager, but because it was practical, I told myself.

"Hi, James."

"Hi, Merci, how did everything go today?"

"Fine, thank you. Mark spilled the beans that you referred me. How did you do that?"

He chuckled. "I still have some pull at my old school, believe it or not. I was a well known alumnus of UChicago at one point, don't underestimate me."

"I know and I don't. For what it's worth, thank you so much. I really like it so far."

"Good. Mark is a cool guy and you'll learn a lot."

"Is he still with Leslie?"

"Oh, you remembered. Yes, they're still together and married. As a matter of fact, he's the one that talked to me about God first when I didn't want to hear it."

"Really? So you had a friend like that too?" I asked, thinking of Teresa.

"Just like that."

"Tell me about California. Tell me about everything." I curled my feet up on my big comfy chair – of course I had to get one – and prepared to listen to James. I couldn't believe I was on the phone talking to James Jansen again.

"Well, I need to start from that day in your dormitory. When you left out, I snorted so much coke that I blacked out. I dreamt that I was dying and I could feel myself struggling to live and I prayed while I was under. I was asking God to help me and if he woke me up after this, I would get help and never touch the stuff or any drugs again. While I was having my dream, I felt something like an angel laying their hands on me and sheltering me, comforting me."

"I prayed over you that night while you were passed out."

He was quiet for a moment. "It was you then. I thought it was an angel taking care of me."

"It was probably both." A tear slid down my check. "Go on." God was truly amazing.

He was quiet for a few moments and his voice was still in awe as he continued.

"So, when I came to, it was about two in the morning. I saw you sleeping at your desk, looking so tired and worried about me that I couldn't bear it any longer. Against my father's wishes, I called and begged Bernard to come pick me up. He took me directly to a beautiful facility called Crossways in Lake Villa, IL, which is about fifty miles from Chicago. It had forty-three acres of beautiful grounds, the staff was very pleasant and accommodating, and the treatment, while difficult, was rewarding. It provided me with knowledge, therapy, counseling and the tools needed to live a life free of drugs and alcohol."

I swiped at the tears that were steadily rolling.

"Wow, that's just...wow. That's awesome, James. How long have you been clean?"

"From any type of drugs? Since I walked out of your dorm. I haven't touched a thing nor wanted to. Now, alcohol was a different story but I've been completely sober for about a year."

"That's amazing. What happened next?" I asked, eager to hear it all.

"I stayed for three months and then, needing a change of scenery, took what money I had left and moved to California. Tim, another college buddy of mine, has an architectural design firm in San Francisco and told me to join him out there so he could show me the ropes on running a firm. I enrolled in California College of Arts to finish my master's. I ended up starting from scratch and received it in Design Strategy which is perfect for running a design business. It was all perfect timing because I needed to be away from everything, especially my family, to try and figure out some things for myself. I knew I needed a church home because I couldn't deny the experience that night in your dorm and how God had taken care of me, how he was still taking care of me out west. I started going to church with Tim and I haven't looked back. I knew I needed to work on me first, before I could be a good man for someone else. What I found out was that God didn't want me to put myself first but Him. That's when everything started to fall in place. When I put Him first, he put me first. Now I understand."

"That's amazing, James, because that's the exact same thing I had to go through." I recounted my story to him, including my experience with Lawrence.

"Merci, I'm so sorry you had to go through that. If I had been right, that would've never happened."

"Don't think that way. While it was a bad thing, I wasn't harmed so it was a learning experience. That's the same way I think about what happened to me with your..." I trailed off.

"I know - with Lorelei."

I continued to speak before he had a chance to dwell. "Yep, so we have to look at it as a way of God developing us. I'd rather have gone through that to get to where I am now instead of floundering where I was."

"That's a great point, Merci. I'm really enjoying talking to you. I hope we can be friends."

"We can definitely be friends."

Talking to James was wonderful and I enjoyed every moment of it, but why was I disappointed that he only wanted to be friends? Well, this was how it was supposed to be, right?

§

The next few days, I worked diligently at Warwick and Sons. Mark and Sienna seemed really impressed with my efficiency and of how quickly I caught on. They told me that my help was sorely needed and that encouraged me that maybe I could get a permanent spot. On Thursday, my phone buzzed while at work.

Want to have lunch?

Smiling, I texted back.

Sure. Where?

I'll pick you up at one. Cool?

Cool.

James was waiting for me when I stepped out of the door, leaning against the car in a pale lavender shirt with the sleeves rolled up, jeans and sneakers. I was also pretty casual with a linen Henley, white skirt and sandals. My hair was loose, blowing in the soft breeze. I added a little more detail to my eyes today. I knew they were a bit dramatic just how he liked them, but how could I know I was going to see him today?

He gazed at me a little too long, but that was James. Or at least that was James when he looked at me. My insides squished under his perusal as I looked back at him smiling.

"Hi, James."

"Hi, Merci…wow, you look great."

"Thank you. So, where are we off to today since you didn't answer?"

He smiled.

"If you don't mind, will you take a ride with me somewhere?" I immediately grew suspect and he noticed. Was this déjà vu?

"No, don't worry. It's just a place I want to show you on the way to lunch. It's right around the corner."

"Okay, as long as it's not downtown," I mumbled under my breath.

Obviously overheard, he laughed, opening the passenger door. Once I was seated, he went around to the other side and jumped in. His seat was pushed all of the way back to accommodate his long legs.

"What - you don't go downtown anymore?"

"No, I don't go downtown with *you* anymore," I mumbled.

He laughed uproariously. "Well, I guess I deserve that. I hope that will change one day."

I just continued to look out of the window as we drove around to Thirteenth and Indiana. He continued to chuckle. James drove up and idled the car in front of a beautiful, orange brick townhome.

"This is where I live now."

"Hey, that's really nice." Sensing that I could get antsy, he took off and turned the car so that we were on the other side of the street, his place visible. He pointed to the side we were on now.

"This building is the location of my new design firm, Jansen Architectural Interiors."

"Really? That's great, James!" He smiled in satisfaction at my response.

I could see that this side of the street had office space as opposed to across the street where residential townhomes lined the block. Inside the window, I could see the faint display of an unlit sign that read, *Jansen Architectural Interiors.*

"You're really close to Warwick and Sons. How does Mark feel about competition being so close?"

"He is the one that encouraged me to set up shop here in the first place. Both of us love exteriors and interiors and this is a relatively new concept of architectural firms that also focus on interior design. He took over his dad's architectural firm and transformed it into what it is now. He wants me to get in on the ground floor and figures that since this area is booming with new construction, I could actually help him alleviate some of the pressure. He is overloaded with clients as it is and even said he'll start referring the overflow to me."

"Wow, that's a great attitude to have. Not too many

people would welcome a competing business."

"Mark is my buddy, plus he's a man of God. He knows that regardless, he'll be blessed for helping me out. That's what we do, look out for one another and know that God has an unlimited supply and will bless us both no matter what - if we're giving. He was just sowing a seed."

"That's an awesome truth. I love it." I wanted to do my happy dance. "When did all of this happen?"

James took off and started driving down the street towards a place to eat.

"I bought both of these places when I got back from California, six months ago. It's another long story."

Since I didn't have much time left on my lunch, we ended up going to Subway and eating our sandwiches in his car. I looked around, taking in the mocha interior for the first time.

"What happened to the red Ferrari?"

"I sold it before I left for California. I needed the money and it was paid for and mine. I used some of it to pay for my master's degree."

"Do you miss it?"

"Not at all. Since I did a lot of drugs in it, it just reminded me of how reckless and immature I was. I wanted to leave the car and everything about that fast life behind me and start over."

I nodded in understanding. "By the way, what kind of car is this? It looks too small to be considered an SUV."

"It's a BMW X4. It's a crossover, which is in between an SUV and a regular sized car. Like it?"

"Yeah, because it reminds me of an M3 on steroids."

He looked at me in amazement. "What do you know about an M3?"

"A friend of mine on campus had one." His smile

hardened a bit.

"A boyfriend?" I played coy because it really wasn't his business anymore.

"Maybe." I sipped through my straw and turned towards the window.

He was quiet for a moment. "Merci, can I call you tonight?" he asked, softly. "I still have so much I'd like to tell you."

I felt kind of bad because of my last comment, and the last thing I wanted to do was scare him away.

"Absolutely."

§

That night, I thought more about James. I was starting to get consumed with thoughts of him again. I wasn't sure if this was a good thing or not. The way he was right now seemed too good to be true. He was drug free, alcohol free and now a Christian. I couldn't deny that my feelings were coming back for him, if they had really ever left. But now I wasn't sure if he liked me that way anymore. I knew he still found me attractive, he made no secret of it from the way his eyes followed my every move. But that was just James. He was a very passionate man and he just loved women, I think. Being with him rekindled my desire for a mate again. I wanted someone just like the way he was now. I recited my prayer again.

"Dear Lord, please continue to mold me to be the perfect mate for my husband. Make sure that I am the virtuous woman that he needs. Please bring me a husband made perfectly for me. Someone who will love and cherish me as Christ loves the church. In Jesus' Name, Amen."

Instead of feeling better, I felt disappointed because all

through the prayer, I could only see James's face. He wasn't interested in me like that - he just said he wanted us to be friends. I prayed for peace and I received it. The Holy Spirit told me to relax and stay in His will.

My phone rang.

"Hi."

"Hi, Merci. How did the rest of your day go?"

"It went fine. A potential client came in and Sienna entrusted me to show them the showrooms on the main floor."

"Oh yeah? How did you do?"

"Afterwards, Mark said I was a natural. They were impressed that I was able to describe the materials in detail. He said I've really done my homework."

"That's my girl."

Both of us were quiet as he seemed to realize his slip up. My heart sped up at his familiar phrase. I couldn't deny that I was delighted about the slip. Could he be feeling like I felt?

My heart dropped a bit when he changed the subject.

"So, I wanted to finish telling you about what happened. We never even got to finish our conversation from the other night."

"You're right. You're supposed to tell me about what was going at JWC when you left."

"That's right. While I was in rehab, I found out that Lorelei's parents were pissed about how we ended things and they still had a deal in place. My dad saw a way out of the mess by coercing my brother, who was now in the running for CEO, to get engaged to Lorelei."

I shook my head. "You're kidding. Poor Andrew."

He chuckled grimly. "'Poor Andrew' is right. So, because he was eager to get into JWC as fast as he could and he knew that if he was with Lorelei, the shareholders would be comfortable - they announced their engagement. They get engaged, Drew takes over my father's spot and everything seems rosy, right? The kicker: On the night of the engagement party, which was this huge society affair at The Drake, somebody runs a reel of a sex tape of Lorelei and some random guy. Lorelei's made a lot of enemies."

"You sure it wasn't you?" I braced myself.

"Ugh, no way. I told you. *That* was not happening between me and her for years."

"Alright." What else could I say?

"So, somebody ran the footage and since the press was there, the tape went viral. I heard she ran out of there disgusted and mortified. On the bright side, apparently, this killed the 'frigid' rumor. But she not only humiliated herself, but her parents as well. It's still going viral to this day - up to ten million views. She tried to get it taken down but it keeps popping up. She's in hiding from what I've heard."

"What? Oh well, you reap what you sow," I said.

"That's for sure."

I know it was bad that it happened, but truthfully at this point in time - I couldn't feel sorry for her. I was going to have to pray on it.

"How did Andrew take it?"

"He was okay with it because he didn't want to marry her anyway. He had been going with his high school sweetheart for years. Since he was already in the company by now and things seemed to be running well, he and Angela are planning on getting married next year. She was crushed and it took him a while to make it up to her, but it looks like it's all coming together." It seemed as if his voice grew wistful about something.

"Aw, good for them. I'm glad things are working out."

"Yeah, I'm glad too. My brother was born for that

position and I'm all too happy for him. It just wasn't for me."

"No, it wasn't. I knew it that night at NeoCon. The way your eyes lit up as soon as we entered the Mart. I was like, who is this man? Where is the arctic, future CEO vampire?"

He laughed. "I know. You would never have seen that joy at JWC."

"I know. You seemed so cold-blooded at first. You actually used to scare me with your glares."

He sounded surprised. "Really? I didn't know I looked at you like that. I had to control myself from looking at you like I wanted to eat you, which I did."

We both chuckled awkwardly. We needed a new direction for this conversation - *next*.

"James, tell me about your new places."

"Well, to finish up the story, all of this was taking place while I was in rehab and when I went to California without alerting anyone, my mom got worried and started calling me almost every day. She apologized to me about everything, including trying to persuade me to get married to Lorelei, especially now that her reputation was shot. I had nothing to hide, so I began to tell her about how much pressure was put on me to take over JWC and my eventual dependence on drugs. I told her it wasn't an excuse, but that was the only way I knew how to cope at the time. I also told her how I had found someone very special to me, but I couldn't be with her because of my so-called commitments and drug issues."

My heart leapt.

James continued, "I let her know that I had a personal relationship with Christ now - take it or leave it. If she wanted to talk to me, she had to hear about my faith and how I was growing and getting well. At first she was reluctant but then she began to ask me more questions about

God and the Bible. I began sharing verses with her."

"That is amazing."

"Yeah, she must've told Dad what I was doing out there and he got on the phone a few times to make small talk. I guess that was his way of trying to smooth things over with me. He asked if this was what I really wanted to do – as if he didn't know before – and I told him, yes. He offered to buy me a place for the business and a place to stay if I wanted to come home."

"That's wonderful, James."

"I refused his offer."

"Why?"

"I didn't want to be beholden to him and I wanted to make it on my own. So, I was able to take out a loan. He called me crazy but I told him that while I appreciated his offer, I didn't need for him to throw it back in my face later."

"Would he do that?"

"More than likely and I didn't want to take the chance. I wanted no parts of it."

"I can understand that."

"Turns out that my mother stashed away some money in a trust account for me. She'd been saving it up for years for me, unbeknownst to my father. I told her I didn't need it but she wired it to my account anyway. I used most of it to pay off the loan and I didn't have to involve my father. She also said he's planning on making sure I get my inheritance. I don't care about that, but I'm just amazed at how God works."

"Yes, that is so awesome. He is good all of the time."

"And all of the time, He is good." We both laughed.

I was astonished that James and I had been on the phone so long. It was almost eleven o' clock when we hung up. I felt really good about our talk. Maybe being just friends would be better than being in a relationship. I don't ever remember him opening up so much before. He always said I was easy to talk to and he obviously still felt the same way. This was a good sign.

CHAPTER TWENTY EIGHT

The next few weeks passed and I talked to James almost every day. He was busy getting his office space together not far from Warwick, so I couldn't help looking out of the window in his general direction. I looked forward to his texts to meet up for lunch. It hadn't happened in a few days due to him being really busy with the construction.

Hey, Merci, you game for lunch?

I wanted to dance with joy.

Sure. Meet you downstairs?

Yep, see you at 1.

Today, we went back to Ameritalia because there were a few other dishes on the menu that had peaked my interest. I ordered Loaded Jojos which were fried potato wedges topped with sharp white cheddar sauce, pepperoni bits, tomato sauce and fresh herbs. Yummy. James ordered spaghetti and meatballs. Famished, I dug in.

"Did you want to see the job site one of these days? It's coming along."

"Sure. I would love to. When is a good time for you?"

"How about after you get off work today?"

"That's sounds fine. I can just drive over there."

After work, I drove around the corner and parked in front of Jansen Architectural Interiors. Today, the huge display window was covered in paper from the inside. James was right at the door to let me in. Once inside, I could see the shape of things coming together. It was a huge open space with nothing but dry wall except on one wall where there was exposed brick. On the dusty floor, samples and boards were in disarray. A construction guy seemed to be gathering his tools to leave.

James smiled and motioned for me to wait a moment. "Alright, Steve, I'll see you tomorrow," James said.

The other guy wiped a dusty brow on his way out of door. "Yep, see you tomorrow."

After a moment, James looked at me in query, waving his hands around. "So what do you think? I know I have a lot to do, but I think it's shaping up pretty well."

"Yeah, this is a really nice space. I can see its potential. How much longer until you're ready to open?"

"It's projected to be finished by next month but I'm trying to hurry it along. I'm anxious for them to be through with the drywall installation so I can start with the design."

I laughed. "Of course you are."

I looked over at all of the materials that were strewn about the floor. Not thinking about it, I put my bag on a nearby chair and started gathering them and sorting them in order by material and color. I was glad today was Friday because I could wear my jeans. Mark said it was okay to wear whatever we wanted, but I didn't want to abuse the privilege. I looked up to see James looking at me in amazement.

"What? You obviously need help and I'm getting good at this." I continued sorting through the stacks.

"You're right, I need help and you are good at it. Don't think I haven't thought about it."

"Thought about what?"

He leaned down on his haunches in front of me. "Stealing you away." I looked up and he caught my eyes with his smoldering ones. That was a familiar look. Startled, I looked back down to my project. I didn't want to think of whether that was a double meaning. James was starting to disorient me, just like back in the old days.

"From?" I didn't look up to see his face. He stood back up and cleared his throat.

"From Mark. Every day that I'm in here, I'm kicking myself for not having gotten things together months ago. That way I could've persuaded you to come help me first."

The thought of working with James again made me positively gleeful, but then I thought about it.

"James, we didn't know that we would be getting along as friends. If we didn't have God in our life, I might not have forgiven you or you may not have wanted to see me. Things are working out just as they should."

He came back down on his haunches.

"That's not true. I would've always wanted to see you. I always had plans on seeing you - and we *do* have God in our life." His eyes held so much sincerity it was staggering. I got up and dusted my hands off on my jeans.

"So what are you trying to say, James?"

"I'm trying to say that, although things are happening the way they should, don't rule out anything."

"What does that mean? Tell me what you really mean." I was starting to get impatient.

He sighed. "I mean that I believe God brought us back together for a reason. He straightened us up and brought us back the way that it should've been in the first place."

My heart filled with joy as I grasped the meaning of what he was saying. He felt the same way I did?

"Are you saying that you still have romantic feelings for me?"

He looked at me as if I was crazy. "Are you seriously asking me that, Merci? I've never stopped having romantic feelings for you. I was just worried you wouldn't accept me again. It was so ugly the way everything ended."

"Why didn't you call me, text me or anything? I received your birthday cards but that was it. You never even left a return address."

"Because I wasn't ready to be the man you needed. I had to make sure I was right with God and myself first, before I could ever be ready for you."

My defenses were starting to crumble. "What if I wasn't available?"

"Seriously, it was one of my prayers that you would be available, waiting for me."

"How did you know I was still single?"

He smirked. "Merci, you know I have my ways. I have a few alumni friends that are now faculty. From what I had found out, it appeared you didn't have anyone – or at least no one serious."

I laughed in amazement. "James Jansen, have you been stalking me?"

"Somewhat. Let's just say that over the past few years, I checked up on you every now and then."

My mind was whirling with his revelation.

"I thought you said you only wanted to be friends."

"I want to be friends. We *are* friends. But friends can be more, too. And I never said *only*. Friends make the best mates." His eyes searched mine for some type of confirmation that his feelings were returned.

"James, I can't deny that I feel the same way, but I cannot make a mistake like I made with you before. That's why I would like to take it slow."

His eyes lit up. "Slow is good for me. Slow is perfect for me." He smiled widely, beautiful teeth gleaming. "So, can I ask? Merci Townsend, will you go steady with me?"

I laughed loudly at his cheesy proposition. "Yes, James, I'll go steady with you." We both grinned as he took my hand and led me around the place, explaining his vision for Jansen Architectural Interiors. I felt like I was floating.

That evening, I went home and fell flat faced on my bed to cry.

"God, is this for real? Is James really the one for me? After all of my asking for a good man, you mean to tell me it's really James Jansen? Did you really separate us to clean us up to be right for each other? You are so amazing. Thank you so much, Lord. Please help me to do what's right. I want to stay in Your Will."

I felt nothing but peace.

§

Over the next two weeks, James and I really went steady. He drove to my place in the evenings and picked me up to take me to the show, out to dinner and wherever else I wanted to go. He never went any further than holding my hand. I basked in his old-fashioned affections. He made me feel cherished. It was just what I wanted.

I remember our first date, when he came to pick me up and saw my miniature abode. I recall him wrinkling his nose in distaste.

"This place is too small. It's almost as small as your old dorm."

"What am I supposed to do? This is all I can afford right now." He looked around shaking his head. I thought I heard him say, *not for long*, but I couldn't be sure.

§

One Saturday afternoon, I figured I would be spending it reading a book or watching television. James was very busy with trying to open for business on schedule and I hadn't yet heard from him today. My doorbell rang and when I opened it, an impatient courier was asking me to sign delivery papers for something. He handed me a big box and scampered away.

Thankfully, the box was light. I took it to my bedroom while I wondered what it could be. I struggled to open the big cardboard box only to see that there was a smaller, elaborately decorated box inside. It was velvet blue and trimmed in satin bows. Inside there was a beautiful, midnight blue gown that looked much like the box. I took it out and held up the stunning creation in wonder. A note fell out.

Please be ready to go to the Ball at 6:30, My Princess.
J.T.J.3

I squealed in excitement and spun around. I knew who it was from even before I read the note. Only James would do something so extravagant. I tried on the dress and wasn't surprised that it was a perfect fit. The sleeveless bodice was dark blue satin and the bottom was a fitted velvet material that fishtailed. It was lovely. I opted to wear my hair up and applied James's favorite smoky eye. Since the dress didn't come with shoes, that was the hardest decision for me. I wasn't short on them thanks to my love for shoes and apparently, James knew that. I decided on strappy, blue four-inch heels that I hadn't worn before. They were a perfect match. At six thirty on the dot, James rang my bell and entered my shabby chic apartment in an elegant tuxedo like he stepped out of GQ magazine. He looked so out of place it was ridiculous. I laughed in delight. He stared in awe.

"Merci Townsend, you look amazing. Did it fit okay?"

I smiled. "You look vey dashing yourself, James Jansen III. It fits perfectly." He grinned in return. Then he cleared his throat and upturned his nose, extending his hand to me.

In a posh British accent, he asked, "Shall we?" I placed my hand in his and stepped over to him, barely missing my trash can in the tight space.

"Yes, we shall," I replied in a pitiful Cockney accent. We chuckled at the hilarity of the moment as he assisted me in my beautiful, luxurious gown down the dirty, unstable, damaged stairs of my apartment.

James drove us downtown to Navy Pier to a venue called *Grand Ballroom*. There were plenty of people unloading from their vehicles in extravagant gowns and tuxedos. I hopped up and down in my seat as James laughed at my exuberance. A valet came and took the car. I clutched James's arm excitedly.

"Wow, James, a real ball!" I reached up and kissed his handsome cheek.

"This is only what you deserve. The best for my baby." I melted. "I noticed you didn't have a problem with us hitting downtown. Am I making up for it?"

"Yes, most definitely!"

§

We went inside and were assigned tables for a meal before dancing. The ball was entitled *White Receptacles*, an affair honoring ground breaking architect, Niles Larson, and a presentation regarding design with the community of architects. I was thrilled that James thought to include me. This was obviously, a very big deal to him. We sat down at a table with four other couples that James seemed to know. He introduced me as his girlfriend and they responded politely. I warmed inside at his introduction. We made small talk as we ate and they were all very cordial. Afterwards, James led me to the floor. He placed his right hand on my back and held my right hand in his left one. He instructed me to place my left hand on his shoulder. We looked like something out of a movie and I felt silly.

"I'm not sure what to do. I don't know how to ballroom dance," I said nervously.

"Look around. Do you see anybody else doing anything fancy like from *Dancing with the Stars*?"

I looked around and laughed. Everybody was just swirling and swaying. Immediately, I relaxed. The music was an old song that I'd heard my father playing.

"That's Duke Ellington's "Take the A Train.""

He smiled, impressed. "That's right. You know your music, don't you?"

"I know some, but not like you."

He laughed. "You remember my list, huh?"

"Yep, how could I forget?" I buried my head in his shoulder to blot out the memories that were surfacing about what happened later that night. He seemed to be remembering too, and held me much tighter.

"Have you done any songwriting, lately?" he asked.

It warmed me that he remembered. "No, I hadn't really felt inspired in the past few years." I looked at him with a coy smile. "I believe inspiration is coming back, though."

He smiled tenderly. After dancing quietly for a few moments, I looked around the room and observed. I could see the big arched ceiling that had glowing red lights that turned everything a pinkish hue.

"I remembered reading that one of the original uses for Navy Pier was as a cargo facility to house huge ships. And for a while, it was considered underutilized."

He looked impressed and his eyes narrowed in interest.

"Yes, until major renovation and construction followed in the 1990s. They transformed it into an excellent attraction and source of revenue for locals and tourists alike."

I kissed his cheek. "I've never been here before, but I've always wanted to. Thank you."

He looked at me in disbelief. "Really, not even for the summer fireworks or to ride the Ferris wheel?"

"No, I hadn't had a chance, yet."

I knew what he was thinking. He pulled me close and kissed the shell of my ear.

"I'm so sorry, baby. You missed out on so much because of me."

I pulled my face back and gave him a cheerful kiss on the lips. "Like I said earlier, you're more than making up for it."

§

After two songs, as we were making our way towards the Lakeview Terrace, we ran into Mark and Leslie Warwick. I flushed with embarrassment as James held my hand tightly, guessing that I was ready to bolt by the way I hid a little behind him. Mark didn't look the least bit surprised and Leslie smiled warmly. Mark laughed in delight.

"Hey, man! Hey, Merci."

I mumbled a timid hello and with his other hand, James shook Mark's hand, never letting go of mine.

"Mark, good to see you." He turned to Leslie and gave her cheek a kiss. "Leslie, this is my girlfriend Merci. I'm not sure if you remember her from NeoCon a few years ago."

I smiled shyly.

"Of course I remember. You two looked so happy that night. I should've known." She surprised me by giving me a small hug. "It's good to see you again, Merci."

"You too, Leslie. I didn't know if you'd remember me."

"Yes, Mark's told me all about what a great help you've been to Warwick and Sons. He told me he brought on James's girlfriend that recently graduated from UChicago."

I was staggered by this information. I had no idea Mark knew that we had been involved and were involved again.

"Yeah, and I'm on to you, man. You're trying to steal away my good help before she can even join the company," Mark said. James, Mark and Leslie laughed loudly while I stood there nervously chuckling, blushing like crazy.

We finally made it out to the beautiful terrace. The nighttime skyline was simply outstanding. James pointed out the faint outlines of old buildings that his grandfather constructed. The dark lake looked still, except for the flurry of lit boats that converged. There were many people milling around as if they were waiting for something. I leaned over the railing while James snuggled behind me, chastely holding me close. It felt so good to be in his strong arms again. They felt like home. All of a sudden, a bright plume shot towards the sky and popped. I gasped in surprise along with a few other people. Fireworks? Wow, this was one of the happiest nights of my night. After the finale, James turned me around. He noticed the tears threatening to fall down my cheeks. Oh no, I didn't want my makeup running. I dabbed at my eyes to stop them and to get a hold of my emotions. He held my chin in his hand.

"What's wrong, baby."

"Nothing's wrong - everything's right."

We hadn't had a passionate kiss since we started dating again. I thought this would be the moment, but James chastely kissed me on the cheek. Then he rocked my world with his words.

"You know that I love you, right? I never stopped. I told you that I wanted to show you." He gave me another quick kiss. "Even if you don't feel quite the same, I just wanted you to be sure of my feelings."

He hugged me as a fresh wave of tears fell, makeup ruined, but who cared?

"I do," I mumbled tearfully against his chest.

He stiffened. "Do what?"

I put my arms around his neck and pulled back to look him straight into his beautiful, chestnut eyes.

"I love you." I gave him a kiss back and half expected him to deepen it. Instead, he held my face in his hands and looked at me with deep emotion. Gently, he put my head back on his shoulder and we just hugged tightly and rocked for a long time.

Thank you, God. Praise God.

He took me home and walked me up the stairs to make sure I got in safely. After he left, I was overcome with emotion as I got down on my knees to thank God again for this wonderful, turn of events.

CHAPTER TWENTY NINE

One Saturday, we casually strolled down Michigan Avenue, his arm around my shoulder and mine around his waist. I had on a tank and blue jean shorts and he had on a t-shirt and board shorts. It felt so good to be able to be with the one I loved without having to hide.

One lady we passed smiled brightly at us. "You two sure make a lovely couple."

We both beamed in surprise. "Thank you," we both replied in unison.

Apparently, we made quite the pair as I could see a few others passing us by with knowing smiles. After all, James was beautiful, and I guess I was okay. According to James, I was the most beautiful woman on earth, but I knew he was biased.

"You know why people keep staring at us?" He turned and gave me a kiss on the nose.

"Because you're so good-looking?" I gave him a kiss on his jaw and he laughed.

"No, because they can clearly see we're in love and God's light is shining on us."

I smiled in agreement.

As I looked around, I remembered zipping down Michigan Avenue in a cab with an arrogant James at our first business lunch. Laughing, I reminded him of his bad attitude.

"In the beginning, you were horribly cold. At Fogo de Chão, I couldn't figure out where you were coming from."

He laughed. "That's because you were stirring up feelings I'd never had before. Truthfully, I was a little scared of how you affected me and you were so young, too."

As we crossed the bridge towards Jansen Worldwide Capital, I thought it would give me a feeling of foreboding but it didn't have that effect. I looked at James out of the corner of his eye. I caught him doing the same to me, as if he knew what I was thinking.

"You okay?" he asked.

"I was going to ask you the same thing. Actually, I was wondering how I would feel, but I feel fine."

"Me too. You know why? It occurred to me that we probably would've never met if it wasn't for this place. So," he tossed his hands up in a salute, "hats off to JWC."

We laughed as we got closer. A few yards up towards the entrance, I spotted a flame of hair eyeing us from a distance. Could it be? OMG, it was Jasmine. She must've decided to come in to work on a Saturday. I remember how devoted she was to her job. She was stock-still as she waited until we got closer, no doubt trying to see if her eyes were deceiving her. James tightened his hold around my shoulder, purposely giving me a kiss on the temple as we got closer. He wasn't right for that but I loved it. She had her hands on her hips, scowling.

"Hi, Jasmine," I said cheerfully. I had no hard feelings against her.

She rolled her eyes at me and it looked like her bottom lip was trembling. James looked at her and smiled congenially.

"Hello, good to see you again."

She huffed. "So, I see you two are together. You sure caused a scandal a few years ago."

I was taken aback by her words and started to get upset, but

James squeezed to let me know he would handle her.

"Yes, we're together and we love each other very much. So you can spread the word, if you must. But Jasaline-"

Her eyes turned to fire and she looked accusingly at me. I shrugged.

"It's Jasmine," she gritted out. I wanted to laugh at the déjà vu.

"I'm sorry. *Jasmine*. You would do well to remember that my brother is the CEO and you could still get into trouble for insubordination if I give him the word. So please, watch your tone."

I glanced at James and saw that familiar, impassive expression that he used on employees of JWC. Brrrr - I'm glad it wasn't directed at me.

She looked dumbfounded at his rebuff. Her back straightened and her eyes widened in uneasiness as she took heed of his warning.

"Yes, sir, I apologize." Then she turned to me, looking me up and down, no doubt trying to figure out how I snagged James.

I gave her a genuine smile. "You take care, Jasmine. God Bless."

Arm in arm, we walked on and I could feel her eyes on us in outrage. No, I didn't sway my hips or anything like that to make her mad. I learned that just because she was nasty didn't mean I should be. She had seen enough to make her mad, anyway.

Once we were further enough away, I laughed. He looked at me in confusion.

"What?"

"You did it. That cold, frosty glare you always gave - you did it to Jasmine."

He chuckled in surprise. "Did I? Well, she deserved it."

§

277

The next few dates were amazing, but I could tell there was something else creeping in. I felt that same jolting sensation that made my knees weak whenever he got very close to me. I was starting to get frustrated about not being able to show our rekindled love for each other. Remembering how our passion for each other could be, I was amazed at his restraint. Not once did he try to persuade me to come back to his place or suggest that he come up for a "night cap" at my place.

Tonight, we had just finished seeing a movie and we were getting in the car to leave. He drove in the direction of the new business space.

"Where are we going?" I asked.

"I want to show you my place." Alarm bells softly rang. Honestly, I was happy to hear them but I should put up some type of resistance, right?

"Um, this late? Maybe I should see it some other time…"

He laughed and tried to reassure me. "I just thought you might have wanted to see my place and how it's laid out. I didn't mean anything by it."

I felt like such a dummy.

"Alright. Actually, I'm very curious to see your place." He smiled and held my hand across the console.

Once we arrived, we walked up a few steps where James opened the door of the rich, burnt orange brownstone. The entry way had luxurious cherry wood flooring and the dining area was visible beyond the foyer. Around the corner, steps descended into a large living area with a beautiful décor in warm tones. Most of the accents were apple green, lemon yellow, burnt orange, brown and pewter. The white sofa that faced the wall mounted TV, looked comfy and cushy. Adjacent was a chair that looked just like my comfy chair from the hotel. Could it be? No way. His eyes followed mine, knowing what I was thinking.

"Yep, I bought one just like it. It was one of my favorites too."

I laughed in delight. I spun around, taking everything in at once.

"James, this place is awesome. It feels like a real home."

"It is a real home, my home." His eyes bored into mine in intensity. I looked away.

"Was your place in Buck Town like this?"

"It was getting there but something was missing. I think the fact that my dad owned it made me feel a bit detached." He looked around. "But not this place, this feels like mine because it is."

"That's great. I love it." I smiled tenderly.

"I'm so glad you do." He shook his head as if to clear it. "Would you like something to drink, some lemonade or tea?" Wow, James was really serious about staying away from alcohol. I was very impressed.

"Lemonade would be great."

He took off to the kitchen to get my drink. He called out, "Would you like to come see the kitchen?"

"Sure."

It was painted in a bright cheery yellow with cobalt blue accents. It was filled with stainless steel appliances and blue and gold mosaic tiles lined the backsplash. I loved it.

"James, this kitchen is *boss*. I love it! I would've decorated it the same way."

He grabbed my hand and spun me around into his arms, holding me there while I looked at him like a frightened mouse that had just gotten caught. He looked like he was ready to devour me. I hadn't seen this look in a while. My heart hammered out of my chest. His penetrating chestnut eyes held mine.

"I know you would've, because we're perfect together. You

were made for me. I knew it all along."

He slowly closed in and sensually kissed my lips. This was the first time our lips had connected like this in over two years. Sparks and fireworks went off as they met. My head was in a fog as I thought about what we were doing. Nothing wrong with kissing – eh, Lord?

His lips molded to mine, begging entrance. I slowly opened my mouth and his tongue invaded my mouth, plundering the depths of it while it begged a similar response from mine. I responded like a phoenix, rising up and taking his face in my hands and kissing back with equal fervor. I saw myself losing control as I shifted to his neck, giving it butterfly kisses. What was wrong with me? James's eyes were closed and he was groaning in ecstasy. *Too much, too much - pull back*, a voice whispered.

I wrenched myself out of his arms, grabbed my lemonade and rushed back into the family room. I sat down on the sofa, digging through my purse to look busy since the TV wasn't on. I was mortified that I attacked James in that manner. Here I was worried about him, and *I* was the one ready to jump his bones. We had a problem.

A minute later, James came in with his cup of tea. He had an amused look on his face as he sat down next to me which made me feel worse. I grabbed a nearby magazine off the table, *Architectural Digest* no doubt, and began sifting through it.

"Merci, we need to talk."

I plastered nonchalance on my face. "About what?" I asked as I continued to flip the pages.

He chuckled and then sounded serious. "You know about what? About us and the direction of our relationship."

I put the magazine down and looked at him. "Alright. Look, I'm sorry if I lost control in there, it's been such a long time-"

"Don't apologize. I started it. It's been a long time for me, too. I guess it's nice to know that we still have that fire, but it's also not a good thing at this time."

I felt my stomach plummet. "Why not?"

"Because we both know that we want to take it further, and with me and you, it would be really easy to fall back into that, but I know both of us want to be in the will of God."

My heart was ready to combust over where I imagined we were headed with this conversation. Was it over already?

"Alright, so what should we do?" I asked apprehensively.

"Well, I want you and you want me, so the only logical next step is for us to get married."

My eyes bugged out of my head. *Oh My Goodness.*

James got down on one knee in front of me and pulled a ring box from under the sofa by my feet. *Oh My Goodness.* I was shaking like a leaf, I was so nervous and excited. My eyes began to tear up and my heart was about to burst. I couldn't believe it. He was trying to hold my left hand but I was trembling too much. He looked up at me with misty eyes. I remembered how emotional James could be. This made me want to start bawling.

"Merci Townsend," his voice shook, "I thank God that He brought you back to me. That He saw fit to split us apart until we were both ready to be the best we could for each other." He actually let out a small sob and tried to gather his composure.

"Oh, James," I cried.

"I am so thankful for all that you've done for me. How you stood by my side when I put you in a bad situation, corrupted you, made you feel embarrassed, made you feel humiliated, and made you unsafe. You almost died because of me. The only one I've ever loved in my life endured so much pain and shame for me. Then on top of that, prayed for me when I was drugged out of my mind. And the greatest gift of all, you *still* love me and forgave me. I don't deserve you, but when it comes to you, I'm selfish. I want you anyway."

I was shaking and trying not to wail out loud.

"Merci, will you do me the honor and blessing of becoming my wife?" He slipped a beautiful, five carat, princess cut diamond ring on my finger and I sobbed and hugged him.

"Yes, yes, yes. All you had to do was ask."

CHAPTER THIRTY

The following Sunday, James joined Living Life and we started pre-marital counseling with Pastor Lawson. We divulged all of our past to him. He took extra care to grill James with plenty of questions about his spirituality, relationship status, substance abuse, commitment, and his devotion to me since he was made aware that James was the "engaged man" from my big testimony. He inquired as to whether we were abstaining from pre-marital sex and we told him we'd already made a decision to do that.

He also taught us that a marriage was not fifty-fifty. We shouldn't expect each person to hold up their end because if they fail, was this grounds for a separation or divorce? The truth was that marriage is one hundred-one hundred. A person should enter into marriage thinking that he or she will give everything they can as often as is needed to make sure their marriage is good. Human nature being what it was, there would be times when a partner would stumble and be unable to carry his or her end of the load. James and I agreed that this was very valuable to know and we were both glad we decided to go to counseling.

§

James and I were married in a small, private affair one month later. My parents flew in along with Layla. Also in attendance were James's parents, his brother Andrew and fiancée Angela.

Mark and Leslie were there along with his friend from California, Tim, and his pregnant wife, Mary. Of course, Teresa and her parents were there.

We were married at our church where Pastor Lawson was the officiator of the ceremony. I had on a simple Tulle & Chantilly ivory colored sleeveless lace dress that flared slightly at the bottom. My hair was down without a veil and I held a simple bouquet of orange roses and cream lilies. James had on an ivory tuxedo with a matching shirt and silk tie, and an orange rose in his lapel. He looked like he'd stepped right out of a magazine. James said I'd never looked more beautiful.

I tried my best not to cry as we read our vows, looking deeply into each other's eyes. We knew that a lot of people used 1 Corinthians 13:4-7 for their marriage vows, and I admit that I initially thought it was corny. Now that we understood its true meaning and how it applied to our experience, we couldn't think of anything more poignant in its place. We had been through something that had us appreciating every word.

We recited it together.

"Love is patient, love is kind. It does not envy, it does not boast, it is not proud. It does not dishonor others, it is not self-seeking, it is not easily angered, it keeps no record of wrongs. Love does not delight in evil but rejoices with the truth."

James's eyes watered as he read the last verse.

"It always protects, always trusts, always hopes, and always perseveres."

We exchanged rings.

"You may kiss the bride," Pastor Lawson said.

James lovingly took my face into his hands and we tenderly kissed. We held back as we both knew how heated we could get and we didn't want to embarrass our families. Our lips separated and his warm eyes continued to penetrate mine. This beautiful man loved me and now he was my husband. Was I dreaming? This was truly the happiest day of my life. We smiled at each other and remembered that there were others in the room. That's the effect we had on each other. Pastor Lawson closed his Bible and cleared his throat.

"This is a union that is sanctified by God. It didn't start that way. It started off wrong, sinful, out of God's will and headed for destruction. But God saw fit to separate them so that He could fix them up, straighten them out and mold them into who He wanted them to be."

Smiling, we continued to stare into one another's eyes.

"The key was that they each had to make a decision to call on God and to put Him first in their life. It was only then, that merciful God saw fit to reconnect them. From what they've told me, they didn't know that they would be back together. But God always knew. Even though the devil meant it for bad, it was already in God's plan for their reunion, but only in the right way - His way. He turned it into good and brought them back for this Holy union of matrimony."

He turned to us and smiled warmly. "I now pronounce you man and wife, and may God continue to bless this union in the Name of Jesus, Amen."

I heard Teresa shout, "Amen."

§

Afterwards, my dad came over to greet James and I. James had called my dad on the phone to properly ask for my hand in marriage. My dad found that hilarious, but appreciated the gesture and immediately took a liking to James. However, after what my pastor just said, dad was eyeing us suspiciously. James was turned around greeting one of his friends while my dad took me aside.

"Baby girl, what in the world did your pastor mean about it starting off the wrong way, sinful and out of God's will?"

Deflecting, I hugged my dad tightly. "Oh, Daddy, I'm so happy you're here. Don't worry, he just meant that our relationship started off wrong because James and I weren't living right in God's eyes. I know you don't want me go into details." I raised my eyebrows in question.

He cringed and shook his head adamantly. "No please - no details."

I laughed. "Just know that now, we are in God's will and we love each other very, very much. Also, James and I both love the Lord."

He hugged me warmly and kissed me on the cheek.

"Well, there's nothing more important than that."

§

When I called my mom to tell her I was getting married, she wanted to know if he was the boyfriend from a few years ago. Leaving out plenty of details, I simply said yes. Last night, over at his place, James met my parents for the first time over a small dinner that he prepared. Everyone seemed to get along fine.

Today, she came over and gave me a big hug, and for the millionth time today, I tried not to cry.

"Mom, I'm so glad you're here."

"Where else would I be? I really like James and I can see that he only has eyes for you."

I blushed. "He is the love of my life."

"Well, he seems to love you very much – not to mention gorgeous, too. You did well, baby."

I laughed. "Thanks, Mom."

"But I have to say, according to that telling message from the pastor, you and James went through some things and you obviously kept a lot from me. When were you going to tell me about that?"

I could detect a tinge of hurt in her eyes. The truth was that I hadn't planned to. I had totally kept it all from her because I was too ashamed for her to know that her "perfect daughter" wasn't perfect. Nor did I want my Ex Navy SEAL dad to come to Chicago and threaten to maim everyone who had done his daughter wrong.

"Oh, Mom, I'm sorry. It's a long story and I just didn't want you to worry, but you're right, I should've shared more with you. The fact is that James and I love each other very much and we're blessed."

She kissed me. "Alright, baby. As long as everything is okay, now."

"It's better than ever."

§

Our reception was held downtown at the Chicago Cultural Center with a massive window overlooking the huge structure, *Cloud Gate*, that was more commonly nicknamed, *The Bean*. Honestly, I had just found out its real name last week. There were more of James's family, friends and acquaintances as insisted on by his mother. I didn't mind, but James wanted me all to himself. His mother and I talked on the phone a few times as I planned out the wedding. She was nicer than I thought she would be. Sofia Jansen came right up to me and gave me a big hug.

"Sweetheart, you look beautiful. I met your parents, they're lovely people."

"Thank you…" I hesitated.

"I told you to call me mom."

"Thank you, Mom."

She smiled happily. "James told me all about how you talked to him about God and prayed for him. I can't be more thankful that he found someone like you. I realized how fragile life was when he said he thought he was-"

She choked up and I hugged her, patting her back and rubbing circles.

"I know, I know. But that's in the past now," I consoled.

She took a deep breath. "I know, but it really makes you realize that the things you always thought were so important in life are really insignificant." She stood away and grabbed my hands with a watery smile.

"I've really enjoyed talking to you these past few weeks and I don't think James could've picked a more perfect person for him. Thank you, sweetie."

She pulled me in for another hug as I tried to hold back tears.

I really, really liked Sofia.

§

Jim Jansen was cordial and welcoming to me, as well. He remembered meeting me at JWC and didn't seem the least bit surprised that I was the one James had decided to marry.

"As soon as I saw you, I knew you were his type. I knew that he was a goner."

I was shocked. "Really, how did you know?"

"Take a look at his mother."

I looked over at Sofia and observed her dark brown wavy hair, olive skin tone and slanted eyes. For the first time, I could really see where James got his dark looks from. And Jim was right -

Sofia and I were sort of the same type.

"You remind me so much of her when she was your age. I knew it was over for him."

I laughed.

§

Teresa came to the bathroom with me to straighten out my dress and help me to reapply makeup.

She hugged me and started to cry.

"Merci, I'm so happy for you. I hope you don't think I was too harsh on you and James in the past. I can see that James has really changed and that he really loves you."

"Aw, don't cry T - I don't think that way at all. If it wasn't for you praying and guiding me in the right direction, do you think we would be here? I thank God for you and how you helped me through. James and I name you along with a few others as brave warriors that helped us in the battle. We honor you, girl."

"Oh, Merci, that makes me feel so good. Seeing you two is such a testament to how God will really answer your prayers. He said 'we have not because we ask not.' Look at you now."

I smiled tearfully.

"Yes, He is so good."

Layla came in too. I had introduced my besties to each other earlier as they helped me get ready. They seemed to hit it off well. Teresa left the bathroom to let me and Layla talk.

She gave me a hug.

"Girl, he is hot! You hit the jackpot."

"Stop it, Layla," I said seriously and then I cheesed, "but I did - didn't I?" We whooped with laughter and hugged as we jumped up and down.

She showed me her left hand that was now adorned with a

beautiful, solitaire diamond ring.

"Josh popped the question, I'm next." I squealed and again, we hugged and jumped around.

"I didn't even see that earlier. Why didn't you tell me?"

"I didn't want to steal your shine. This day is for you. Plus I didn't want to bombard you with all of the stuff I've got planned for mine." She looked around. "While this is all private, quaint and nice, you know I don't do small. My wedding is going to be huge, honey."

I laughed. That was my Layla, never one to do anything simple.

§

James and I were sitting at the head reception table, laughing and joking while guests came up to greet us. There were many beautiful women in the room that looked at us with barely concealed jealousy, probably wondering how we had such a "perfect life." While we were indeed happy, they didn't know what lay beneath the surface. They weren't at the wedding, so most of them had no idea of what we had gone through. They didn't know how much devastation, heartbreak, prayer and transformation went into getting us to this point. They only saw the cosmetic side of a good-looking couple in love - but none of the history, none of the pain. James and I had been through so much.

Suddenly, James looked down and groaned.

"What's wrong?" I asked in confusion.

"Ugh, why is she here? She must've come with Byron." My eyes were about to start searching but James checked me. "Don't look now - but remember the so-called friend of Lorelei's that I saw in Water Tower Place that day – the gossip? Well, she's on her way over – act natural." James protectively put his arm around my waist.

"Hello, Miki," he said politely.

Miki looked and sounded like a screeching peacock.

"James," she sang annoyingly, "introduce me to your wife." She had on a massive hat with plumes sticking out in all of the colors of the rainbow. James seemed to be exhibiting great calm.

"Merci, this is Miki Day. Miki, this is my lovely wife, Merci Jansen." I thrilled at my new name as James took my hand in his and lovingly caressed it. We blissfully stared into each other's eyes and almost got lost in our own little world until I quickly remembered my manners. I turned back to her.

"Pleased to meet you, Miki." I sincerely smiled and offered my hand. Miki took it and smiled at James.

"Oh, I like her, James. She seems way cooler than that *other* one. Obviously, you feel the same since that *other* was a perpetual fiancée and this one became the wife, very quickly." I laughed awkwardly while James's hold around my waist tightened in reassurance.

She cackled and took off, waving disingenuously.

"Toodles."

Our foreheads met as we both cracked up.

§

After greeting more guests, I was shocked to see Marguerite coming our way. She was simply elegant in a vintage, 1950's black taffeta, cocktail party dress. The shoulders were of crushed velvet. Instead of the familiar chignon, her lovely grey hair was down in soft, cascading waves over her petite shoulders. I'd always admired Marguerite's style, she was so chic. She had always been nice to me and I was a little embarrassed about the circumstances and how I never got a chance to say goodbye.

"Marguerite!" I exclaimed.

She beamed as she got closer, hugging James and me tightly and giving us both kisses on our cheeks. She stood back and waved a bright, pink fingernail in admonishment.

"You might've have been able to fool other people, but you couldn't fool me." She looked pointedly at James. "I knew as soon as I saw this young lady that you had *bad* intentions." She drew out the word.

I cracked up and nudged James playfully as he ducked his head in embarrassment.

"They weren't all bad. I married her, didn't I?" he asked, sheepishly.

She smiled brightly and tapped his shoulder. "That, you did. It was the smartest thing you've ever done," then she leaned into his ear and whispered conspiratorially, "that and leaving the company."

He looked at her in astonishment.

"What? You think I didn't see how miserable you were from the moment you got there? The only time I saw you excited was when you would lead the managers around, pointing out design changes – oh yeah, and when she got there." She pointed at me, laughing.

"Wow, Marguerite, you noticed all of that?" I asked in awe.

"Yes, I did."

"How is J.J.?" James asked.

"Oh, last year Jairus went back to New York to finish studying at Juilliard. That's where he attended before coming to Chicago for a while. He is a classically trained actor."

I should've known. I was totally speechless and would have to share my inside joke with James, later.

She grabbed both of our hands. "I'm so happy for you two,

have a blessed life together."

After she left, James and I were still stunned by her revelations.

He turned and gave me a kiss on the tip of my nose.

"More confirmation that we were meant to be," he said.

CHAPTER THIRTY ONE

That evening, we retired to the trendy W Hotel that was a few blocks away from the Cultural Center. We were to spend the night before leaving for our trip to the South of France, tomorrow. I had kissed my parents and Layla goodbye and told them to text me when they got back to New Hampshire. I washed up and changed into my new La Perla lingerie. I wasn't nervous about tonight, just anxious. We wanted each other so bad and it had been so long. I waited for James to come out of the adjoining bathroom.

When he came out, he slowly crawled over me on the bed. He was naked except for a towel.

"Merci, you are exquisite and officially mine. I'll never let you go, again. I love you so much."

"James, you're so beautiful to me. I love you, too. I'm thrilled to be your wife."

His head lowered as our lips met. Our kisses were even more passionate than before, our touches, more electrifying. Over the past few weeks, it had become harder and harder to not lose control. We were so in love and so ready to show one another.

He shook his head at my lingerie. "There will be none of this," he said, fingering the strap of my camisole.

He quickly sat me up to take them off. Evidently, there would be no time to waste. Eagerly, I complied and in turn, boldly wrenched his towel away. He gazed at me with surprise and chuckled at my audacity.

"That's right, baby, take what's yours," he murmured.

James Jansen III was mine, utterly and completely. I was emboldened now that he was my husband, that our union was sanctified, and that the marriage bed was undefiled.

He let me push him back on the mattress and I climbed on top of him. Kissing and tasting my husband's beautiful, pouty lips and strong jaw, I reveled in my new status and power. At thirty-two, James was more masculine and sexier than ever. He moaned with pleasure and it only fueled my passion. I kissed my way down the entire length of his body, missing nothing. I marveled at the perfect specimen of man that was beneath me, caressing, squeezing and kissing every part of him while he gasped and groaned in delight at my audacious conduct. I was a ravenous, mad woman that couldn't be stopped.

What a man.

No longer able to deal with my intense ministrations, James pulled me up from beneath my arms and turned me over onto my back.

"Sweetheart, we don't want to this to be over before it begins," he gasped, chuckling.

I smiled languidly as I reached up to kiss him.

He looked down at my body for moment, taking it all in. His eyes were wild with hunger as I'm sure was reflected in mine. He started with my face, giving me the sensual butterfly pecks that I loved so much and made his way down to my neck. I could feel his appetite increasing as he licked and nipped my throat down to my collarbone. Once he reached my chest, he was feral. Voraciously kissing and squeezing me with both of his strong hands, I started to writhe and thrash on the bed. I groaned in pleasure as I watched the way his tongue meticulously played with me. It was so sensual and it was driving me wild. He held me still.

"Oh baby, this is just the beginning."

James made his way down to my stomach, his mouth not missing and inch and then he parted me without preamble. Still shy about being so exposed, I tried to turn my head away, but he reached up and turned my chin back towards him. His darkened eyes were looking at me in such hunger, such awe and with so much love.

"Don't, Merci. Every part of you is beautiful, and in the sight of God, it's mine. Your body totally belongs to me now, so let me show you how I'm going to take care of it," he rasped.

I moaned as his mouth descended on my thighs and everything in between. I gasped as he kissed and sampled every bit of me, leaving nothing untouched. Watching him was almost too much to take. He paid special attention to that sensitive part of me that almost had me leaping off of the bed as he held me down with a vice grip.

"James..."

"Is it good to you?"

"Yes, *so* good."

Apparently consumed with reacquainting and probing every area that he had missed over the years, he continued exploring as if he were making new discoveries. Overwhelmed by his newly enhanced, lethal and overpowering sensuality, I was on my way to ecstasy. I thought he would've stopped by now for us to unite, but evidently he was taking me all of the way. Stars were about to burst and I was desperately clinging on for dear life.

"James, James, James," I chanted as I fisted the sheets. His attentions picked up in velocity, virtually lifting me off of the bed while he devoured me like a mad man.

"That's it baby, I love you."

And I shattered. I let out a long wail as I disintegrated into pieces. James held me up to him while my body tremored sporadically. He growled and the vibrations prolonged the pleasurable torture. After a moment, my body started to still and James lovingly kissed his way back up my body. I felt like a rubber doll - loose and lethargic.

I put my arms around his neck in gratitude and in anticipation of what was to come next. He burrowed his head into my neck and we joined in one motion. We both gasped in surprise and pleasure. It had been so long since we were like this, but I marveled at how we fit perfectly.

"Merci, I missed this so much. I told you - you were made just for me."

I gasped as he filled me completely, rolling and rocking us gently. I held onto his broad, muscular shoulders to brace myself for what was to come.

I was consumed by him, and felt like I was drowning as he kissed me, caressed me, stroked me and filled all of my senses. All around me was nothing but James. I felt wanton as I allowed James to take me to those dizzying heights that only he could take me. He squeezed my body up to him tight and showed little mercy. I gasped at his overwhelming zeal and like a lion, he slayed me rapidly and repeatedly. Once again, stars were inside the room but they were brighter than ever. We were soaring. I mewled and cried out repeatedly as we went higher and higher.

"Baby, you sound so sexy."

Just from his words, I felt myself building to that pleasure again. James accelerated as he anticipated our impending rapture. Then he stopped to contort us into another position...and later...flipped us again. I was getting fatigued as he kept me from reaching our impending rapture.

"James," I moaned, "I can't take it anymore."

"Hold on, baby," he demanded.

I whimpered as his movements became even more forceful and

erratic. He held on to me, basically holding me up as by now, I was a limp ragdoll. I couldn't hold back as I splintered like a volcano. Pleasure took a hold and didn't release me for what seemed an eternity. He continued rolling, rocking and plundering. I heard him groan in satisfaction as he stilled. We cried out together in ecstasy as his body crashed into bliss. He pulled my shoulders back up and held my entire body to him as he continued burrowing in while kissing and gently biting the side of my neck. Then he laid us back down and I drifted away.

As I regained awareness, I was in his arms while he gazed at me with intense emotion. I reached up to touch his face as a lone tear escaped. He was such a lovely man.

"You are so precious to me and I'm so thankful for you, Merci Jansen." he said.

"I'm thankful to you, too. I love you, James Jansen."

I reached up to kiss him and once again our passion reignited. That night, we continued to give into our every pleasure and our every whim as we loved until the dawn.

This union was truly sanctified because it had never felt so right. The key ingredients that were missing before was God and true love. While we may have loved each other before, there were hindrances and walls dividing that love, so it wasn't pure. Now, I was assured that he loved me, too. He had shown me as he said he would. Now, there was no shame, no worry, no *other*, no humiliation, no drugs nor alcohol. We were high off each other and God's love. There was no greater pleasure to behold...

EPILOGUE

I started working at our new business as soon as we got back from our beautiful honeymoon in Saint-Tropez. I had put in my two weeks notice with Mark before the wedding, and he and Sienna were sad to see me go. But Mark understood.

"You think I didn't see this coming?" He laughed heartily. "You should've heard how he was going on and on about you when he referred you. I'd never heard my boy talk like that, so I knew you had to be special."

I smiled in delight. "I am so grateful that you took me on. It's been a very valuable experience that I'll always cherish. Plus, you helped James and I get back together, so thank you." I gave him a big bear hug and hugged Sienna too.

I easily broke the lease on my apartment since it was in high demand and I explained that I had just gotten married. I was finally able to move in with James and I absolutely loved my new home. He let me add my own designer's style to our bedroom which I felt could use a feminine touch. He was all too happy to let me do whatever I wanted as far as home was concerned.

Now, *working* with James wasn't as easy as I thought it would be. Now that we were a true husband and wife team, I had to learn that he was still in charge because he knew about business and design strategy. I don't know why I forgot how dogmatic and bossy he could be. I started remembering back to his remote attitude when we first started having "business lunches." I dealt with it for a while, but today I put my foot down.

"Alright, dude, you need to chill out."

He looked at me in surprise as his cool façade broke.

"What? *Dude?* That's not very professional Merc-"

"I don't want to hear it! Stop talking to me like I'm a child. I know you're the boss, but I'm your wife so please treat me like an equal and stop talking down to me all of the time," I bellowed. I left the room and went into the bathroom to cry.

Please Lord, help us. Peace pervaded my senses.

A moment later, he knocked on the door.

"Baby, I'm sorry. I'll try to be more patient and speak to you with more respect. Forgive me?"

I opened the door and launched myself into his arms.

§

Later that week, I was talking to Teresa while James patiently waited until I got off. I kept telling him to wait a second and I would be off soon. As soon as I was about to hang up with T, Layla called on the other line to ask me about some wedding ideas she had. Before I knew it, two hours had passed and I had forgotten all about James.

He came back into the room and said a little louder than necessary, "I said I had something I needed to talk to you about."

I quickly got off the phone. "Geez, what is it?" I asked impatiently.

He looked wounded by my outburst.

"I wanted to tell you that Tim called me, devastated, because Mary lost the baby – but never mind."

He stomped away and I felt like a fool. Oh no, poor Tim and Mary. I immediately went into the bedroom and asked James for forgiveness. I was so wrong.

"Sweetheart, I feel so dumb. I'm so sorry that I neglected you when you really needed to talk to me. I feel awful for Tim and

Mary. Will you please forgive me?"

He pulled me onto his lap and hugged me.

That's the thing when God is the head of your life. If you let Him, He'll show you your errors and if you humble yourself and admit them, you can move on. James and I were learning about forgiveness and patience in our first few months of marriage. If people thought this would be a fairytale after the wedding, they were wrong. This was real life. But with God, ALL things are possible.

ABOUT THE AUTHOR

Traci Morris holds a bachelor's degree in Speech Communications and in addition to author, is a graphic artist that's had her card designs carried in Target stores. She is also a songwriter and lives outside of Chicago, Illinois with her family.

www.ingramcontent.com/pod-product-compliance
Lightning Source LLC
Chambersburg PA
CBHW031250170626
46807CB00001B/73